DEATH is a

CABERNET

Also by Ken Dalton

The Bloody Birthright

The Big Show Stopper

DEATH is a
CABERNET

Ken Dalton

Different
Drummer
Press

For more information concerning *Death is a Cabernet*, email the author at ken@kendalton.com

ISBN 978-0-578-09198-3
  1. Humorous—Mystery—Fiction. 2. Pinky—
     Delmont (Fictional character)—Fiction. 3.
     Bear—Zabarte (Fictional character)—Fiction.
     4. Modesto—California—Fiction.. 5.
     Healdsburg—California—Fiction. I. Title.

ACKNOWLEDGEMENTS

This novel came together with the help and assistance of the following:

Bob and Norma Wiltermood, our hard working partners in the great adventure known as Pommeraie Vineyards—seven years of madness that provided me a peek into the wild world of crushing grapes, selecting yeasts, French oak barrel selection, filtration, and the marketing of a world-class cabernet sauvignon.

To my son, Hugh. He reads the first draft of the novel, visualizes the story, and creates the provocative covers to make each Pinky and Bear Mystery unique.

To Wendy Maxham for another exceptional picky, picky job of editing.

To Dr. Ye, and all the staff, nurses and Pharmacists, that dwell in the magical land of room 170, also known as the Kaiser Infusion Center, for giving me many years of complete remission.

To the long suffering members of my writer's group:

Editor-in-Chief Mary Madsen Hallock
Jon Gunner Howe
Norm Benson
Thea Howe
And the divine Sarah Andrews

Finally, to my wife Arlene, for remaining my lover and best friend while we both learn how to live with a cancer in remission.

This book is dedicated to the memory of my great friend and winery partner, Bob Wiltermood.

For years, we would work day after day at the winery and communicate without a spoken word.

But when the day was done, we would pop the tab on a cold beer, sit back, and swap tales of our youth.

ONE

Pinky Delmont-Carson City, Nevada

I had extracted an innocent, but extremely unsavory client from the clutches of the law, so when evening arrived, I had allowed myself an extra cup of cheer before my celebratory dinner. At that moment, the concept seemed to have merit, but I fear that excessive vessels of triumph had now caused the dawn to arrive with more than its usual abruptness. After struggling through my morning ablutions I slowly nibbled at two pieces of dry toast to settle my stomach. Forty-five minutes later, I arrived at my law office with what felt like a tiny carpenter hammering large nails into an area directly behind the bridge of my nose. I could have suffered through that minor complaint, but as Lu, my beautiful, and always smiling secretary, cheerfully greeted me, my digestive system suddenly took a turn for the worse.

Lu, correctly anticipating my frail physical condition, had placed three steaming cups on my desk. The one on the left contained tea, the one in the center beef bouillon, and the cup to my right held coffee. To complement this display of healing libations, a sealed Manila envelope lay to the right of the coffee cup.

I gingerly took a few sips of the hot beef bouillon in a valiant attempt to banish the craftsman who continued his task behind my eyes and focused my attention on the Manila envelope. A cursory glance indicated that neither front nor back contained an address or mark of origin.

I buzzed Lu. "You left an envelope on my desk. I checked both sides and the item lacks a notation of any kind." I hesitated as a rumble of sour gas escaped through my mouth. "How did the aforementioned container find its way to my office in Carson City?"

"It was enclosed in a FedEx overnight package with attached directions to place the envelope, unopened, on your desk."

For a moment I pondered why anyone would go through such an elaborate game. "Thank you," I said, with a touch of curiosity.

After a few more swallows of the scalding beef broth, I opened the package and pulled out an 8x10 glossy photo of what appeared to be a naked male body face up on an autopsy table.

The dry toast I had consumed earlier jumped up my esophagus at the startling sight of a corpse that was colored with an amethyst tint from head to toe.

I quickly turned the photo face down while I willed the disgusting gorge back into my stomach. Slowly, so as to not upset my tenuous equilibrium, I swiveled my chair to the cabinet behind my desk, reached inside, dragged out a bottle of brandy, and poured two fingers of the room temperature alcohol into the broth. After a moment to allow for cooling I took a large gulp of the mixture and replaced the foul flavor of vomit with the cleansing bouquet of distilled grapes.

When the cup was empty, I called Lu.

"Was there nothing else inside the FedEx enclosure?"

"I'll check."

The combination of the warm protein and brandy calmed my stomach. I took a deep breath and waited for Lu's response.

"Pinky, I apologize. A business card had settled to the bottom of the FedEx container. My guess is that the card was paper clipped to the note that instructed me to place the unopened envelope on your desk."

Mystery solved. "Bring the card to me at once."

As I waited for Lu, the image of the corpse flooded back—the head, chest, legs, even the open eyes were stained a deep violet. Until that picture had caught me off-guard, I had assumed that my career of defending the vilest criminals of northern Nevada had inured me against that sort of visual shock.

During an average murder trial, I expected the prosecution to display the goriest pictures of bloody victims to turn the jury against my client. But this morning I learned that even I, the great J. Pinkus Delmont, could be caught unprepared if a photo of a purple corpse crossed my vision so soon after a breakfast of dry toast.

The door to my office opened. I was gratified to replace the image of the colorful corpse with the perfection of Jung Lu, my vibrant Asian secretary. However, at the moment, a supportive crutch was tucked under each of her otherwise flawless arms. Being young and reckless, Lu had gone skiing at Tahoe with a couple of friends over the past weekend. During her final downhill run the poor girl had lost control and skidded directly into a tree, breaking her right leg. According to the doctor her appendage would be encased from ankle to hip for the near future.

Lu said, "Here is the business card and the . . .

3

Pinky your face is as white as fresh snow! Are you sick?"

"All things considered, I am fine. Let me see the business card."

She handed it to me. It read:

Charles H. Godwin III

Sonoma County District Attorney

I nearly allowed a surprised expression to cross my face, but years of courtroom experience had taught me to conceal my emotional state from the jury so I retained my mask of stoicism. "Thank you, my dear. That will be all."

After Lu limped out and closed my office door, I grabbed the bottle and poured some brandy directly into my mouth—then a second mouthful.

Charles H. Godwin the Third, indeed! For some inexplicable reason, my law school nemesis had returned to my life with what I assumed to be a schoolboy prank—a fake photo of a purple corpse!

During my legal matriculation at Hastings, the finest law college on the west coast, Charles and I had jockeyed back and forth for the honor of top-of-the-class. One month he would end up number one, the next month I would achieve the exalted position. What is most important is that by the final ranking, when the first-in-class position mattered, I ended up at the top. The problem was that Charles, a man whom I had once counted as one of my few friends, had refused to acknowledge my achievement.

On the cusp of graduation, I was besieged with offers from most of the top law firms in the country. However, before I made my decision, an obscure attorney by the name of Murphy had entered my life.

I was sitting in my tiny apartment reading Dostoevsky's Crime and Punishment, when he phoned me the first time. "Mr. Delmont, Padriag

Joseph Murphy here. The Dean gave me your number. I have a proposition that I trust you will consider."

I said, "Are you the same Murphy who presented the outstanding guest lecture on jury selection two months ago?"

"Guilty as charged."

"Mr. Murphy, I want you to know that I learned more from that lecture in three hours than I had—"

"Mr. Delmont, I am truly gratified to hear that you gained some knowledge from my efforts. Now, the reason for my call. Each year I invite the top Hastings student to spend the summer months with me at my law practice in Carson City. I am a trial lawyer and—"

"Mr. Murphy, I—"

"My boy, your first assignment is learning that you should never interrupt me. Now, as you recall, I am a trial lawyer, and as such, I endeavor to protect the constitutional rights of the accused in northern Nevada. Would you be interested?"

"Mr. Murphy, I—"

"Mr. Delmont, I presume as the number one at Hastings, you are considering positions with the some of the most prestigious law firms in our great country. Please note I applaud your youthful zeal. I believe that accepting my offer could keep you from making a misguided decision that you would regret for the remainder of your legal life."

I was on the verge of attempting, for the third time, to tell Mr. Murphy no thank you when his final admonition sunk in. "Are you trying to tell me that I could become lost in the corporate morass if I signed on with one of the top firms?"

"I see that the Dean was correct in his assessment of you. Mr. Delmont, you are direct, and in this case, spot on. Yes, my boy, that was my point exactly. Come and spend three months with me. After ninety days, if you still want to go with one of the big firms, I will use my considerable influence to pave the way for you."

So now you know the story of how the premier member of the Hastings class ended up working with Padriag Joseph Murphy, in Carson City, the half-baked Capital of Nevada.

During my initial week, Murphy pulled a few strings and after a day of questioning from a panel of local judges, I was fast-tracked and became the newest member of the Nevada Bar.

Half way through the second week, I found myself seated at the defense table next to Murphy, as his second chair, defending a man accused of killing his estranged wife by lopping off her head with an antique sword.

From the initial moment of the trial, I marveled at Murphy's ability to comprehend every nuance of testimony, and anticipate all moves made by the prosecution. I observed intently as he slowly, but surely, created a cloud of doubt around the prosecutor's case. In my mind there was little doubt that our client was on his way toward an acquittal when disaster struck.

On the final day of the trial, while running his closing statement past me in his office, Murphy clutched his chest and pitched to the floor, as if a bolt of lightning had struck him. Moments later, when the ambulance arrived, he was pronounced dead.

As the attendants rolled my mentor's body out of the office, I snatched the closing statement notes from Murphy's still warm fingers. While jogging the two blocks to the courthouse, and using Murphy's final thoughts, I mentally mapped out the closing argument that I would present to the jury. I should note to those who do not know me, or my legal abilities, that most of the sparkling concepts had come from the young, but brilliant mind of J. Pinkus Delmont.

Murphy's client—a sniveling wretch named Hubert Heyenga—was less than pleased to discover that the words of a recent law school graduate were to be his only bulwark against a state-sanctioned execution. After the jury had been dismissed, I talked with members of the jury and they agreed that it was the closing statement—delivered by J. Pinkus Delmont, a young, untested lawyer —that had moved them to a not-guilty verdict.

The press and television cameras met me on the courthouse steps and eventually followed me back to my modest motel room where I did my best to handle their endless accolades with my usual humility.

The following morning, when I left my motel room for my morning repast, seven potential clients stood on the blacktop, clamoring for me to represent them. Within a twenty-four hour span, I had become the most sought after defense attorney in northern Nevada.

Less than a week later, acknowledging the kismet that had led me to Carson City, I took over the office space left vacant by my beloved mentor, the now deceased Padriag Joseph Murphy, and opened my law practice.

And what happened to the Hastings number two after graduation? The last news I had concerning Charles was that he had relocated from San Francisco to southern California, disappearing into

7

the land where only the elderly recall the days of sweet orange blossoms and clear skies.

I turned to my daily schedule and noted a gap of twenty minutes before my first appointment of the day so I relaxed and contemplated the gross photo Charles had sent me.

The big question remained: why? Was it a prank? I pulled out a magnifying class and scrutinized the photo. The body looked genuine. I studied the face and saw no feature I recognized. Eventually, curiosity got the better of me and I dialed the telephone number on the business card.

"District Attorney Godwin's office."

"Good morning. My name is J. Pinkus Delmont. I would like to speak with the District Attorney."

"One moment, please."

"Pinky, it's been years. I'm pleased you called. How are you?"

"Now that my stomach has settled down, I am fine. What compelled you to send me that grisly photo?"

"I'm embroiled in a sticky situation here, one that I don't feel comfortable talking about over the phone."

The anxiety in his voice was palpable. I said, "Charles, considering the distance between us, I fear the phone is our only viable method of communication. What are you suggesting?"

"Pinky, please give me a few minutes to hear me out."

"I am a very busy man. You have three minutes."

"Three minutes? I can't complete—"

"Charles, you have two minutes and fifty-five seconds left."

"Now I recall why we didn't part as friends."

8

"I am not sure that was the only reason."

He paused, and then said, "You're not still hung up that I didn't acknowledge your class ranking after all these years?"

"You are correct, but I need to warn you that you have used up another thirty seconds of your allotted time."

"Damn it, Pinky, you're not making this easy."

I fully understood that I was making the moment uncomfortable for my former classmate, but this could be my last opportunity to clear up his long-standing lack of acknowledgement. "Charles, to quote our old law school dean, no one told us life was going to be easy."

"Okay, you win. I sent you the photo because I'm seeking advice, and assistance, from the top student of our class at Hastings."

"Charles, although the tone of your voice indicates a true lack of sincerity, I will accept your belated acknowledgement of my outstanding accomplishments. Now, in what way may I assist you?"

"As I told you, I can't discuss the matter over the phone. Break free and come to California for a couple of days? We need to . . . Pinky, did you hear that noise?"

"What noise?"

"That click on the line a second ago?"

"I heard nothing but your ridiculous request that I come to California. Charles, do you think that click was an indication that someone could be eavesdropping on our conversation?"

"In my present situation I think that is a possibility."

"Oh what a tangled web we weave, when first we practice to deceive! Give me a moment to check my calendar . . . I'm sorry but my schedule looks very tight at the moment."

"That may be, but the Pinky Delmont I knew at law school would never turn down a friend, especially if it included a free vacation in the heart of the wine country."

God! What a memory he had. During our final year at Hastings, Charles and I had discovered the wine country, and the quaint town of Healdsburg. At every opportunity we would drive seventy miles north of the Golden Gate Bridge to indulge in our newfound appreciation of great wine. From Healdsburg's central plaza, we were a short drive from winery after winery, and free samples of the best vintages.

"Charles, as you so aptly pointed out, we did not part as friends, and unlike some, I do not have the luxury of spending my precious idle hours revisiting what you call the good old days."

"Come on, Pinky, turn everything over to one of your underlings and get away for a couple of days."

"I do not have underlings as I have not yet discovered an attorney as capable as myself."

Charles chuckled. "I can see that the years haven't changed J. Pincus Delmont one iota." Then the joy faded from his voice. "Pinky, I need your help, and I need it now. How about spending a week at The Red Rose Bed and Breakfast in Healdsburg."

"Charles, that was presumptuous of you. We have not even discussed my fee."

"Once you've checked in, call me at this number and we'll meet at the Downtown Pub."

"The Downtown Pub? You know how to get to me, but I will not drive a mile west of the Nevada border until you give an idea of why I am going to all this trouble."

"Pinky, you don't understand. I'm an elected official and I am up for re-election in a few months. One of my deputies is after my job and the office is filled with spies, his and mine. At this juncture I'm leading in the polls, but if I blow my next . . . what the hell, I'm wasting my breath. You private attorneys don't have a clue of the problems I face and—"

"Charles, do not assume anything. My favorite ex-wife, Willow Stone, is the District Attorney of my county."

"Willow Stone's your ex-wife? I met her last year at a convention in Las Vegas—capable and beautiful—and I thought smart enough to avoid marrying you. What madness made you divorce a gem like her?"

I said, "Charles, I am going to ignore that last remark."

"Pinky, at Hastings you had your pick of the females. Willow proves to me that time hasn't changed your good looks."

"Thank you for your kind words. For the compliment, I offer you a final opportunity before I hang up to give me more information. Why should I drop everything and travel to California?"

"I can tell you this much. It's a matter of life or death."

"Yours, or some one else's life?"

"All the above including my political life. I can't discuss any more over the phone."

I pondered the situation for a moment. Charles was asking me for an enormous favor, especially for a man I had not spoken to in years. However, an all-expense-paid vacation to the wine country in northern California was a positive aspect. I could

11

take advantage of the opportunity to restock my wine cellar.

I said, "All right. I will check into the Red Rose and contact you."

"Bless you, Pinky."

My office door opened and Bear burst through in a fair imitation of the creature for which he was nicknamed.

"Excuse me, Charles, something has come up. I need to put you on hold for a moment."

Lu pushed past Bear. "Pinky, I'm sorry. I tried to stop him."

I hit the hold button, dismissed Lu with a wave, and demanded, "Damn it, Bear, were you raised by a pack of wolves? My departed mother, may she rest in peace, taught me to knock before entering a room."

Bear glanced over his shoulder, as if he just realized he had gone through a door. "Sorry Boss. But you told me the minute I hit Carson City I was to give you the . . . ah . . . stuff you sent us to Vegas to get. You remember? The crap me and Flo grabbed when she hacked into that—"

"Stop right there. Do not allow another word to pass between your lips."

"But Boss—"

I clapped my hands to my ears. "Cease! Just place the printout on my desk and leave. I have an important call to complete."

Bear placed a small stack of paper onto the corner of my desk.

"Is that everything? And do not respond. Just nod your head."

"Boss, there's something about this last job that bugs me. I spotted a name—"

"My boy, the names of my clients are not your concern."

"But, Boss, you told me his name was Martin. While I was taking the picture off the dude's wall, so I could get to the safe, I spotted one of those fancy nameplates, sort of like the kind you got on your desk, and the name was Macario."

"Martin, Macario, what is the difference to you?"

"Me and Flo's ass, that's the difference. The story you fed me was that you were helping some broad named Martin to get the goods on her rich husband who lived in Vegas. But if you made up that name, and the babe's real name is Macario, then me and Flo just waltzed through a mine field without a map."

"My boy, I will admit to a minuscule fabrication concerning the name of my client, but you have to understand that—"

Bear backed away from my desk as a flash of something that looked like apprehension crossed his eyes. That was unusual. In all the years I had know Bear Zabarte I had never known him to exhibit fear of any nature. "Then me and Flo did dodge the big one in Vegas. Boss, Alberto Macario is not the kind of dude people clip stuff from, especially his financial records."

"But I required those records so I can correctly identify the man's true assets. Now if you are concerned about your safety, I can assure you—"

"Hey, once my truck cleared the city limits of Vegas, me and Flo were scot-free. You're the one who's now lined up in Macario's sights. Sooner or later, he'll figure out the name of his wife's attorney and once he finds out you've got the goods on him, your ass will be grass, and trust me, that dude has a garage full of power mowers."

The hair on the back of my neck tingled at Bear's description of my possible future, but the huge retainer from the lovely Elena Macario consisted of more than money and made the risk acceptable. "In case you didn't notice, I was on the phone when you burst into my office. If you are through, remove yourself at once."

"Okay, just as long as you know that your ass is hanging out there in the wind."

"Out! I have a phone call to complete."

"One more thing. I promised Flo that I'd tell you that she was the one who figured out where the dude had hidden all this crap. The stuff was on his computer in something she called a procrypted file."

"I am reasonably certain that the proper word is encrypted."

"Whatever. I don't have a clue how she knows where to look, but she finds the procrypted stuff every time."

While Bear rattled on I mentally considered what he had told me concerning Elena Macario's husband. But what he did not understand was that Elena was both beautiful and rich, a rare and irresistible combination in a woman.

"Boss, me and Flo make a great team. Remember when we were in LA? Shit, I got us into that bean counter's office but it was Flo who found the secret files in the computer. And that reminds me, Flo told me to tell you—"

"My good man, I am not the least bit interested in what that woman has to say. Now clear out! I have an extremely important caller placed on hold."

"But Boss, you don't understand. Flo's really pissed off and if you don't talk to her real soon she'll get more pissed off. She wants you to know that the computer work she did this time was the last job you're getting for free. From now on, she gets paid for her work or no more procrypted stuff."

14

Once again, the tiny carpenter's hammer began to hit those nails in that area behind my eyes. "Get out of my office and stop calling me boss."

"Okay, Boss. I'll tell Flo that you agreed to think about paying her. See you later."

The thumping behind my eyes grew to an unacceptable level. "I have not agreed to consider any sort of compensation for that woman." My office door slammed shut.

I required an investigator with the physical appearance of Bear Zabarte. The man was big, strong, fearless, and possessed the obligatory low standards needed for investigative work. However, he lacked basic computer knowledge, and in this age, computer savvy was an essential attribute for an investigator. Then there was his girlfriend, Flo. Other than her over-developed mammary glands, and her witch-like disposition, she contributed nothing except her skills with computers. When I first met the woman I could not abide her and my opinion of her had not changed. But she did fill in some of the gaping chasms in Bear's knowledge and that was something to consider in the future. For the present, I had to complete an interesting, and a potentially lucrative discussion with Charles. I slipped the Macario printout into my briefcase and tapped the button to reconnect Charles.

"Charles, I apologize for the interruption but as I told you, my practice is a one-man operation, and as such, my input is needed on a regular basis. Now, for a concluding word on the subject of my generous offer to help you out, I have one full-time investigator on my payroll. His name is Bear Zabarte. Mr. Zabarte has killed one man that I am aware of, but so far, I have been able to maintain control by keeping him on a short leash. However, if I discover

15

you have exaggerated your present situation, in any way, I will be forced to turn Mr. Zabarte loose to resolve any misunderstandings you may have given me during this phone call."

"Pinky, it's truly amazing how little you've changed during all these years. Call me as soon as you've checked in."

TWO

Pinky-Carson City, Nevada

I buzzed Lu and sat back to evoke the fond memories of my nights at the Downtown Pub. Since my move to Carson City, my taste for the brewpub life has diminished for two reasons. First, Carson City does not possess a decent brewpub. Second, my lifestyle has modified somewhat since my college days. Those evenings during my misspent youth were passed with friends and fellow students, arguing over a pint of IPA. Today, I look forward to a quiet evening by the fire with a great book and a glass of world-class cabernet. The reason for my self-imposed isolation? I assume it is the result of maturation along with my commitment to represent the downtrodden. My profession has caused me to become insular due to the lack of idle time required to cultivate—

Lu knocked first and then entered my office.

I said, "I have to leave town immediately due to the sudden illness of an old college friend in California. The poor soul is on his deathbed and has asked me to help him slip from this mortal coil to whatever lies beyond. Contact the court clerk and have him postpone all my cases for a week."

Lu blinked. "A week. That could be difficult. The last time—"

"My dear, inventing new and interesting ways

17

to adjust my court calendar is one of the reasons I pay you so well. Any further comments?"

She shook her head and left my office.

I had spent a few moments reviewing my calendar when Lu buzzed me. "Willow is on line one."

"Willow my darling. All I have to do is close my eyes and your beautiful—"

"Cut the crap. What the hell are you trying to pull this time?"

"Pull? My dear, I do not have any idea what—"

"The Puzzo trial, damn it. I was just informed that your girl, Lu, called the court and requested a postponement."

News does travel quickly these days. "That is correct. I just received tragic news concerning a fellow Hastings graduate, perhaps you know him, Charles H Godwin, the Sonoma County District Attorney. He called and begged me to travel to northern California. He requires my immediate assistance in a delicate life and death situation that I cannot discuss any further."

Willow said, "Yes, I recall meeting Charles at a conference a year ago. What do you mean you can't discuss the situation? Is he ill?"

"As I told you, I cannot answer your question. What I can say is that Charles, my old school chum, and friend, needs me, and his needs are immediate. "

"Pinky, I apologize. Here you are, consoling a friend in an obvious time of need and I jumped all over you. I'll talk with the judge and I'm sure he'll move out the Puzzo trial a couple of days."

"My sweet, could you make that two weeks? You never can tell how fast or slow these things move. I've heard of a few similar cases taking a month before the end came."

"Four days are the best I can offer. And you take

care of yourself."

"He could linger. Perhaps ten days?"

"Okay, a week."

"Thank you my love. I owe you a dinner when I return."

I buzzed Lu and pulled out the Las Vegas paperwork I had placed in my briefcase.

After scanning through a few pages I realized that Lu had not knocked on my office door in response to my command. I jumped up and walked into the front office. Lu was sitting at her desk crying softly.

I walked to her side. "Lu, what is wrong?"

"My father . . . the nursing home called . . . it's . . . he . . . he's—"

It was not like Lu to stutter. She was deeply upset.

"Deceased?"

"Yes."

"My condolences. Sorry for your loss."

"Pinky, I don't know what to do next."

"I'll call Bear. He will take care of everything."

"But he's so big. He scares me a little."

"Not to worry. The man is all bark and no bite. Now, I will call him and you sit here and wait for him. Once I place my call to Bear, I will stop by my house, pack a few things, and leave for California."

Lu nodded. "I'll do what you say."

I returned to my office and called Bear.

A few moments later, with all the loose ends tied up, I returned home, filled my suitcase with casual clothing, and by noon I was cruising through Sacramento in my bright red, 400 horsepower, 4.4-liter V-8, 550i Gran Turismo BMW. I could not wait to show Charles my car and watch him turn green with envy. Without question, even he would have to admit that a civil servant would never be able to afford to buy a sixty-five thousand dollar vehicle.

THREE

Bear Zabarte-Carson City, Nevada

Me and Flo were in my Pickup heading back down highway fifty to our apartment, and just like I told Pinky, Flo was pissed and all over me, like flies on a ripe road apple.

"So what exactly did Pinky say about paying me?"

"I don't remember exactly. Something like he'd think about it. Flo, we've got to talk about something else. Pinky forgot—"

"Not interested."

"Hey, cut me some slack. You remember that office in Vegas where I opened the safe, you figured out the secret code, and printed out those files?"

"Of course I do. What does that have—"

"It has to do with Pinky and some babe who wants a divorce."

"What's a divorce got to do with our Vegas trip?"

"The babe's name is Elena Macario."

"So?"

"Her husband is Alberto Macario."

Flo's mouth stopped flapping for a minute while she thought over that name. "Isn't that the name of one of those big-time mobsters?"

"Yup."

"Hold on! You're not telling me that the computer I hacked into belonged to—"

"Yup."

21

"Oh my God! Are we in any danger?"

"I don't think so, but if I was Pinky, I'd hire a stupid dude to start my car for a couple of months."

"Does Pinky know he's in danger?"

"Sort of, but the little bastard lives in some kind of world where he thinks he can outrun a bullet."

Flo sat back and stared out the window for a second. "Okay, enough about Vegas. Just how much is Pinky going to pay me for my computer work?"

"He told me he'd think about it."

"Think about it! That's it? You turn this truck around. It's about time I looked that little pipsqueak in the eye and told him what—"

My cell phone buzzed. Saved by the bell! "Hello."

"Bear, I have a situation in my office that requires your immediate attention."

"I just left. What's up?"

Flo poked me in the side and said, "Is that Pinky?"

I nodded.

Flo grabbed for the phone. "Bear, let me have that phone! I'm going to settle this pay question right now."

I held the steering wheel with my knees and blocked Flo with my elbow while Pinky said, "A problem concerning Lu."

"What'd she do?"

Pinky said, "Nothing! Cease your incessant interruptions and listen to me."

I elbowed Flo back to her side of the truck. "Sure."

With one eye on the road and the other on Flo I switched the phone to my left hand while I kept the truck between the lines with my knees.

Pinky said, "A few minutes ago Lu received a phone call informing her that her father had passed away."

"Jeez, that's tough."

"I told you to stop interrupting me."

"Okay. Go ahead, Boss."

"Return to my office and drive Lu to the nursing home where her father's earthly remains await her arrival."

Flo got tired of trying to get the phone so she grabbed the steering wheel. The pick-up jumped to the right and I damn near wacked a dude getting out of his UPS truck.

She screamed into my right ear, "Damn it, give me that phone."

Pinky yelled into the phone, "What was that noise?"

"Nothing. Hey, Lu works for you. Why don't you take her?"

"Because I make the decisions here."

"Oh."

I couldn't peel Flo's fingers off the steering wheel so I put my big paw on top of her hand, cranked the wheel, and forced the truck back into my lane.

Pinky said, "My good man, I pay you an enormous sum to do my bidding, and at the moment, that means accompanying my bereaved secretary to her departed father's side."

"Hey, we both know you pay me big bucks, but that's for doing important and dangerous shit, not driving your secretary somewhere to look at a stiff."

Pinky rattled on and on about my job duties, like I never heard that crap before. But he had me between a rock and a hard spot, and the bastard knew it. Working for him was a pain in the ass, but he paid me more than twice what I'd get mopping up barf off the floor at The Old Globe Saloon, where I used to work, and that was enough for me.

I barked, "Okay. We're on our way back to your office."

Flo let go of the steering wheel and smiled. "It's about time you listened to me. I'm ready to confront that little pipsqueak. He's used my computer expertise for the last time for free. Next time I will charge him . . . hey, how much should I charge Pinky for—"

"Flo, we're not heading back to the office to talk to Pinky. Lu's Pop kicked the bucket and I've got to drive her to the nursing home so she can look at him."

"Oh my God, that's terrible. Hurry up, she'll need to talk to me."

"But she's suppose to talk to me."

Flo grabbed her purse and shook her head. "She'll want to talk with another female."

"Oh."

I had figured out a while ago that living with Flo was no piece of cake. The broad, when she was naked, was a lot of fun. But other times, like now, she could be real pain.

We arrived at Pinky's office and as we walked through the front door Flo pushed me to the side, threw her arms wide open, and headed straight to Lu's desk. "Lu, I'm Flo, Bear's friend. What you need now is a big hug."

While the two blubbered on each other's shoulders I peeked inside Pinky's office. Thank God, the little creep was gone. Two crying broads were about all I could handle for the rest of the day.

Finally Flo stopped hugging Lu and said, "It's time we go to the nursing home. I've been through all this before. First you'll want to say good-bye to your father. Then we need to take care of the

24

arrangements. Do you have any other family in town?"

"No, just my father and myself. My parents and I lived in Reno while I attended the University of Nevada. After my mother died, my father started to fail, and when he became more than I could handle I found that Carson City had the best places for him to live, and that we could afford."

Flo said, "I understand. Lu, we're your family now, and we'll help you take care of all the details. From now on you call me if you need a shoulder to cry on. Bear will take care of all the heavy lifting, understand?"

Lu started to cry, and before I knew it they were both sobbing away again.

While I pushed both of them toward my pickup, I thought how weird it was that Flo could be so nice to a Chinese broad she didn't even know, and sometimes so nasty to me, the guy who paid her rent. My Pop had warned me that when he married my Mom he had found the last perfect woman in the world. At the time I thought he was just blowing smoke, but lately, I'd begun to think that he could have dished me the straight scoop.

FOUR

Pinky-Healdsburg, California

While I drove my car down Center Street, close to Healdsburg's central plaza, I was reminded that some memories from one's youth are worth a revisit. As a starving student, I would occasionally pass by the Red Rose B & B and dream of the day that I would be able to afford to spend the night in what looked to be absolute luxury. Today, thanks to the generosity of the District Attorney's office, I would achieve my goal.

A short female minion who had smeared a deep red gloss across her lips greeted me at the door. "Can I help you?"

"J. Pinkus Delmont. I have a reservation."

She gave me a perfunctory nod causing her obviously dyed-black hair to bounce about her furrowed face, picked up a clipboard and I watched her fingers walk past a list of names. "Right here," her fingernail pounded a name on the list. "A single reserved under the name of Delmont. Oh, you're one of those."

The woman's insipid expression tumbled into disgust. "Mind you, I don't have anything against all you government folks, but the last time we had a county worker stay here, Albert was forced to make a dozen phone calls to track down the person in the county government who was responsible for the payment."

She opened the door wider and I walked into a beautiful entry hall. In front of me was a carpeted stairway. To my left, a dining area, to my right, a sitting room with marble topped tables. The furnishings looked antique but seemed fully functional.

She swept her hand and arm to the right, as if she was granting me access to a magical land. "Welcome, Mr. Delmont. Are you visiting Healdsburg on business or pleasure?"

By that point I had taken more than I could stomach from the female. I raised myself to full stature. "Madam, I would have addressed you properly if you had extended me the courtesy of providing me a name. However, since you have not introduced yourself, I will continue to use madam, an accepted form of respectful or polite address to all females. Madam, rest assured that I am not, nor will I ever be, an employee of any governmental organization. Next, my reason for spending time in this area is none of your business. Now, assuming we have completed all of the preliminaries, show me to my room. "

Her penciled-in black eyebrows arched and her open mouth informed me that she realized she was dealing with a man who demanded deference. "Follow me."

We walked past a second woman, obviously a maid, who was pushing a vacuum across the sitting room, and made our way up a flight of stairs to my room.

"Mr. Delmont, your room, one of our finest accommodations, is named for Cyrus Alexander, the pioneer who built his home in an area a few miles northeast of where you stand. The Alexander Valley now bears his name, and produces many of the world's finest wines."

A perfunctory glance informed me the room was tastefully decorated in a manner I fully expected for one of the more expensive tourist destinations in the wine country.

She handed me a room key. "Please remember that I am here to answer any question you might have concerning the—"

"Thank you. That will be all."

With a second look of aversion, she stormed out and slammed the door behind her.

Before I had completed unpacking, I heard a light knock on my door. I opened it and stared at the head of a totally bald man. He had no hair, no eyebrows, and from my close view, no visible beard. A classic case of alopecia!

"Mr. Delmont, I stopped by to apologize for not greeting you with my sister, Agatha." His razor-thin lips twisted into a shape that oscillated between a smile and a grimace. "Let me welcome you to your home away from home in the heart of the wine country. My name is Albert Bliss. I am the proprietor of The Red Rose."

"Thank you, Mr. Bliss. Now if you will excuse—"

"Pardon my interruption, but there are a few items of vital information that I feel every guest requires to make their stay at the Red Rose comfortable. We serve breakfast in the dining room between seven and ten each morning. At five in the afternoon, wine and cheese are available for your pleasure in the sitting room. And for the pièce de résistance, at eight each evening, we offer homemade desserts, coffees and teas in the library. Are you here on business, or to tour the wineries?"

"Before I respond your inquiry, Mr. Bliss, you

and I need to establish a few ground rules. First, I do not suffer being interrupted while I speak, so in the future, wait until I have completed my sentence. Now, to answer your final question, I see no reason to inform you, or your sister, as to my reasons for spending a few days in Healdsburg."

"But Mr. Delmont, you don't understand. I am here to assist you in all your endeavors. You can count on me if you have any questions concerning the best local restaurants, points of interest, or maps to the many wineries, please—"

"Mr. Bliss, as I previously indicated, my reasons for visiting your charming village are mine, and mine alone. I have just completed a five-hour trip in my car and need to take care of an urgent bodily function. Now, short of being evacuated due to a fire, I expect to be left alone until breakfast. Do I make myself clear?"

Mr. Bliss' expression was one of mild shock, as if he had not been set straight by a guest for at least a decade.

"Mr. Delmont, please accept my sincerest apology. I will be in my office, the room opposite the dining room, if you have any further needs or questions."

The hairless innkeeper scurried away and left me alone to complete my personal tasks.

An hour later I walked through the door of the Downtown Pub. Before my eyes became accustomed to the dim light within, my nose told me that nothing inside this establishment had changed since my last visit. The air consisted of a curious combination of cooked cereal, stale beer, and that staple of pub snacks, French-fried everything. I scanned the room and Charles was nowhere in sight. I sat down at one of the few empty tables.

While I concentrated on the menu of available brews, a sensuous female voice asked, "Can I get you something?"

Even in the low light of the room, the figure standing to my right exuded the full flush of femininity. The top of her head was covered with a straw hat that had been spray-painted aqua and beneath the hat hung blonde pigtails that flowed down to her shoulders. Her face was an impish, girl next-door cute. Wrapped around her more than ample upper torso was a clinging, peach colored cloth that somehow merged into the same colored leggings. Around her neck she wore a long aqua scarf. Frankly, she dressed like an old-fashioned "hippie" who had been updated through modern dress. But hippie or not, I could not take my eyes off of her.

I said, "Ah . . . not right now. I am waiting for someone."

"My name is Arianna. Just give me a wave and I'll come running cause I think you're kind of cute."

I was mulling over what she meant by 'kind of cute' when Charles walked in. I regret to report that unlike myself, he had not successfully endured the passing years. His once-handsome face had widened but his waistline had won the race of expansion. I stood, and when he reached my table, we had one of those awkward male moments when we were not sure if we should shake hands or cautiously attempt a hug. As I abhor direct male bodily contact of any sort, I solved the dilemma by thrusting my right hand in his direction.

"Pinky, you don't look as if you have aged a day. Have you made some sort of a pact with the devil?"

"Charles, I would like to offer you the same compliment, but I am positive that it is just as obvious to you as it is to me that all of your growth has not been intellectual."

"Same old Pinky." He shook his head. "How about I buy you a pint of Berger Brown, for old time's sake?"

I had tasted a multitude of beers and ales since my college days, and nothing had ever come close to a Berger Brown, poured directly from the tap at the Downtown Pub. "Sounds excellent." I waved to Arianna. "Two pints of Berger Brown."

"You've got it, cutie."

Charles and I both focused on the gyration beneath Arianna's tight pants as she walked toward the bar.

"Pinky, that makes me wish I was young and single again."

"I feel the same way, and it just so happens that I am single. Now, tell me why I had to travel all this way."

"Are you familiar with the name, Paul—" Charles stopped when Arianna reached our table with tray in hand. He handed her a twenty and as soon as she left, he finished, "Paul Hellman?"

"Charles, earlier, on the phone, you stated you were afraid to talk because you were concerned about office spies and phone taps. Does your fear extend all the way to a lovely blonde serving a libation at the Downtown Pub? If so, your present state of paranoia is greater than I had thought."

"I'm sorry. I guess I'm just a little jumpy."

I took a sip of the beer and was overjoyed to discover that the years had not diminished my favorite brew. "Fine. Now, back to your question concerning the name, Paul Hellman. Of course I know that name. He is the winemaker at St. James Winery who each year crafts one of the world's greatest cabernets."

"Was the winemaker. The purple corpse in the photo was Paul Hellman after he had floated for hours, head down, inside a tank of cabernet sauvignon."

I set my glass down. "Paul Hellman is, no, was a winemaking artist. I have twelve cases of the St. James Bench Land Cabernet slumbering in my cellar as we speak. I find it hard to believe I missed the news of Hellman's death. But then, Carson City, Nevada, is not the center of wine news. The production of that Bench Land-designated cab is very, very limited and is only sold to a list of charter members of their exclusive St. James Club Cabernet."

"And you're a charter member?"

"In good standing of course, but Hellman's death changes everything."

"What do you mean?"

"Wine making is an art form and in the world of cabernet Paul Hellman was a Picasso." The news of Hellman's death had depressed me a touch, so I took a large sip of beer. "There is no guarantee that the next winemaker at St. James will be up to the task." I drained my glass. "Charles, up to this point the beer is excellent and your story is interesting. However, other than learning that I will be cautious concerning my next wine purchase from the St. James Club Cabernet, the reason for my visit remains elusive."

I waved and Arianna appeared at my side. "Two more, my dear."

"I'll be right back, cutie."

Charles sipped his beer. "I shouldn't have a second. I have to get back to work."

I laughed, "Then I will be forced to finish both pints. Please continue with your story."

"Months ago, the night of the murder a young Hispanic cellar worker named Enrique Flores was working at the winery. The following day he was arrested for Hellman's death and goes on trial for murder one in a few days." Charles downed the rest of the brew. "And . . ."

"And what, Charles?"

"Frankly, I'm not convinced Flores committed the crime!"

"My good man, you are the District Attorney. If you feel the evidence does not merit a trial then set the man free."

"I wish my life was that easy. In this area winemaking is a religion, and Hellman was a high priest. Also, he was white. In the minds of many voters in this county, a Hispanic accused of murdering a white man is guilty until proven innocent."

"So it comes down to your personal preservation. If you let the Mexican go—you could lose some of the white support and be voted out of office. Am I correct in my assumption?"

Charles sighed. "Yes."

I said, "All right, let us cut to the chase. What exactly do you think I can do?"

He said, "I've heard of your exploits in Nevada—more than twenty murder trials without a loss. I could use some of your magic arrows in my quiver."

Arianna appeared and placed two full pint glasses on our table. "Thank you, my dear. That will be all for the moment." I hesitated until Arianna was out of earshot and said, "My good man, we are faced with two predicaments concerning your present train of thought. First and foremost, my retainer for a client accused of murder begins at sixty-five thousand dollars and all that would buy your man

33

would be some sort of plea bargain. If I mounted a full-blown defense the cost could set the Mexican lad back five hundred thousand, and that is the ground floor. Occasionally, my fees and expenses will reach a million, or higher. As I recall, you told me the accused worked in the cellar."

"You are correct."

"And that means he clears in the neighborhood of twenty thousand a year?"

"Around that figure would be right."

I lifted my glass and sipped the wonderful brew. "So who will pay my fee?"

"I will."

"Charles, I know that California is the land of milk and honey, but we both know you cannot afford to hand me half a million dollars."

"I agree with your assessment. But I have a person with deep pockets—someone who can afford to pay your retainer and more."

"That is encouraging. Now to my second quandary. I have never attempted to pass the California bar, and as such, I am not allowed to practice law in the Golden State."

"I understand that, but you could act as an interested party of the accused who desires to right a grievous wrong. That way, any money you receive for your time and expenses should not create a legal, or an ethical, conundrum for my office."

I sat back and considered Charles' proposal. Except for the Puzzo trial, my present caseload was light. If an accused required the best legal mind available, and there were sufficient funds to properly compensate me, I could see no rational reason to turn down his request. "Fine. Under those circumstances I accept. However, I need to make one final item perfectly clear. Before I do anything on the lad's behalf, I will require a deposit of five hundred thousand dollars into the bank of my choosing, along with the understanding that there is no guarantee that I will be able to extricate . . . what was the accused's first name again?"

"Enrique."

"I cannot guarantee that even I will be able to extricate the aforementioned Enrique Flores from his present incarceration."

Charles reached into his breast pocket and pulled out a card. "That's all anyone could ask. Here is the name of the man who will cover your retainer."

I glanced at card. "Before I talk with this man I think a visit to the St. James Winery, to view the site of the murder, would be in order."

Charles leaned forward and whispered, "Considering my tenuous position, don't say another word. What happens from this moment on must remain between you and the man named on the card. Under no circumstances can my name, or my office, be connected with anything you do."

"Then who will pay my bill at the Red Rose?"

"Tell the proprietor to send the bill to my office. Why?"

"Would not the bill tip off your office spy that something was going on?"

Deep creases twisted their way across my old friend's forehead. "I hadn't thought about that."

"Not to worry. I will have the bill sent to the name on this card."

"Pinky, you're a genius."

"I know that. Now, considering this could be our last opportunity to talk over old times for another twenty years, would you care to consume your second round of Berger Brown?"

"No, thanks. I have to get back to my office."

35

"Charles, during this clandestine affair I might need to contact you. Do you have a cell number?"

"Of course. I should have thought of that."

"Do you often receive cell phone calls at your office?"

Charles paused, as if trying to figure out where I was going. "No, not often."

"I have an idea. If I feel the need to contact you I will call your office, inform the person who answers the phone that my name is Padriag Murphy, and leave a message to call me. I'll leave my cell phone number and you can call me when the coast is clear, so to speak."

Charles jumped up. "As I said, you're a genius. Got to go now." He sprinted out of the pub as if a tsunami loomed in the distance.

I waved in the general direction of Arianna. She said, "Can I get you another Berger Brown?"

"No thank you, but I could use some information."

"Fire away."

"My dear, what time is your shift over?"

She twirled one of her pigtails for a moment, as if she did not know where my line of question was headed. "Eight o'clock. Why?"

"I am offering to take you out for a gourmet dining experience at the restaurant of your choice."

She glanced at the bar where a large man with a full black beard, a nose ring, and arms the size of beer kegs glared at her. "I don't think so. You could eat here. They've got some great pub food. You know, burgers, onion rings, fries, and the hottest Buffalo wings in town. The food's a little greasy, but everything tastes super great."

"I think I'll pass on that offer."

Arianna smiled. "What's your name?"

"J. Pincus Delmont, but my friends call me Pinky."

"Pinky? That's a cute name."

"Arianna, I am truly sorry that I will dine alone. Could you suggest the best establishment?"

"If you gave me my choice, I'd go to the Plaza Bistro, but it'll cost you a bundle because of the linen people."

"Would you be so kind as to define a linen person for me?"

"You know, the tourists that wander around town wearing those fancy duds. They all have tons of money so all the good joints charge a bunch of bucks."

Her response made me ponder what the locals wore. But a cursory glance at my server reminded me that any outfit was possible in Northern California. "Allow me to reiterate my offer. Can we meet tonight, eight o'clock, at the Plaza Bistro?"

"Arianna," The big man behind the bar yelled, "Get your shapely butt over here."

She leaned toward me. Her taut nipples pressed hard against the thin fabric wall that fought to restrain them. "Sorry, Pinky, I don't think Thor wants me to talk to you anymore. Bye now."

FIVE

Pinky-Healdsburg, California

I found a tattered phone directory hanging by the public phone at the Pub, looked up the number for the St. James Winery and placed a call.

"St. James Winery. Home of the world famous Bench-Land Cabernet Sauvignon."

"Good morning. My name is J. Pinkus Delmont. I wish to speak with Martin St. James."

"Mr. Delmont, I'm sorry, but Mr. St. James is unavailable at the moment. May I pass on the reason for your call?"

"My dear, as a charter member of Club Cabernet I feel it is about time I met Mr. St. James and toured his winery."

"Please understand, Mr. Delmont, we do not offer public tours, but as a charter member of the club you do receive special privileges. I will pass on your request to the Club Cabernet coordinator and ask her to return your call."

"But according to the information your winery sent me concerning my charter membership some twenty years ago, the special privileges, to use your words, were a winery tour, and some barrel samples from future vintages."

"I'll pass your concerns to the Club Coordinator."

I gave her my cell number and hung up.

I wasn't sure what I could possibly discover during a short visit to the winery, but I had an obligation to Charles to at least visit the site of the murder before I returned to Carson City.

My cell buzzed.

"Hello."

"Mr. Delmont, our club coordinator asked me to inform you that the winery no longer does tours for charter members, and due to circumstances beyond her control, she will be unable to accommodate your request for a barrel sample today."

"That is dreadful news."

"I apologize but—"

Allowing a touch of anger to enter my tone, I said, "As a valued client of St. James Winery, a man who has purchased more than twenty-five cases of your Bench-Land Cabernet, I find it inconceivable that someone at the winery cannot accommodate my request for a barrel sample."

"One moment, please."

The muffled voices I detected informed me that the phone minion was discussing my request with someone close by.

"Mr. Delmont, I have just been informed that the coordinator is leaving on an east coast public relations trip this afternoon. If you can arrive within the hour she will meet with you for a short period. Will you be able to make it here in time?"

"I will leave immediately and arrive at the winery as soon as possible."

"Fine. When you turn into the winery follow the left fork to the main winery building."

"And where does the right fork go?"

"Ah . . . the right fork goes up the hill to the St. James home."

"Thank you, my dear. I will be at the winery in

thirty minutes."

I jumped into my car and drove north.

The Alexander Valley was as beautiful as I remembered—grassy hills to the east and oak studded knolls to the west. In between there were ten to twelve miles of vineyards that marched in symmetrical patterns toward the Russian River that bisected the valley floor.

As estimated, I passed through the St. James Winery gate in less than a half hour, followed the road and prior to taking the left fork as instructed, I paused and noted the opulent home at the top of the hill. A hundred yards later I parked my vehicle in front of a large wooden structure. As I killed the engine, a man whose physical stature was close to Bear's approached my car.

"Mr. Delmont, I'm Luciano Botarri, the cellar master here at St. James and I'm pleased to meet you. Please follow me."

He opened the door and we entered a small space. On my left I glanced through an open door into an empty office with two desks and a few file cabinets. Before I could shift my view from the vacant office a delicate jasmine-based perfume hit my nostrils. As I turned in the direction of the perfume, Luciano said, "Florianna, I would like to introduce you to Mr. Delmont, a charter member of Club Cabernet."

She faced me and my heart literally skipped a beat. For a brief moment I thought the woman standing before me was Arianna, but as I viewed her more closely I realized it was not she. The woman Luciano introduced to me had Arianna's classic face, but her makeup was under-stated. She had Arianna's blonde hair but each strand was styled in a business-like way. She had Arianna's perfect

40

breasts, but they were trapped inside a tailored silk blouse. She had Arianna's shapely body, but those hips were covered in a light-gray worsted business suit.

She smiled. "How do you do, Mr. Delmont? My name is Florianna. Come with me. Luciano, our cellar master, and I, will provide you with the exclusive charter member barrel tasting from the three latest vintages of the world's greatest cabernet sauvignon."

"Thank you, but before we do the barrel samples, I look forward to meeting your winemaker, Paul Hellman. I am curious to learn how he seems to be the only man in the world who can accomplish what he does year after year. Will he meet us in the barrel room?"

Both of them recoiled, then Florianna said, "I wish that we could all ask Paul that question."

"I am sorry. I do not understand."

The woman struggled to hold back any emotion from her expression. "Paul Hellman, our esteemed winemaker, is dead. He was murdered!"

"Oh my God. That's terrible. Ah . . . I am not sure how to broach the subject, but how could you ever hope to find another winemaker with the talent he had?"

"At this point, we're not sure."

"Please accept my condolences concerning your irreplaceable loss."

Her emotional reaction to my request to talk with Paul Hellman seemed genuine, but it seemed to me that her grief vanished too quickly. Or had the passage of time allowed her to put the shock of Paul's murder behind her. I said, "I am curious. How did you get into the wine business?"

She shook her head. "My story is very dull. I'm

41

sure you'd be more interested in how our owner, Martin St. James, got into the wine business. Thirty years ago Martin started the winery. Twenty-five years ago he planted the special Cabernet Sauvignon clone in the Bench-Land section, the vineyard situated on flat land above a creek. A few years later Martin hired Paul Hellman." She lowered her voice and hissed. "Now that goddamn Mexican has murdered him." As quick as her smile had disappeared it returned. "This afternoon I'm flying to the east coast to promote the St. James brand. Public relations used to be one aspect of Paul's job, but now that task is mine." She glanced at her watch. "I'm running late. Did you still want a barrel sample?"

"Yes, but one last question before we start. I was hoping to ask Paul if it was the grapes, or the winemaker, that make an outstanding wine."

"Mr. Delmont, you have asked the question of the ages. First, you must start with a perfect cluster of fruit, along the lines of the old saying you can't make a silk purse out of a sow's ear. However, a poor winemaker can ruin an outstanding crop of grapes."

"I see. By the way, in the future, I would appreciate it if you would address me as Pinky. My full name is J. Pinkus Delmont, so as you can see, my nickname Pinky fits."

Florianna did not respond to my attempt to promote a closer level of intimacy between us. "Now, if you will excuse me, I have to leave. For the barrel samples I will turn you over to Luciano. He will pour you samples from each of the last three vintages of the Bench-Land section."

"Was that the Bench-Land section I passed when I drove in?"

She hesitated for what seemed to be longer than I would have expected, then shrugged. "No. Those are cabernet vines but not the Bench-Land section."

I said, "Where is the Bench-Land section?"

"In an area near the west border of the property. The vineyard is not accessible to the public. Mr. Delmont, I took the liberty of reviewing our sales records and noted that you have purchased a case of the Bench-Land cab every year for the past twenty-two years. And every year, attached to your order form, you have included a note requesting that we increase your allotment. The amount of wine allotted to each customer is based on the amount of wine we can make and that is predicated on the amount of grapes we pick. I tell you this so you'll understand that my hands are tied, so to speak, concerning an increase in your existing allotment. Reguardless, I am happy to meet with a charter member of Club Cabernet. Luciano, will you escort Mr. Delmont to the barrel room."

I was pondering why the Bench-Land vineyard was hidden away from public view when Luciano grabbed my right arm and steered me across the room.

"And after the barrel sample I trust Luciano will take me on a tour the winery." My male escort stopped and looked back at Florianna.

She said, "I'm sorry but that's not possible. Except for this room, the office, and the barrel room, all remaining areas of the winery are closed to visitors."

I considered pursuing the near paranoia concerning visitors in the winery but decided to drop it for now. "Luciano, what does a cellar master do?"

He laughed, "You need to ask Florianna. She'd tell you I'd give you an overblown description."

Florianna said, "Luciano's a good cellar master, and loyal, but no matter what he says he'll never

43

replace Paul Hellman."

I took a long look at Florianna. She was beautiful to a fault and obviously better educated than Arianna. However, she had a spitefulness about her that Arianna seemed to lack. I directed my next question to Luciano. "Have you asked to be considered for the position of winemaker?"

Florianna butted in before Luciano had the chance to answer. "Yes he has, but he'll never do. I've tasted some of his sample wines and everything he makes is heavy-handed—too bold—the man has no concept of subtlety."

"He makes wine? I thought you said Luciano was your cellar master?"

Florianna said, "Mr. Delmont, you need to understand that every man, woman, and child in Alexander Valley makes a barrel or two of wine. In my opinion, Luciano's wines don't measure up to the high standards laid down by Paul Hellman."

Luciano cried out. "That's not fair. I didn't have access to the same quality of grapes that Paul had."

Florianna shook her head. "I'm afraid I haven't made myself clear. Mr. Delmont, there are the technical aspects of winemaking. Some would call it the janitorial details—keep the winery clean—get rid of bad barrels, that sort of mundane work. Luciano has that part of winemaking down. However, the rest of making a great wine is an art. Trust me, Paul Hellman was the Michelangelo of winemaking."

"Has the winery advertised for a replacement?"

"Of course. Excuse me, but I have to leave now. Luciano, offer Mr. Delmont his barrel samples, answer any questions, and then escort him back to his car."

I said, "Is there a reason that the Bench-Land section is closed to the public?"

Florianna blinked, then she said, "Yes! The Bench-Land vines are so valuable that we cannot take any risks of contaminating the vines by the public—I'm sure you understand. Luciano, after you finish the barrel sample tasting, please follow Mr. Delmont's vehicle to the highway, just to be sure he doesn't get lost."

After a few barrel samples of the excellent Bench-Land cabernet, I drove my car away from the main winery building. As I passed the fork I took my foot off the gas, to get a better look at the house atop the hill. Luciano, following behind me, honked his horn, so I drove onto the county road with my head buzzing with questions.

Later that evening I dined alone at the Plaza Bistro and as Arianna promised, the experience was outstanding. The food titillated my taste buds and the wine exceeded my expectations. All I missed was a date—a properly frocked Arianna—to make the evening perfect. As I walked back to my room I considered my curious visit to the St. James Winery. Although I had failed to visit the murder site, there was something about the demeanor of Florianna and Luciano that demanded further investigation.

SIX

Pinky-Healdsburg, California

The following morning, after an outstanding breakfast of fresh fruit, a spinach frittata, and homemade banana-nut bread, I returned to my room and called Bennett Hamilton, the name on the card that Charles had given me.

A female voice said, "Law offices of Hamilton, Berman, Berman, and Churchill."

"My name is Delmont and I would like to speak with Mr. Hamilton."

"Good morning, Mr. Delmont. Mr. Hamilton's been waiting for your call. I'll put you right through."

After a moment a male voice said, "Mr. Delmont, Charles told me he gave you my card. Thank you for being so prompt."

"No thanks are necessary. Business is business. Now, before we discuss your situation, there is the matter of the retainer for my investigative time."

"I understand. Charles informed me that I would have to transfer five hundred thousand into the bank of your choice."

I gave Hamilton my bank information.

He said, "Everything looks in order. I will instruct my banker to make the wire transfer. The transaction shouldn't take more than a few minutes."

"Excellent. I will call my bank, and once the transfer has been completed, I will call you back."

"Mr. Delmont, perhaps we could continue our discussion over lunch. That might create a more collegial atmosphere."

"An excellent idea. Meet me under the gazebo in the Healdsburg Plaza tomorrow afternoon at one."

There was a pause, and then Hamilton said, "It is nearly eleven. Is there a reason we cannot meet today?"

My cell beeped indicating I had a call waiting. "Mr. Hamilton, I have another call. Give me a moment."

I pushed a button. "Hello?"

"Pinky I have to talk to you." The caller was Lu and she never interrupted me unless there was an emergency. "I need—"

"Lu, as we speak, five hundred thousand dollars are being transferred to my bank account. I have no reason to assume that the gentleman I am dealing with is untrustworthy, but neither am I foolhardy. Call my bank manager and find out if the transfer has been completed then call me back."

"Hold on a minute, I called you. I need to take a—"

"Lu, you will have to excuse me. I am extremely busy at the moment. Good-bye."

"DON'T YOU DARE HANG UP ON ME."

What had happened to my inscrutable Asian secretary? It was not like Lu to raise her voice. "My dear, what is wrong?"

"I'm attempting to complete the final instructions given to me by my father before he died."

I glanced at my watch. This discussion was distracting from my valuable time but I was three hundred miles from home and could not afford to upset Lu, as she was the only representative in my office. "And what did the document say?"

"First, my father requested his body be immediately cremated. Second, his ashes must be buried next to Pyramid Lake before the sun sets tomorrow."

Somewhere between immediate cremation, digging a hole by a lake, and a potentially disgruntled client, I had to make a decision. "Hold on a moment, Lu, I have another call."

I pushed a button. "Hamilton? I have managed at great expense I might add, to clear my afternoon. Meet me in the Healdsburg Plaza in an hour and we will discuss your situation."

"I can see why Charles thinks so much of you. See you in an hour."

I pushed the button to return to Lu but her line was dead. A touch shocked, I sat down in the overstuffed chair by my window. Below, in the garden, there was a line of large pink camellia shrubs in full bloom, but the brilliant display of color did not distract me from my dilemma. In an hour I would met with Ben Hamilton. Before my meeting, I would require confirmation that the bank transfer had been completed. However, the confirmation call had to come from Lu, and a few moments ago she had exhibited outright insubordination and less than rational behavior.

I decided to give Lu another ten minutes to call me back with the confirmation. During the interim I checked the phone list my pocket calendar to be sure I had the number for the Rapid Replacement Agency in case Lu did not meet my time limit.

More than seven minutes passed before my cell buzzed.

"Pinky, this is Lu. The bank transfer has been completed."

Restraining my anger, I said, "You sound much calmer. Now, please inform me what burying your father's ashes next to Pyramid Lake, before sunset tomorrow, has to do with managing my law office in my absence?"

"When I talked with you a few minutes ago, I was afraid that I would fail to accomplish my father's final request, but somehow, in the last few minutes everything worked out."

"Lu, stop talking in riddles and explain to me what is going on!"

"You were right. I put my faith in Bear and a couple of minutes ago he handed me the urn that contains my father's ashes."

"Ashes? How could your father's remains be ashes? I thought he died less than twenty-four hours ago."

"He did. I don't know how, but Bear took care of that part."

With breakfast still fresh in my stomach, I refused to speculate how my investigator could have achieved that bit of madness. "What do you mean, that part? Is there more to this sordid tale?"

"My father's last wish was to have his ashes buried on the shore of Pyramid Lake before tomorrow's sunset."

"You told me that before, but you neglected to explain to me why that is so important?"

"In his request, he wrote that many years ago he proposed to my mother by Pyramid Lake as the sun was setting. He wants to sleep in peace, throughout eternity, with that wonderful memory."

"My dear, I find all this hard to believe."

Lu's voice took on a hard edge. "What you believe is not important. We are talking about my father's eternal memory."

I sighed. "Is there more?"

"There was, but Flo's taken care of that problem."

"Are we now talking about Flo, Bear's woman?"

"Yes. She told me that she would cover for—"

"Are you suggesting I let that woman—"

Lu said, "Pinky, stop right there. I'm not suggesting anything. The decision has been made. She covers your office tomorrow morning or I'll tell Willow that you told me to lie to get the judge to reschedule the Puzzo case."

I will never understand where the little people of this world suddenly find the courage to rise up and attempt to smite their superiors. "My dear, I fear that is not going to work. My need to remain in California is truly a matter of life or death, and my client, Ben Hamilton, will testify to that fact to the judge. Willow will not have—"

"Then I'll tell Willow that you stood her up last month so you could sleep with Brady's widow."

I hesitated. This situation was becoming sticky. "Come, come, my dear, we both know that occasionally I expect my employees to—"

"In case you don't recall, I was standing in your office when you lied to Willow about having to meet a client. We both know who that client was and what you were going to do during that meeting."

This might be the perfect opportunity for a compromise. "Fine, Flo covers for you. How long are you going to be gone?"

Lu paused, and then said, "Bear will drive me to Pyramid lake. We'll bury the ashes, and return to Carson City. According to Bear, it shouldn't take us any longer than four hours. And don't forget, you have to pay Flo my salary while she is covering my job."

I took a big breath to calm down. At this point it would do me no good to argue. "Fine. Flo covers for you and I pay her. And who came up with this outlandish plan?"

Lu sniffed, "Flo did. She's like finding a big sister."

"Why do you feel the need to take Bear with you?"

"Because Flo told him to go. My leg is in a cast and I'm on crutches, so she figured I'd have trouble driving that far and digging a hole for the urn once I got to the lake. And Flo reminded me to tell you that you'll have to pay for Bear's gas."

"Pay for Bear's gas! That old pick-up must average around eight miles per gallon."

"That's why I gave him fifty dollars from the petty cash box."

Without question, my half-million dollar retainer trumped all of these trivial expenses and Lu's day of retribution would come. I glanced at my watch. If I was going to meet Hamilton in the plaza, I needed to leave soon. "Lu, Bear is a giant of a man, but in truth, he is nothing more than an overgrown child. He means well, but frankly, you should consider driving. I wouldn't trust the clumsy oaf to drive me across town, much less transport your revered father's ashes almost a hundred miles."

"He picks me up in an hour. Are there any final instructions you want to give me before I leave."

"Yes! Lock up the petty cash box and do not, I repeat, do not give Flo the password to our computer system."

SEVEN

Bear-Carson City, Nevada

Once I heard that I was going to piss away a day driving Lu to Pyramid Lake, and using Pinky's money to pay for the gas, I figured the boss would come up with a really nasty way to get back at me. Besides, my grandma told me that for thousands of years the Basque people have had to fight for everything they had and if they ever took something for free, like Pinky's gas money for a four-hour joy ride, bad times would follow. Granny Zabarte lived to be ninety-seven and I can't remember the last time she was wrong.

"Flo, this Pyramid Lake thing scares me."

"What's wrong with a morning off?"

"Granny Zabarte, that's what."

"What's to worry about? Lu just lost her father. She needs our assistance to dispose of his remains and we offered our help."

"But I don't think—"

"For the first time since you rolled out of bed you're correct. You don't think. What else could we tell her?"

"I can't believe that she got Pinky to pay for the gas. I know that man and he's tighter than a wedding ring on a fat bride's finger."

I climbed in the truck, turned the key, and the engine sputtered a couple of times, like it was too damn tired to fire up. "See there? Now something's wrong with my truck. Now I'll have to spend a bunch of bucks on the engine."

"Don't try to pull that old one on me."

"What do you mean?"

"Last time I checked we had four thousand left from Pinky's bonus. That means we've got lots of cash."

"Babe, I'm afraid we're a little short of the four grand mark."

Flo glared at me. For a second it looked like she was going to let fly with a right cross. "How short are we?"

I backed away to get clear of her fist. "About a thousand, or maybe fifteen hundred. Remember? I had to buy that new set of tires for the truck."

"Don't remind me of how much you spend on that bucket of bolts. The first garage had tires for sixty bucks. But was that good enough for you? No, you had to buy better tires than President Obama has on his pick-up."

"I don't think the President has a—"

"Whatever. We still have enough to fix the engine and buy you a new pair of pants."

"Why do I need to do that?"

"Forget I brought it up."

"Forget what?"

"Bear, you are so dense. We're Lu's only support. You're driving her to Pyramid Lake to bury her father's ashes. You have to wear something better than blue jeans to do justice to the solemnity of the occasion. That's why people have emergency funds, to take care of this sort of situation! And that's why I have to buy a new outfit. So I'll look good while I'm covering Pinky's office."

"But you're only going to be there for a few

hours."

"That makes no difference." Flo slammed her hand on the truck's hood. "Let's get going. We have an appointment at the outlet mall."

"I still think Lu could drive to Lake Pyramid by herself."

"There you go, thinking again. Her doctor told her to rest her broken leg—driving that far—digging a hole in the dirt to bury the urn—all that physical exertion could lead to medical complications, including deep-vein thrombosis."

"So?"

"That's bad! Some people die from a pulmonary embolism."

"Are you telling me that pulemblem thing could kill Lu?"

"Yes! The poor girl needs your help or her father will not rest peacefully for all eternity. Is the free gas that much of a problem?"

"Babe, it's not the gas. I think the shit's going to hit the fan when you cover Pinky's office."

"Humph! I'd like to think Pinky would wish you and Lu a happy trip and be glad I'm willing to break away from my busy life to watch his phones."

"Okay. But whatever you do, don't play around with anything in the office. Babe, you don't know Pinky like I do. Just answer the phones. Take down the time and names of the people who called and don't touch anything more."

"Bear, I'm doing the little bastard a big favor."

I knew that arguing with Flo could end up causing me as much pain as pissing onto an electric fence. I said, "Okay, I'll take Lu but while were gone, and you're watching Pinky's office, you've got to promise me that you won't do anything stupid—like screw around with his computers—or count the

54

money in the petty cash box—or go through Pinky's desk—or anything else that'll piss off the boss."

"I promise. Now let's head to the mall."

EIGHT

Pinky-Healdsburg, California

After quelling the latest peasant rebellion, I went downstairs and walked through the front door of the restored Italianate Victorian B & B. The porch was lined with rocking chairs. On a small table sat a pot of coffee, cups, and copies of the local newspaper. The air temperature was cool, but fresh and invigorating. I poured myself a cup, sat down and spent a few relaxing moments catching up on the contents of my briefcase.

"Would you care for more coffee, Mr. Delmont?"

I looked up and there stood the omnipresent Mr. Bliss. "Yes. I think so."

While he poured I noticed that his eyes devoured the paperwork that covered my lap.

He said, "Hard at work I see."

"Yes, and I would appreciate it if you would not hover about. The items that you are desperately attempting to read are confidential."

"Mr. Delmont, I cannot imagine why you would make such an accusation."

"My good man, straighten up and act accordingly when you are caught red-handed. Now, go away and don't come within ten feet of me for the rest of the day. And do not bother searching my room while I am gone. The only items I have left for your scrutiny are my underwear, socks, toothbrush, and a razor."

Frankly, I lacked any factual evidence to mistrust the man, but he was, without a doubt, one of those grotty characters who spend their waking hours hovering close enough to listen in on a private conversation, or to read confidential documents lying upside down on a desk or table.

"As you wish, Mr. Delmont." He bowed and scuttled around the corner of the porch.

Refreshed by the coffee, I walked the short block to the plaza that was the heart of Healdsburg.

The mature flora that filled the square was an interesting, if not curious combination of trees: palm, redwood, oak, and citrus. Two orange trees, fully loaded with brightly colored fruit gave the town center a festive feeling on that sunny, late January day.

Standing beneath the gazebo roof was a broad-shouldered man in his fifties or sixties. He wore a perfectly tailored gray sharkskin suit—in his right hand he held a black leather briefcase—the figure personified the portrait of a successful attorney.

I thrust my right hand toward him. "Mr. Hamilton?"

He smiled and grasped my hand. "Mr. Delmont. Can I get you something to eat?"

"No thank you. I am staying at the Red Rose B & B, and between their breakfast, and dinner last night at the Plaza Bistro, I will be lucky to find room for anything the rest of the day."

He guided me toward a bench. "I understand. Now, Mr. Delmont, can we get started?"

"Yes, but in the future, please address me as Pinky."

Hamilton hesitated. "As you know from my card, my given name is Bennett, but my friends call me Ben."

I glanced at my watch. Not because I was the least bit interested in the exact time, but I wanted to signal to the man at my side that my time was valuable and to move along with his story.

"Ben, the ball is in your court."

He sat back and I was surprised to see a tear pool in the corner of his right eye.

He said, "We all have family skeletons hidden away from the harsh light of public scrutiny."

"Excuse me, but I have left an extremely busy law practice in Carson City, Nevada, that is presently cruising the stormy legal seas without its captain at the helm. I trust a review of your family's sordid history has something to do with the supposedly innocent man being held behind bars for murder."

Ben's jaw tightened and the knuckles on his right hand turned white, as if he wasn't used to being addressed in such a direct manner. Then his fingers relaxed and he said, "I understand. I will attempt to make the pertinent background information as brief as possible. My sister Jennifer is the black sheep of my family. Before her eighteenth birthday she ran away. We found her six months later in a drug rehab center in San Francisco. While Jenny worked to kick her habit, she fell in love with a Mexican named Juan Flores, a counselor at the rehab center. When she was clean and sober, Jenny announced she and Juan were going to get married. In my parent's circle of friends, Anglos did not marry Mexicans. My father, short of attempting to deport Juan, did everything he could to break them up, but eventually my sister married him. A year and a half later they had a son."

I checked my watch again. "That was a very interesting story, perhaps an Emmy contender on one of the daytime soaps, but you still haven't explained the connection between—"

"Their son, Enrique Flores, is the young man charged with the murder of Paul Hellman. The trial starts very soon. Pinky, from my view, Enrique's Public Defender has been worthless. Other than a couple of futile attempts at a plea bargain, the lazy bastard hasn't done a thing."

"It is possible that the plea bargain the PD pursued was the only viable alternative for your nephew."

"But you don't understand, plea bargains are for the guilty. My nephew didn't murder Hellman!"

"Ben, your card indicates you are an attorney. If your nephew is innocent and you are displeased with his legal representation, why not take over his defense?"

"I'm a corporate attorney. I review contracts and try to keep my clients out of court. In fact, as poor a job as the PD is doing he's likely done far better than I could. The last time I stood in a courtroom was ten years ago when I fought a speeding ticket."

"You understand that I am not licensed in California, and as such, my efforts would only be investigative."

"Charles explained that to me."

"And that I cannot guarantee a thing."

"I understand. Pinky, I've already gone through two private detectives. All they accomplished was to waste a lot of time and a large amount of my money."

"What did they come up with?"

"They found nothing. My God, they never saw the murder site because Martin St. James does not allow anyone, outside of the police, the DA, and the PD, access to his winery. If you can't find the truth my sister's son could spend the rest of his life in jail, or . . . he'll be . . . no, I can't allow myself to contemplate that alternative."

"Ben, as I stated before, my legal practice is a one-man operation. At present, I have many clients who face long-term prison sentences. They cannot afford to have me gone for more than a few days."

"In this," Ben placed his large briefcase on the bench. "I have all the information concerning Hellman's murder."

"If finding a better suspect was that easy, the DA would have—"

"I told you that Enrique was half Mexican. Trust me, in this county once a Latino is behind bars the Sheriff stops looking for suspects."

His observation was correct with one exception. All police, in all jurisdictions, cease looking for a suspect, regardless of race, ethnic background, or religion, once they are confident they have arrested the man or woman they feel could have done the crime. If Enrique was innocent, I would be hard-pressed to find support from any member of law enforcement in the county, other than the present DA.

I sighed, "Legally, I could drive away from Healdsburg this minute, return to Carson City, and retain the fee you transferred to my bank."

He opened his briefcase and pulled out a large manila envelope. "I understand. All I ask is that you review the contents of this envelope before you decide there's no hope. Pinky, your legal brilliance is all that stands between my nephew and the death penalty."

In truth, my present caseload back home was light, and if needed, I was positive that Lu could squeeze out another week's worth of postponements—and I was curious as to what was enclosed in the envelope. Besides that, returning home with Ben's retainer, without a cursory glance at his information, could be construed as stretching the accepted ethical standards of my profession.

I thrust my right hand in Ben's direction. "I will review the contents."

"And then what will you do? What will be your plan of attack?"

His question took me by surprise. At this point I did not have a plan of attack. But I was dealing with an attorney, so I knew better than to create a stratagem out of whole cloth. "Yesterday I visited the St. James Winery, but as you stated, I was unable to gain access to the site of the murder."

"Pinky, I'm pleased to see we're on the same track. I feel your investigation must start at the scene of the murder."

"I agree with your logic, but at the moment, I'm not sure how—"

"I don't know if you believe in serendipity, but this morning I received a phone call that I believe will solve our problem. In addition to my law practice I own the Yosemite View Winery located outside of Modesto. This morning my general manager received a tip that Cal OSHA will conduct a surprise inspection tomorrow."

"I can see that receiving an advanced notice of a surprise government safety inspection would be a fortuitous event for any business."

"Come, come, I would expect nothing less for one of the major contributors to the Governor's campaign fund."

"Ben, I am happy for you, but I fail to see how that helps."

"Don't you see? The OSHA inspection is the answer to our problem? If you can send one of your investigators to my winery in Modesto I'll set everything up so your man will have the opportunity to observe what an OSHA Inspector does during a safety review."

I was pleased to note that the mind of a corporate attorney also functions on the edge of the law. To say I was impressed would be an understatement. "Ben, that's a brilliant concept. You may not feel comfortable in court, but from what I have observed today, you are extremely quick on your feet."

"Thank you, Pinky. From an attorney with your reputation that is a major compliment."

The mental picture of Ben's idea was coming clear. I said, "Let me finish your scenario. After a day in Modesto, my man will arrive on the doorstep of the St. James Winery for a surprise OSHA inspection that includes the murder site. This should be easy because I'm sure no one takes a long and careful look at the OSHA credentials."

Ben grinned. "Correct."

"Just a moment, I need to call my office to set up the Modesto trip." I turned my back and walked a few paces away.

Lu answered. "Law office of J. Pincus Delmont."

"There has been a change in plans. Bear has to visit a winery in Modesto first thing tomorrow morning."

"But he's here now—to drive me to the lake—to bury my father's ashes."

"I understand that, but a man's life now hangs in the balance. Do not worry. I will come up with a way to solve your family crisis."

"But what about your promise? How am I going to properly dispose of my father's ashes?"

"Lu, as your friend I feel a bit of advice is in order. Your personal life is important, but it should never be as important as your position as the major-domo of the J. Pinkus Delmont legal empire. Have I made myself clear?"

I heard her sob, "Will Bear and Flo return soon?"

"I am afraid not. After Modesto I will require his immediate presence in Sonoma County. I will fax you his instructions within an hour."

There was a momentary pause, I assumed to give Lu time to adjust her priorities. "Okay, you win. Is that all?"

"No. I told you I would take care of your personal problem and I will. As soon as I hang up, place a call to Harry, the jail guard. Tell Harry that Pinky has a job for him. His task? To immediately pick you up, drive you and your father's remains to Pyramid Lake and bury them before the sun sets."

"But what if Harry doesn't want—"

"Don't concern yourself with something that is not your problem. Remind Harry that I will be sending him a case of his favorite beverage once the job is complete. Lu, now that your personal complication has been solved I expect you to concentrate one hundred percent of your energy on your job. When I return, after your leg has healed enough so you can drive, I will arrange some time off so you can drive to Pyramid Lake and spend a full day by your father's final resting place. By the way, make a map so you can find the site where Harry buries the urn so you can find it on your return trip."

I closed the case, slipped the cell into my pocket, and turned to face my new client. "Hamilton, as you can see, I have set the wheels of our plan in motion."

"Very impressive. Now, I—"

That was the moment I heard Arianna say, "Hi, Pinky."

She was a vision in red, gold and white. A scarlet scarf was woven through her long blonde hair. My eyes slipped down to a gold top that literally caressed her generous feminine attributes. Finally a pair of white silk harem pants gently fondled her perfect hips.

I introduced her to a stunned Bennett Hamilton.

She flipped her head and her blonde hair bounced off her alabaster shoulders. "Got to go to work now. Don't forget to stop by for a pint of Berger Brown."

Ben's jaw dropped as we watched her cross the street and enter the Downtown Pub.

He said, "Did you tell me when you arrived in Healdsburg?"

"No, but it was late yesterday afternoon. Why?"

"My God man, that female is living proof that you are quick on your feet. Now I understand why Charles was so positive that you'd find Hellman's killer before Enrique goes to trial. Here's the file, and God speed."

NINE

I returned to my room at the B&B, pulled out a legal pad, and wrote:

Bear:
While Lu travels to the lake, and my office is unattended in the normal method, I expect you and Flo to cover all the bases. The moment Lu returns from her trip to Pyramid Lake to bury her father's ashes before sunset, both of you are to drive to the charming central valley village of Modesto, California.
Tomorrow morning you will call on Meade Mobbs, the General Manager of the Yosemite View Winery. You are to participate with him during a CAL-OSHA inspection. Maintain a close-on watch of the OSHA inspector because you will be impersonating one in the near future. After you complete your assignment at the Yosemite View Winery, you will proceed to Sonoma County and move into the first inexpensive motel south of Healdsburg.
Now read the following very carefully. Once you cross the Sonoma County line, you will assume a clandestine modus operandi! That means that when you take on your sub rosa

65

persona, you are to discuss your investigative assignment with no one.

Included with your instructions is a check for $750. That will cover your expenses for ten days.

You will contact me once you have checked into your motel in Sonoma County.

In anticipation of your next question, I do not care a whit concerning your thoughts that seventy-five dollars per day is not enough advance to cover your expenses while on assignment. I pay you a princely sum to do my investigative work and you are free to seek other employment at any time. If that is the case, please give me the courtesy of letting me know that you have decided to resign so I can immediately seek a replacement.

And that brings me to a final item. This fax authorizes Lu to compensate Florence Sonderlund a lump sum of one thousand ($1000.00) dollars (one hundred per day for ten days) for her computer expertise during the California investigation.

J. Pincus Delmont.

Instructions completed, I walked downstairs and knocked on the office door of Mr. Bliss.

A bald head with beady eyes popped out. "Ah, Mr. Delmont. And what service may I perform for you today?"

"I need to send a fax."

His fingers reached for the sheet but I pulled the paper away. "Mr. Bliss, I believe the pronoun used was I, not you. Direct me to your fax machine, instruct me how to use it, and then vacate the area so I can conclude my affairs with absolute privacy."

The man's eyes flashed a touch of disappointment. "As you wish, Mr. Delmont."

As the innkeeper scuttled away I decided it was time to call Charles.

"District Attorney's office."

"My name is Padriag Murphy. Please inform the District Attorney I would like him to return my call."

"Your number?"

"He has my number."

"Thank you. I will give him the message."

Fifteen minutes later my cell rang. "Charles, are you in a position to talk?"

"I am. Is there a problem?"

"Not exactly. We need to discuss the present situation at the Red Rose B & B."

"Situation?"

"Either the proprietor, a Mr. Bliss, is inquisitive to an extreme, or he is working for you opponent."

"Has something happened?"

"No, I am a just laying the ground work in case he is a concern."

"Oh."

"Not to worry. If Bliss turns out to be a spy, I was thinking that you could use the situation to your advantage."

"How?"

"I could accidently leave an important document in my room, something with specific information. If that information gets back to you then you know you have a conduit to your opponent—the perfect opportunity to conduct a mis-information campaign."

"That's brilliant, Pinky. Let's try this. How about I fax you a note informing you that, without a large infusion of cash, my campaign media account will run out of money in two weeks."

"That should bait the hook."

"Call me after you've planted the misinformation."

TEN

Bear-Carson City, Nevada

While Flo was adjusting Lu's chair to her height, I stared at the seven hundred and fifty dollar check Lu handed me. "What's this for? Why is Pinky paying me big bucks to drive you to Pyramid Lake?"

Lu's gaze dropped down, like she'd just noticed that there was a message from George Clooney tied to her shoelaces. "Bear, read Pinky's fax and then we'll talk."

I set the check down on Lu's desk. "What's that short bastard doing to me this time?"

Before I could stop her, Flo grabbed my check, stuffed it into her purse and said, "Okay, Lu, give me the scoop on how Pinky wants his calls handled."

"Hold on, Babe. Let me read this fax first. We've got a new assignment."

"But I have to learn Lu's office procedures before you two take off for the lake."

I gave Flo one of my killer stares. She clammed up and sat down.

I read the first part of the fax. "Hey, Pinky's sending us on a trip to sunny California to some burg called Modesto."

Flo snorted. "Modesto? That's somewhere in the central valley between Sacramento and Fresno. Count me out."

"Babe, Pinky wants you to go with me."

"You're kidding!"

"Nope."

"I'm not sure I want to go."

"I'll find us a really slick motel with a great pool so you've got something to do while I nose around."

"Not good enough."

I kept reading. "What the hell is CAL-OSHA?"

Lu said, "I believe that has something to do with occupational safety."

Flo snorted, "Sounds like the three most boring words in the English language."

I said, "What's that?"

"Modesto, occupational, and safety."

I said, "Come on, Babe. Give me a break."

"Whatever."

"Hey, help me with this . . . When you cross the Sonoma County line, you must assume a clan-de-stine mo-dus opera-n-di! . . . What the hell is Pinky talking about?"

Flo turned her chair around so her back was toward me. "Didn't you hear me? I'm not listening to you."

"And I have to become a sub rosa person and not talk to anyone about my assignment. Babe, I need help with all those big words, like clandi-pus operation and submarine rose."

"How many times do I have to tell you? I'm not going to get involved if I'm not going to be compensated for my work. You'll be on your own in Modesto."

"Babe, I can't go without . . . wait, you'll love last part. 'This fax authorizes Lu to compensate Florence Sonderlund a lump sum of one thousand ($1000.00) dollars (one hundred per day for ten days) for her computer expertise during the ten-day California investigation.'"

Flo's chair spun around and big smile crossed her puss. "A thousand bucks! Now that's more like it. It's about time that pipsqueak paid me my due. Hold on, what about Lu's trip to the lake?"

Lu said, "Harry the guard will pick me up in a minute to drive me."

Flo said, "Great. Okay, while you're gone burying those ashes, Bear will have time to run to the mall and pick up a few things for our trip to sunny California."

The door opened and a big dude, about six-six and a solid three hundred pounds walked in. He wore an overcoat and it wasn't that cold outside so I was pretty sure he was packing some heavy stuff under all that wool.

"Is the lawyer in?"

Flo said, "Do you have an appointment?"

The big guy's eyes drifted from Flo's face to her rack and he said, "Nope."

Flo said, "I'm sorry sir, but Mr. Delmont is not in at the moment. Would you care to leave a message or make an appointment?"

"Not interested. The lawyer's got something important that belongs to my boss."

I said, "I'm not sure when he'll get back."

The dude glared at me, like he was trying to decide if he was going to kill me now, or drop hot lead in my eyes for an hour, and then kill me.

Finally he said, "I'll call my boss man to find out what he wants me to do."

He pulled out a cell phone, and while he stared at me, I watched his lips move for a couple of seconds. He closed the cell, and said, "Tell the lawyer that Mr. M's man stopped by. I'll come by tomorrow about the same time and pick up the package."

He turned and as he walked toward the door,

Flo said, "But sir . . . "

The door slammed and Flo said, "Well, he was not very polite."

I said, "Babe, I'd bet a year's salary that was one of Macario's goons."

Flo's eyes got as big as a half-dollar. "Oh my!"

Lu said, "What do you mean, Macario's goon?"

I said, "Pinky's in a pot full of shit. That dude is a strong-arm for the husband of that broad Pinky's representing in a divorce case and Pinky's got something the husband wants real bad."

Lu jumped up. "I'll call Pinky, tell him what the man wants, and maybe FedEx can ship it overnight."

The door opened and Harry the guard stuck his head in. He said, "Lu, let's go."

Flo put her arm around Lu's shoulder. "You go and bury your father's ashes. Bear will take care of this little problem."

Lu grabbed the urn, waved, and limped out of the office.

The phone rang. Flo picked it up and said, "Law office of J. Pinkus Delmont. Please hold for a moment."

I said, "What the hell are we going to do?"

Flo shrugged, "At this point I'm not sure, but whatever it is, we have to finish it before we leave for Modesto. And don't forget, we have to go to the mall before we go. I'm not traveling to California without at least two new outfits."

Pop told me that babes were hard to figure out. That dude from Vegas damn near blows us away and all Flo talks about is a trip to the outlet mall.

Flo plastered a smile on her face, pushed the hold button, and said, "Thank you for holding, how may I help you?"

ELEVEN

Pinky-Healdsburg, California

My buzzing cell phone jolted me from a peaceful and well-deserved nap. I glanced at my watch and it showed two thirty-five.

"Lu, I assume that hell froze over because nothing short of that occurrence would qualify for this phone call."

"Listen up, you're speaking to Florence Sonderlund, and no, hell did not freeze over. However, this could be nearly as bad. You have two major problems. The first one? A judge is demanding your appearance in his court in less than an hour."

"Oh my God! What judge and what is his reason?"

"His name is Judge Anderson and it concerns a client's DUI."

A pulsing began to throb behind my left eye. "Did the name George Sterling enter into the discussion?"

"Yes, it did. I took the liberty of checking your database and I am scanning through the George Sterling file as we speak. Is there anything in the file you'll need during you're your court appearance?"

"Flo, I am a four to five hour drive from Carson City and I have a splitting headache."

"In other words, the situation is hopeless?"

"I would not go so far as to—"

"Pinky, take a quick shower. By the time you are squeaky clean I'll call you back."

"Hold on. You said I have two major problems. What is the—"

"Damn it. Shut up and take your shower. I'll call you back in thirty minutes."

Before I could respond the line went dead. I sat for a moment and considered the worst possible outcome. If I were unable to show up in court, Judge Anderson would assign George Sterling a new pro bono attorney. That might help George but the judge's action would strip me of my perfect pro bono client—a man who took none of my valuable time, yet allowed me to fulfill my obligation of free legal advice to the poor and downtrodden.

As the hot water flowed over me I pondered what I could possibly accomplish three hundred miles from Judge Anderson's court. After I finished drying off, I decided to tell Flo to call the judge's clerk and beg for a continuance. If that failed, then my one and only pro bono client would vanish and I would have to begin the long and arduous journey of finding a replacement.

My cell buzzed. "Flo, I know I don't have much time. This is what I want you to—"

"Calm down, Pinky. Bear and I have everything under control."

"You and Bear have . . . explain yourself."

"I would if you'd shut up. First, I printed out the complete file on George Sterling. Pinky, this is only an opinion of a layperson, but your client is a drunk and a danger to the law abiding citizens of Carson City. However, I understand your job is to represent Mr. Sterling no matter how big a scumbag he is. I called the judge's clerk and explained that your appearance in court was out of the question due to your sudden onset of a contagious illness. Next, I convinced the clerk to accept a statement from you stipulating that you feel Mr. Sterling should reside in jail for a week or two so he will better understand the implications of his latest drunken rampage through the streets of Carson City. I typed out your statement, signed it, and faxed it to the clerk ten minutes ago. Finally, if the judge doesn't believe your claim of sickness, I have contacted a doctor, one I've used in the past who, for a small fee, would be happy to send a fax to the court verifying your claim of the contagious illness."

I sat for a moment, stunned at the brilliant solution that witch had come up with. "My good woman, it looks as if you've saved my bacon. As soon as I return to the office, Lu will receive my instructions to cut you a five hundred dollar bonus check."

"Pinky, I appreciate the thought, but we haven't discussed the other problem yet."

"Right. Go ahead."

"About an hour ago a man walked into the office and demanded the item that Bear removed from that safe in Vegas. We told the man you had the item, and that you were out of town, but would return in a couple of days. After a quick phone call he told us that he'd be back tomorrow at noon, and if the items weren't ready to hand over then, as Bear so aptly put it, the shit was going to hit the fan. The second the man left, Harry picked up Lu. That left Bear and myself. We checked the desk in your office. It didn't take us long to come to the conclusion that you must have the printout in your possession. Am I correct?"

"Yes, I have it in my briefcase."

"You'd better FedEx everything to your office along with a note that you haven't had time to look at anything because Bear's afraid, if you fool around with this guy, he'll do something drastic."

"Relax, all you have to do is call Willow. She'll send over an army of cops."

"And what happens to us when the cops go home? You sure are a brave little shit when you're three hundred miles away. That guy could wait another day, or a week, or a month. Pinky, this dude is big and Bear is sure he's carrying a weapon."

"Right. I'll FedEx the printout as soon as I can make a copy."

"No copies damn it! If you use any information off those papers, that guy's boss, you remember, your client's husband, will know it and our friend from Vegas will come back to Carson City and stuff you, feet first, into an oil drum full of wet concrete and drop you into Lake Tahoe."

"Right. No copies."

"Okay, and remember, if that guy comes in here tomorrow, and that FedEx envelope isn't here, and Lu's all alone, he might lose it and do something to her. If that happens, when we get back from our trip to California, I guarantee that Bear will chain you to the steering wheel of your fancy BMW and we'll both drive your car into the nearest river."

I always knew that Flo was a dangerous woman. "Fine. I will not look at, or review in any way, the printout, and the FedEx envelope will arrive at my office before noon tomorrow."

"Sounds good. Lu will return in an hour from her journey to bury her father's ashes and once she gets back Bear and I are off to the charming village of Modesto. Have a nice evening."

TWELVE

Bear-Modesto, California

After four hours of driving, me and Flo cruised past Modesto's city limits sign. At least that's what I think the sign said.

Flo said, "Damn it, slow this truck down, the fog's so thick I can't see the curb, and if I can't see the curb, I know you can't either."

"Babe, I'm worried about a crazy truck driver rear-ending us."

"Wake up and smell the coffee. A little tap on the rear end of this old pile of junk is a lot better than crashing head-on into an eighteen-wheeler."

Flo was right but I wasn't about to let her know that. She'd been bitching at me ever since we dropped out of the clear mountain air and into the cold valley fog just east of Sacramento.

Flo said, "Just once I'd like someone to explain to me why we get the crappy end of the places to go while Pinky gets the pick of the litter. I'll bet at this very moment he's sitting in a fancy restaurant and downing an expensive glass of red wine."

I said, "I wonder if we can find a good breakfast joint in Modesto?"

"This is a truck route and you know what they say about . . . hey, slow down, that looks like a motel sign on the right."

"Nope, that's a Seven-Eleven. Jesus, it's so foggy out there that I'm not sure we're still in Modesto."

"If it was up to me I'd pull into that Seven-Eleven and ask the guy behind the counter if they could recommend a clean motel. I don't know what it is with you men. Never want to ask anyone for help. Like you're afraid someone will think you're—"

"If you'd stop ragging at me I'd be able to think."

"Too late to pull in and park, the Seven-Eleven sign's disappeared."

"Babe, how's this for an idea. I'll head for the first motel we see. Tomorrow morning, when the fog has lifted, if you don't like the joint, we'll look for a better place that has a nice swimming pool."

"What makes you think this fog will be gone in the morning? When I lived in LA I'd read newspaper stories where they had to close the schools from Visalia to Lodi because the school busses couldn't find the kids in the morning and the kid's parents couldn't find the schools because of the thick fog."

"Shit! How long does something like that last?"

"Days on end. Sometimes a week. But don't worry about my comfort. I'm just here for the computer work. If you can't find me a motel with a nice pool, I'll spend my day watching Oprah on TV."

"Oprah's not on TV all day."

"Whatever. I'm cold, tired of riding in this old truck, and need to pee. If you can't find a motel, the least you can do is find a gas station, but first, make sure the bathroom is clean. The last station you stopped at had a filthy bathroom. If I've told you once, I've told you a thousand times that—"

"Hey, there's a motel sign on the right, and you know, from here it looks pretty good."

"I don't know how you can see anything through this damned fog, but let's take the chance. God knows I'm tried of wandering around Modesto in this cold muck."

THIRTEEN

Bear-Modesto, California

Driving mile after mile in fog as thick as cold pea soup was not easy and once my head hit the pillow I slept like Flo had hit me with a sledgehammer. The next morning I peeked through the shutter and everything was still wet and gray. According to the motel dude there was a truck stop joint across the street so me and Flo dodged cars and trucks and managed to get there in one piece. Flo told the waitress to bring her an order of oatmeal and dry toast. I was starving and ordered chicken fried steak and hash browns.

The waitress, a cute little thing with nice boobs, said, "Do you want the usual on the steak and potatoes?"

"What's that?"

"White gravy with bits of pork sausage."

"Sounds good and don't forget a couple of cups of hot coffee."

Forty-five minutes later, with me feeling like I'd just swallowed a basketball, me and Flo found our way through the fog back to our room.

A belch and a fart fired off at the same time. "Sorry, Babe, but I do feel better."

"If you didn't eat so much you wouldn't feel the need to get rid of excess gas. Besides opening the door to let in some fresh air, what happens next?"

"I'm about to head to the winery. You ready?"

"Not really." Flo put her pouty look back on. "Remember, I'm here for the computer work, not impersonating an OSHA Inspector. I'll find something to do even if Modesto is the drain pipe for the world's fog."

"Hey, I could tell Meade Mobbs that you're my assistant. If we worked together we could wrap this up early and get out of this bad weather."

"Not interested."

"Come on, Babe, I might need your help. Who knows, I might have to get into a computer."

"Little chance of that happening. However, I'd consider changing my mind if you will guarantee that I will not be involved in anything that could be construed as illegal."

Shit. She had me there. At this point, I didn't have a clue what was going to go down, so I decided to feed her a little bull. "Babe, you know me, I never do anything illegal."

She grabbed her coat. "I guess wandering around with you would be a lot better than staring at these gray, concrete block walls all day."

I glanced around the place. The room wasn't bad for an any-motel-in-the-middle-of-the-fog joint. There was a little desk, not big enough for me to use, but it fit Flo okay. A TV that worked pretty good. A chrome rack for Flo's suitcase. And a really cool painting of a sunset behind a tropical island hung behind the king-sized bed. "Hey, I've slept in worse."

"Maybe, but not with me you haven't."

"Jesus, Flo! Do you want me to check out and look for another motel?"

"No, I'm a strong enough woman to put up with anything for a night. Where do we go after Modesto?"

"Somewhere in Sonoma County."

"That takes me to the obvious question. Is that far enough away from the central valley to get clear of this damned fog?"

"I think so. According to my map Sonoma County is about three hours west of here and it's near the ocean."

"So you're telling me that I get to trade dense valley fog for some salty ocean fog. Wow, you really know how to show a woman a good time." She threw her coat on. "I give up. Let's get this caper over with."

I drove south on the old highway, spotted Yosemite Boulevard, turned east, and after a couple of signals, Flo yelled, "There it is, on the left, The Yosemite View Winery."

I pulled into the parking lot and we walked into the tasting room.

A short, young broad with a perky rack stood behind a counter. She showed us her pearly-whites, and said, "Welcome to Yosemite View. Did you have any problem finding the place? I hear it's pretty foggy out there."

Flo snorted.

I pushed Flo aside and said, "We're here to meet with Meade Mobbs."

She must have been working on a hundred percent commission because her smile shut down faster than a kid's brain during summer vacation.

"Wait here. I'll try to find him." She walked through a door at the end of the tasting bar and left us standing in the empty room.

After a couple of minutes, the door opened. An older, bald dude, about the same height as the young broad walked in.

Before he moved, his eyes locked on Flo's assets. Then, still staring at Flo, he stuck his hand in my direction and said, "Good morning. I'm Meade, and you are?"

"Bear, Bear Zabarte and this is Flo, my assistant. We're here to—"

"Mr. . . a . . . Mr. Zabarte, I don't recall having a meeting scheduled with—"

I stepped between the dude and Flo so he could get his mind back to business. "Hey, call me Bear. Your boss told us to come to the winery to follow a CAL-OSHA inspector during a safety review. Now do you remember?"

"Yes, but he didn't tell me that you would be accompanied by such a beautiful assistant. This way."

Flo pushed me aside. "Excellent. Now, Mr. Mobbs, while my partner follows the CAL-OSHA man, I've been instructed to review all the records of your previous inspections. Where do you store those forms?"

Did I say anything about checking OSHA forms?

Mobbs said, "The old forms are in my office. After we find the inspector, and drop off your friend, you follow me and I'll make those records available along with a fresh cup of hot coffee. These foggy mornings can suck the marrow right out of your bones, don't you agree?"

As we walked through the winery, Mobbs ignored me and rambled on. "Flo, what I don't understand is why CAL-OSHA is inspecting us. My God, this winery has the best safety record in Modesto, if not the whole central valley."

We rounded a corner and Mobbs damn near ran into the inspector guy. The dude was wearing jeans, a sweatshirt, and around his neck hung a big CAL-OSHA identification badge.

"Gary, this is Bear. The owner, Mr. Hamilton,

wants him to work with you while you make your inspection."

I said, "Gary, glad to meet you, but before we start, my boss told me to check out your badge."

He flipped the lanyard over his head and handed it to me. "No problem. Happens all the time. Take it and call the head office if you want. I realize that a CAL-OSHA inspection can be a pain in the butt, but trust me, I'm one of the good guys in the department."

I looked at his badge. It had his name, a number, and a photo taken when he had a little more hair. All I needed was a few seconds and a copy machine. Then I noticed something smeared across the dude's picture. "Gary, if it's okay with you, there's a blob of crap on your photo. My assistant, Flo, would be happy to take your pass and clean it up for you. Right Flo?"

She flashed me a blank stare for a second, and then nodded. "Sure. I'll shine it up better than new."

Gary's attention, along with Mobbs, had settled on Flo's bodacious boobs. To tell the truth, at that point I could have lifted Gary's wallet and he wouldn't have noticed until he tried to buy a beer after work.

Mobbs said, "Flo, you're in luck. There's a restroom with a sink located next to my office. I'll show you the way."

Flo said, "Thanks, and don't forget, I'm dying for that cup of fresh coffee."

Mobbs moved closer to Flo. "I didn't forget my promise. You know, there's a lot to learn about the wine business. I can show you all sorts of things."

Flo gave her head a little flip. "I'll bet you can. Bear, I'll be back in an hour."

Gary didn't say anything, but he almost dropped

his clipboard when Flo turned and brushed her best parts across his arm.

She sure knew how to work the dudes. I clapped Gary on the shoulder and said, "Okay, let's get this inspection crap on the road."

Six hours later, after returning to our motel room, I poured a big slug of red wine in Flo's glass and opened a brew for me. "Great job, Babe. For a second I didn't catch on about the past inspections."

"I just figured that a couple of old forms would help you understand what OSHA was looking for."

I said, "And then I got worried that you wouldn't pick up what I wanted when I asked you to clean the badge, but you figured out that we needed a copy of the damn thing."

Flo grabbed her glass and downed half the wine in one gulp. "Frankly, my job would have been a lot easier if you had told me beforehand everything you wanted me to do."

"Babe, that's not the way this investigative stuff works. Do you remember last year, inside that bean counter's office in LA?"

She took another swig and damn near emptied the glass. "You mean that time when that roly-poly night guard hit on me?"

"And I had to hide under the desk."

Flo poured herself some more wine and smiled. "I remember."

I said, "I didn't expect to find a key taped under the drawer. In fact, I didn't even plan on crawling under the desk. When you've done investigations as long as I have, you learn that things just sort of pop up. You've got to be ready for anything. Just like what happened with the CAL-OSHA pass. You took it to clean off the crapola on his photo, and then you figured out how to make a couple of copies while you were drinking coffee in the office."

"Hell, guessing we needed a copy was the easy part. Getting rid of that bald guy was tough. He stuck closer to me than stink on manure. He showed me a computer program, and the forms they use to follow grapes to a bottle of wine. I had to accidentally spill some of my coffee on his white shirt to get him to back off."

"Jesus, I hope you didn't burn the dude."

"Get real. The coffee had cooled down, but he had to go into the men's room to clean up. That coffee dump bought me enough time to copy the badge, grab a few forms, some old OSHA inspections, and the program disk before he came back. Anyway, wineries push around more paperwork than any business I've ever seen. How about you? Did you get all you needed from Gary?"

"It was a piece of cake. I learned that all you had to do was say 'I'm from CAL-OSHA' and most people will crap in their jeans. Now that I have a badge, and a couple of the OSHA forms you copied, I'm ready to cause soiled shorts all over Sonoma County. Let's see if we can find a decent place to eat in this dumpy town and tomorrow morning we'll check out of here."

Flo downed her wine. "Before we eat, let me see if I can find us a better place to stay on the Internet for tomorrow night."

I sat down, popped open another brew and watched the Lakers pound the crap out of the Warriors. Pro basketball games are boring and pro football is over and the Red Sox haven't started playing baseball, so there wasn't anything else to watch on TV and—

"Bear, check out this place."

Flo carried the laptop over to me. The screen

showed a picture of a dozen cabins alongside a gentle river. Behind the cabins was a stand of tall redwood trees and between the cabins and the river was a brick BBQ grill, and a bunch of lounge chairs filled with good-looking babes lying in the sun. "Where's this joint?"

"Along the Russian River in Sonoma County. Looks really nice, doesn't it?"

"Yeah, but I'll bet those cabins are real expensive. Don't forget we only have—"

"No buts and there's an internet special rate for only fifty-five bucks a night. Hell, that's less than we're paying for this dump."

"Yeah, but I'll bet they're too far away from the winery. I'll have to drive there every—"

"According to the map the cabins are less than fifteen miles from where Pinky's staying. All you have to do is drive north on Westside Road and bingo, you're in Healdsburg."

I knew better than to argue with Flo after she'd downed a half a bottle of wine. After a couple of glasses her brain was sort of like wet cement, soft and workable, but after the fourth or fifth glass of red, it turned as hard as a rock. But there was something wrong with that picture.

I said, "Let me take a closer look at—"

Flo grabbed the laptop, slammed it shut, and dropped it onto the bed. "Bear Zabarte. I did everything you wanted today without a single complaint, and another thing, I'm not positive that pouring coffee on a man's shirt is legal. All I ask of you is—"

The cement had hardened. "Babe, I don't know what I was thinking. The fog must have leaked into my brain. I'll open another brew while you make the reservation and then let's go to dinner. I'm starved."

FOURTEEN

Pinky-Healdsburg, California

Rejuvenated by the knowledge that Bear would soon be wandering through the St. James Winery in the role of an ersatz OSHA inspector, I collected the paperwork that Ben had given me and walked downstairs to the porch. On the southwest corner a wicker chair in the afternoon sun called to me. I sat down and placed the paperwork on a small table.

"Mr. Delmont, I trust you are comfortable. Would you care for a glass of wine?"

I glanced up and the owner of the Red Rose B & B was hovering over my left shoulder. Like a jungle cat, the man had an uncanny way of silently closing in on his prey without creating alarm.

He fawned and added, "Courtesy of the house, of course."

A moment later, as Bliss handed me a glass of wine, I noticed the eight by ten glossy of the corpse was lying face up, on the top of the stack, and quickly turned the photo over. "Mr. Bliss, I am amazed that even at this time of the year, the ambient temperature in Healdsburg is perfect."

"I'm happy you are pleased with your stay, Mr. Delmont."

I completed running through the stack of documents and pondered why Charles felt Flores was innocent. The young man had motive, opportunity, and he was at the winery the night of the murder.

While I sipped the last of my wine I ruminated over my general ignorance concerning the actual process of making wine. Was there an element of that procedure that could have caused Paul Hellman's death? I realized that my lack of knowledge was hindering my investigation. To move forward I required more detailed information on the process of winemaking.

At that moment I detected the sound of light breathing over my right shoulder. Damn it, Bliss again. I jerked my head backward and smacked the tip of his nose. "Pardon me, Mr. Bliss, I did not realize you were standing behind me. I was just about to call you. I require a phone book."

"Of course, Mr. Delmont. I'll bring you one from my office."

A moment later, his bloodied beak wrapped with a handkerchief, the toadying wretch handed me a phone book and a sheet of paper.

"This fax came in for you, Mr. Delmont."

With a flair for the dramatic, I quickly turned the fax over, face down, and placed it on the tabletop. "Thank you."

I waited for Bliss to leave, looked up the number for the Arroyo Verde Winery, and dialed the number. Twenty years earlier, the owner, Bill Mazzerella, had taken me under his wing and had taught me the glories of zinfandel wine.

"Good morning. My name is J. Pinkus Delmont. I am a long-time member of the Arroyo Verde Zin Club. Please put me through to William Mazzerella."

"One moment, please . . . "

"Mr. Delmont. Good to talk to you. I see by the sales records that you continue to buy your five case allotment of my top zin each and every year."

89

"Bill, this is Pinky."

"Pinky?" He laughed. "Oh, I remember now. The budding lawyer. Okay, Pinky, what can I do for you?"

"I aspire to learn some of the finer details of winemaking, and who better to teach me than the maker of a world-class zinfandel?"

"My pleasure. I'm free this morning."

"I will be there in fifteen minutes."

I glanced at the fax and noted it was from Charles concerning his lack of campaign funds and pleading with me to come up with some clever ways to raise money. When I picked up my paperwork, I 'accidentally' left the fax on the table and walked to my car.

After a short drive through the verdant Alexander Valley, I parked my car by the tasting room of the Arroyo Verde Winery. I opened the door and the pungent aroma of spice blended with the bouquet of aged red wine flowed past my nostrils. A very thin, elderly man greeted me. The top of his head was bald surrounded with a well-trimmed crop of white hair. He jumped forward and shook my hand as if we were long lost relatives.

I said, "Bill, if I recall, the last time we talked you had more hair."

"Always the observant lawyer. And the hair I had was a lot darker. So what brings you to Sonoma County?"

"A few questions and a taste of some of your excellent wine."

"Fire away."

"In your opinion, how long could a premium winery function without a winemaker?"

"That sounds more like a lawyer talking than a lover of fine wines."

"Let us say I am on a working vacation."

"Okay by me. Now, I can't speak for everyone, but without a full-time winemaker my place would shut down in eighteen months. Pinky, I'm going to let you in on a little secret of the wine business. Most customers, even lawyers like yourself, think my business is a glamorous profession. In reality, a winery is not much different from any business that produces a sellable item, except a winery makes a fragile, living product out of grapes and yeast and that product could perish at any moment. The winemaker understands that concept. During the crush the grape juice is pumped into stainless tanks to begin fermentation. Then the juice is separated from the skins at the optimal moment. If the winemaker waits too long, he will overwhelm the wine with tannin. If he separates the juice too soon, the final product will lack color and fruit. Next, after a period of time in bulk storage to settle out dead yeast cells, the fermented wine is transferred into barrels. The aged wine must be bottled at the right moment to avoid extracting too much oak flavor from the barrel. The winemaker makes all the important decisions from the crush to bottling. So the job is a complex set of logistical judgments that must be made at the precise moment. Why the question?"

"Bill, I am going to impose upon our twenty-year relationship to ask that you keep our conversation between us."

"I guess I understand, but first, how about a glass of my private reserve."

"Thank you, and while you pour, I have a couple more questions."

"Shoot."

"When I was at the St. James Winery I met a woman named Florianna. Does she have a sibling?"

"You mean Arianna? Hell yes. That's her

identical twin."

"I thought I had spotted a female in town—"

"At the Downtown Pub I'd bet."

"Correct."

"Pinky, those twins are famous around here for their antics but you need to be careful. Take Arianna for an example. Her boyfriend, that big guy behind the bar, doesn't like competition."

"And Florianna? She came off as a cold businesswoman. Is that a correct assessment?"

"Perfect. Although there's a rumor floating around the valley that she's not that frosty around everyone."

"Any names?"

"One name that keeps popping up is Martin St. James."

"That is interesting."

"And he's a married man. Now it's my turn to impose upon our twenty-year relationship. What I told you is just winery gossip and I shouldn't have mentioned Martin's name."

"Bill, my lips are sealed. Now, is there any reason you would not allow one of your customers to tour your winery?"

"None that I can . . . oh, I get it now. Are you pissed because Martin St. James wouldn't let you into his winery?"

"Now that you mentioned it, yes I am."

"It's nothing personal, Pinky. Since the Hellman murder, Martin's place has become tighter than Fort Knox. Come to think of it, Martin implemented the no-tour policy about two years ago."

Bill topped my glass with more wine.

"Are you familiar with Luciano Botarri?"

"Yes. He's one of the top cellar masters in the county."

"Bill, could Luciano take over the winemaking responsibilities at the St. James Winery?"

"You know, that's a great question." Bill took a sip. "He could, but I don't think the Bench-Land cab would have the same finesse that Paul gave the wine."

"Thanks for the wine and the discussion. Now, would you give me a tour of your tank room?"

"Sure."

We walked through a door behind the tasting bar and a wave of frigid air flowed over me—the identical experience that happens when you open your refrigerator on a sweltering summer day. Not fifteen feet away stood what looked like a ten foot tall Popsicle—a big cylinder covered with a heavy blanket of ice.

I reached out and touched it. "Why the ice?"

"That's a stainless steel tank covered with a layer if ice. The tanks are built with double walls so we can run chilled glycol through the walls to control the temperature."

"But why do you need to freeze wine?"

"We cold stabilize the wine to precipitate out Tartrates. The Tartrates crystallize and fall to the bottom of the tank. We also maintain the temperature of the wine during fermentation. That gives us better control over the final product."

"A moment ago you mentioned Hellman's murder." I shivered. "Did the poor man freeze while precipitating Tartrates?"

Bill stared at me as if I had spent the last year living in a cave without a newspaper. "No, Paul didn't freeze, but before I talk about Hellman's death, you need to understand that all stainless steel tanks are dangerous. The tanks have to be cleaned out after the wine has been pumped out. In the tank room, if a cellar worker makes a mistake and forgets to open the top and bottom ports to vent the tank, that cellar worker has made his last mistake."

"Are you telling me that Hellman died because he forgot to follow proper venting procedures?"

"For God sakes, Pinky, he was found drowned inside a tank full of cab."

"My God, that doesn't sound like an accident to me."

"You've got that right."

"Bill, any idea how a man could end up drowning inside a tank of wine?"

"No, and I don't want to think about it."

"Okay. How many tanks do you have in this room?"

"Twelve. Four five-thousand gallon and twice as many ten-thousand gallon tanks."

"Are your tanks identical to the tanks at the St. James Winery?"

"Pinky, where are you going with this?"

I knew that sooner or later Bill would ask that question, and for Charles' sake, I was trusting that he was the apolitical type. "I am attempting to understand what happened at the St. James Winery the night of the murder."

He laughed. "Why didn't you come right out and ask me?"

Bill grabbed my arm and we walked between a row of tanks until we reached one without a layer of ice. He stopped and knocked on the steel with his knuckles. "This is an identical tank to the one where Paul was found." Bill pointed to the top of the tank. "The only difference is that Martin has a catwalk up there so a cellar worker can walk from tank to tank. I'm too cheap and don't have as many tanks as Martin does so we do the same job moving around a couple of ladders."

Bill took a ladder, leaned it against the tank, and said, "If you really want to know what happened the night of the murder? Go on, climb up the ladder."

I have never been comfortable on ladders. "You'll hold the ladder?"

"Sure."

After five steps I reached the top of the tank and stared into an 18" porthole. Connected to the base of the port was a top with a rubber seal that swung on a hinge from right to left. I ran my finger around the inside of the porthole and felt the sharp edge. Now I understood how Hellman's head could have been damaged if the team pulling his body out of the liquid became carried away with their task.

Bill called to me. "Relax, Pinky. I've got a hold of the ladder. Now stick your head into the opening. I'll open the bottom port and you'll see my hand waving at you."

I looked down, into the porthole, and felt a touch dizzy. About ten feet away was a shaft of light, and Bill's hand moving across the floor of the tank.

Bill yelled, "Now, envision this. The tank is three-quarters full of wine. Someone walks up behind you, dumps you in headfirst, and holds you down by your feet until you stop struggling. That's how they found Paul Hellman. Got it?"

I shuddered. As much as I savored a great cabernet, drowning in the liquid would not be a pretty way to die. "Don't let go of the ladder. I have seen enough. I am coming down."

Once my feet reached the floor, Bill said, "Now, let's head back to the tasting room. I'll bet you're ready to buy some wine."

"Actually, I have all the zinfandel I need at the moment."

Bill flashed a hard smile. "Pinky, pull out your checkbook. A couple of cases of my top zinfandel will go a long way to help me forget your questions concerning the Hellman murder."

FIFTEEN

Bear-Rio Nido, California

The thick ground fog disappeared about the time we hit the Sonoma-Napa county line. The warm sun coming through the windshield was so damn bright I had to put on my dark glasses.

A good hour after the first blue sky we'd seen since we were east of Sacramento, I pulled into the Chapman's Riverside Resort parking lot just off the highway.

Flo jumped out of the cab and a big frown twisted across her forehead. She hauled in a breath and shouted, "Hold on, where's the river, and those cute little cabins I saw in the internet pictures?"

"Don't know, Babe. You'll have to ask in the office."

We walked into a dark lobby. On the right stood a dude behind a counter. On the left was a rock fireplace with a couple of logs that put out more smoke than heat and a couple of tired looking chairs. The air inside the room smelled weird, like somebody had figured out how to mix wood smoke and sour milk.

I could see where the wood smoke came from, but the sour tang seemed to be floating up from somewhere, but because this joint was Flo's pick, I knew better than ask too many questions.

That's when I spotted the strap of a floor length

white cane looped around the dude's wrist, and then I noticed he was wearing dark glasses inside the dark lobby. Jesus, the poor bastard was blind!

"Howdy, folks. Welcome to Chapman's, the outstanding destination resort on the Russian River. My name's Oliver Chapman but most folks call me Ollie. Do you have a reservation?"

Flo pushed her way past me. "Yes. Last evening I made a reservation on the Internet. One double room with a river view at $55.00 per night."

I watched the dude. He didn't seem to let his blindness bother him, but he didn't know he was missing one of the world's great sights, Flo's super melons.

"Madam, you were indeed lucky. The Internet special rate is only available during this month and is an unheard of value in this day and age. However, I must remind you that the Internet special rate is non-refundable. Once you made the reservation I charged your credit card for five days at $55.00 per night for a total of $275.00. Now, I'll imprint your card so I can cover any further room-service charges you might make during your stay, along with the County hotel tax."

"Hold it right there, buster! I don't remember seeing anything about the rate being non-refundable and—"

That was when I remembered what I spotted when Flo showed me the computer screen in Modesto, the word non-refundable. "Babe, it's okay. The web site said the reservation was non-refundable if—"

"Well, I don't remember seeing anything about charging the card for the five days. What if we don't like this place?"

Damn, she could be a pain. I grabbed her

shoulder, pointed at the dude's white cane and growled, "Flo, I told you I saw it. End of story. Now hand the man the credit card."

She glared at me, and then followed my finger down to the dude's white cane. A light finally went on. "Oh, I apologize. Here is the card."

So Flo got us locked into staying at Chapman's River Resort for five days, and knowing her, she'd figure out a way to make it my fault before long.

Suddenly a girl-kid popped out from behind the blind guy. "Mister, now that you're checked in, I'll show you to your cabin."

The kid was skinny, not much more than four feet tall, with a tassel of rusty hair peeking out from under a Giants baseball cap. She had on orange jeans and a pink lacy thing that draped over a purple shirt. An oversized pair of ruby slippers covered her feet. The poor kid was dressed like a clown who'd escaped from the circus.

Flo said, "What's your name, little girl?"

"Ettamae Chapman. What's your name, big girl?"

Flo blinked a couple of times. "Florence Sonderlund, and my gentleman friend's name is Bear Zabarte."

The kid gave me the stink eye. "Gentleman friend? Sorry to hear you're not married! Florence, we get a lot of this kind of business on the weekends during the summer. But since you've checked in for five days I guess this is not an afternoon stand. Grandpa Ollie has put you in the Bluebird Cabin. We name all the cabins after birds. The Red-Tailed Hawk cabin's my favorite, but we don't book it during the winter."

I said, "Why not?"

The kid said, "It's sort of built too close to the

river."

Flo said, "I love to listen to the water at night. Move us to that cabin, please."

The kid said, "Not safe. Twenty years ago, during the last big flood, we lost that cabin."

Flo said, "How old are you?"

"I'm ten."

"How do you know what happened twenty years ago?"

"Grandpa Ollie told me."

Ollie said, "She's right, miss. The couple staying in that cabin lost all their luggage and they nearly lost their lives."

"I don't care. I want to stay in a cabin next to the river."

The kid shrugged. "It's your funeral."

Flo said, "In my day, little girls didn't address their elders that way."

Ollie said, "If I was you I'd get used to the way Ettamae talks. She's been working with me since her parents were killed in a dreadful car accident a couple of years ago."

"Two years, three months, and five days to be exact, Grandpa."

"And then your grandma passed."

Ettamae nodded. "One year and six days ago."

Ollie said, "Her Grandma was one of the top exotic dancers in San Francisco. Ettamae loves to rummage through her Grandma's old costumes. I can't see what she's wearing today but I'll bet she's a colorful sight."

Flo said, "She's colorful, all right."

Ollie said, "Like I was saying, Ettamae is ten going on twenty-nine and I'm afraid there's nothing she hasn't done or seen while helping me out at the resort."

Flo said, "How come she isn't in school?"

Ettamae grabbed Flo's small suitcase and started to push us toward the door. "I'm home schooled. There's this lady from the county that comes around every other week to be sure I'm learning how to read, write and do math. Grandpa Ollie teaches me everything and the resort guests take care of the rest of my education. Right, Grandpa?"

Ollie kind of smiled. "Darling, we do the best we can under the circumstances."

Flo said, "Ollie, based on my brief observation, Ettamae is definitely receiving a well-rounded education. Now, if you're ready, can someone show me the way to the Red-Tailed Hawk cabin? I need to pee."

It wasn't very often that I ever saw Flo back down, or apologize, but somehow that skinny little broad had pulled it off. I made a promise to myself to keep an eye on Ettamae to try and figure out how she did it.

The kid grabbed Flo's hand and the two walked down the road toward the river while I followed them in the truck. Just like the picture on the web site, there were a bunch of cabins, but there was one big difference. The white lounge chairs that had been filled with the good-looking babes were now empty—no cars—no dude cooking stuff on the BBQ. In fact, except for the line of cabins, the Chapman River Resort looked deserted.

I followed Ettamae up a couple of stairs. "Hey, kid," I said, "How come the resort is so empty?"

"The joint really jumps in the summer, but January and February are dead months."

I handed her a couple of bucks but the kid shook her head. "As one of the proprietors, I don't accept tips."

I put my money back in my pocket. "Kid, you got any idea what's causing that skanky smell in the lobby?"

"I'd put my money on a momma possum and her babies. The momma has her nest under the building near the fireplace."

"That'll do it."

"Almost forgot to tell you. We serve a continental breakfast every morning between seven and nine in the lobby. Bye." She turned and ran back up the hill to her Grandpa.

Flo came out of the bathroom and her cell phone beeped. "Lu, I was just about to call you. We are now staying at Chapman's River Resort. If I sit on the steps and stretch my leg out my toes can almost touch the river. You can reach out the bathroom window and feel the bark of a giant redwood with your hand. Across the river there are green hills covered with trees. This place is so much better than that dump in Modesto. Trust me, Lu, this is a perfect location for a vacation and—" She stopped and listened for a second. Then she said, "Right. I'll pass that on to Bear. Bye."

I said, "What's going on?"

"Pinky needs to talk to you immediately."

"Okay." I dialed his cell. "Hi, Boss."

"Damn it, stop calling me Boss."

"Okay, Boss."

"Where have you been?"

"In Modesto, why?"

"I thought you would arrive in Sonoma County yesterday afternoon?"

"It was late when we finished the OSHA scam and the ground fog was so bad that we had to wait for morning to find our way out of Modesto."

"Sounds like a weak excuse to me but that is water under the bridge."

"Boss, I forgot to tell you that Flo made me an OSHA badge that looks like a real one."

"At least she is earning her keep which is more than I can say for you. Tomorrow morning take your fake Cal-OSHA badge and go to the St. James Winery. There you will meet Luciano Botarri, the cellar master, and you will start to nose around, as you so aptly describe your investigative process."

"What's a cellar master do?"

"That's not important at the moment. Once you are inside the winery you are to follow your inspection routine until your reach the site of Hellman's murder."

"Who?"

"Paul Hellman. You will find out more concerning his death tomorrow when you talk to Botarri."

"Okay. Let me make sure I got everything straight. I go to the St. James Winery. Hook up with Luciano Botarri. Do a fake OSHA inspection of the joint. And find out who killed Paul Hellman."

"That is correct. Now if you will excuse me I have an important—"

"Sorry, Boss, but I'm going to need a lot more from you than that."

"What do you mean?"

"Like I asked you before, who the hell's Paul Hellman?"

"My good man, I pay you a large amount of money to do investigative work for me and I expect you—"

"Hey, I'm not a mind reader. I go to the winery with my fake OSHA badge, and meet up with this Botarri dude, and do a phony safety inspection. Boss,

103

I still don't know what the hell I'm looking for."

I heard Pinky sigh. "Some months ago Paul Hellman was found drowned in a tank of cabernet sauvignon. A cellar worker, Enrique Flores was arrested for Hellman's murder because they'd had bad words over growing dope on the winery property. Enrique's uncle is paying me to find the real killer, and the Flores trial starts in a few days. We have a limited amount of time to come up with a second murder suspect, someone better than Enrique Flores."

Jesus, he doesn't want much. "Is that all?"

"And whatever you do, don't forget you are going to the winery as an OSHA inspector because no one, and I mean no one, can discover that you are investigating Hellman's murder. For example, you could tell Mr. Botarri that you are investigating Hellman's murder as a possible accident."

"Okay boss, now I understand what the hell is going on."

"Call me the minute you finish your visit at the winery."

"Right."

SIXTEEN

Bear-Alexander Valley, California

The next morning me and Flo walked up the road to the main building a little after seven and inside the dingy lobby stood the little kid, Ettamae. On her head was one of those tall white hats fry cooks wear in restaurants. The rest of her outfit looked like a rainbow on dope—a purple shirt, a feathery pink thing that wrapped around her skinny shoulders, grass green pants and a pair of Minnie Mouse slippers.

Flo said, "How about a Denver omelet?"

"Sorry, Florence, don't do omelets. What you see is what you get for breakfast."

Ettamae was standing next to one of the ugliest continental breakfasts I ever saw—six bananas, all covered with ugly black spots, a couple of really green apples that looked harder than a rock, a pile of boxes with those little powdered donuts inside, white plastic cups, and coffee that smelled like it could strip spar varnish off an old sailboat.

Ettamae gave us the old Vanna White move and said, "Sorry the spread is a little skimpy, but as I told you yesterday, this is a slow month. You should see what this table looks like in July."

I could tell that Flo was about to blow. She loved her continental breakfasts and had worked out a sort of rating system for each place we stayed based on the pool, lounge chairs, bathrooms, and continental breakfasts. I guessed that in Flo's mind, the Chapman Russian River Resort had just about reached the bottom of the list, and this joint was her pick. In case you don't know it by now, Flo doesn't like ending up on the bottom of any list, anytime, anywhere, even when it's something as dumb as picking a dippy motel.

Flo flashed me her stink eye. "You've done it again."

"What did I do?"

"Anyone with half-a-brain should have know better that agreeing to a non-refundable charge for an unseen motel in a place you've never been before."

Before I could think what to say to Flo, Ettamae ran behind the counter with her pink feathers flapping behind her.

"Whoops. Forgot to set the juice out."

She ran back in a second carrying a jug of juice that was almost as heavy as she was. "Florence, I'll pour you a glass. How about you, Bear?"

I watched a stream of fluorescent orange stuff fall into Flo's cup. "No thanks, kid. I'll stick with something real, like the coffee, as bad as it smells."

Flo moved between me and the kid. She patted the kid's baseball cap and for a second looked like she was going to cry. Why did she do that? Ettamae was cute, pure and simple.

Flo said, "Don't let what that old grouch says bother you. The spread looks perfect to me. How about some more of that juice, Ettamae."

With those two females ganging up on me there was no way I was going to come out ahead. I stuffed a couple boxes of those little powdered donuts into my jacket pocket, poured some coffee into a plastic cup and said, "I'm out of here. Have a good day."

Dreaming of a three-egg cheese omelet with a side of ham, I jumped in the truck and hauled my ass to the St. James Winery.

On my drive north I took the time to catch the scenery. Sonoma County was a pretty place with lots of green hills, trees, and what looked like a billion grape vines. In the forty minute drive I must a passed about two million of them, all planted in nice rows, and most of them had yellow and green stuff planted between the rows. Compared to all this, my hometown of Carson City was a dusty, brown desert.

I arrived at the winery around eight-thirty, about the same time a guy got out of his truck. He was a good-sized dude who looked like he could do about fifty chin-ups without breathing hard. His dark hair matched his eyes and I was glad Flo had stayed at the motel because I was pretty sure she'd think this dude was a keeper. I flashed him my Cal-OSHA badge. "What's your name?"

"Luciano Botarri. Mr. Zabarte, what do you want?"

"Take me to your tank room."

"I'd be happy to do that, but tell me, what's the reason for the sudden inspection? We had an OSHA inspection about six months ago."

I said, "Call me Bear. I know all about that, but since then one of your guys fell into a tank and drowned."

"You don't understand. He didn't fall in. He was murdered. The cops arrested a guy and—"

"Hold on, has anyone from Cal-OSHA done an investigation concerning the unfortunate incident?"

"No."

"Then the final decision of what happened to that poor dude is up to me to decide. Until I've completed my investigation no one, not you, me, the police, nobody knows if that dude died from an accident or if he was murdered."

"Really? I didn't know that."

"Don't worry, not many people in this state understand the power of Cal-OSHA. Now take me to where the incident occurred."

"Right away." He unlocked a door with a sign, 'Tank Room', and said, "Follow me, sir."

"Hold on. Drop that sir crap. I'm just a state grunt doing my job."

Botarri's face relaxed into a smile, like we were now grunt buddies. "Okay, and you can call me Luciano."

"Like that big-time opera dude, Luciano Pavarotti?"

"Yes. My dad thought he was the best tenor since Caruso."

"Why was the tank room door locked?"

"The boss put locks on about two years ago. Now that I think of it, I'm not sure why."

The tank room was a big room, like half a football field big, colder than a meat locker, and nearly two stories tall. The floors were concrete with little drains that ran down the center. Rows of stainless tanks that looked ten to fifteen feet tall sat on concrete pads about three feet off the floor. Ladders leaned against a couple of tanks. A bunch of clear-plastic hoses lay on the floor. Some were empty and some were moving wine from a tank to somewhere else. I wasn't a real OSHA inspector, but with all the water all over the floors, the hoses, and the ladders, the tank room looked like an accident waiting to happen.

"Why's it so cold in here?"

"Paul weather stripped the doors so the room was as air-tight as we could make it."

"Luciano, I'm trying to be nice, so don't bullshit me."

"Bear, I'm telling you the truth. He wanted to keep out the outside air so he could control the temperature in the wines stored on these tanks."

I scribbled something on a note pad.

"Bear, what are you doing?"

"Just writing down there are no windows. Let's move on to the tank where the tragic incident happened."

I took a step and damn near tripped over a couple of hoses when Luciano stopped walking and pointed up. "This is the tank where the murd . . . ah, that incident you're investigating took place."

I stood back, scribbled more notes so the dude would think I was hanging on his every word. The bottom of the tank was bolted to a concrete pad about three feet off the ground. The top was a good ten to twelve feet above me with a catwalk that connected the killer tank to a row of tanks going left and right. "Luciano, were you at the winery on the night of the unfortunate incident?"

"I've already told the sheriff. The crush was about to start. I was behind schedule clearing space in the warehouse so I had to work late, to get caught up."

I didn't have a clue what this dude was talking about. "For my final report, what's stored in the warehouse?"

"After we bottle the wine, the bottles are put into cases and then the cases are placed on pallets. We stack the pallets, two high in the warehouse for further ageing and storage until they are shipped to our distributor. I'll take you through the warehouse after we leave here."

"Don't bother, I get the warehouse part. Now, a

109

minute ago you said something about a crush starting soon. What does that mean? I need to be sure my dumb boss back in Sacramento doesn't get confused and start to think your guy was crushed in that tank."

"The crush happens after the grapes are picked. Bins of grapes are dumped into a machine that literally crushes every little berry to release the juice, color and flavor."

I scribbled on the pad, like I was really taking notes. "And how do you know when the crush is supposed to start?"

"That's easy. We measure the sugar content of grapes through sampling before they're picked. Past histories and sugar measurements should give us a good estimated date for the crush."

"So you had to be at the winery on the night of the accidental death to get everything ready for the crush that was going to start soon. Am I correct?"

"You've got it. Bear, do you really think it's possible that Hellman's death was an accident? I mean the guy was floating upside down in a tank full of cabernet sauvignon."

"As I stated earlier, that's why I'm here. Now, do you get paid by the hour or is your position salaried?"

"I'm paid a salary. Hey, what the hell does that got to do with anything?"

"Just answer my questions."

"Okay."

"So you're like a manager at the winery."

"I guess you could say that."

"And because you don't have set hours, you need to be at the winery as long as you're needed."

"That's right. You know, I've worked up to twenty hours straight during the crush."

I decided it was time to push this dude a little harder. "Did you see anyone else at the winery the night of the unfortunate incident?"

"Yes. The night guard and I spotted Enrique Flores, he's the guy in jail for Hellman's murder."

"Was he a salaried employee, like yourself?"

"Hell no. He's just a cellar rat."

"Cellar rat?"

He laughed. "That's what all cellar workers are called. Martin St. James, the owner, pays all his cellar rats minimum wage."

"Was it normal to see this cellar rat that late at the winery?"

"Yes and no. Enrique would pick up a few bucks by working extra shifts for the owner—landscaping, building walls, that sort of thing."

"Did you leave the winery on the night of the accidental death?"

"No, I was here . . wait . . . yes, I did. I went home about seven-thirty, ate a quick dinner, and returned a little after eight. That's when I saw Enrique while I was parking my truck. A few minutes later I fired up the forklift in the warehouse and moved pallets until the sheriff's deputy walked in."

"Luciano, now think before you answer this question. Do you think the Mexican murdered the dude or was the death accidental?"

He didn't say a word for a few seconds, like he was trying to figure out how Hellman could have been working at the top of the tank, slipped and then fell in headfirst. Finally he said, "I don't see any way but murder, but I don't really know. I was in the building next door stacking pallets. I wasn't here when Hellman died. Besides, the Sheriff arrested that Mexican. Between you, and me, and the gatepost, I'll admit I didn't shed a tear when I heard that Hellman tried to drink five thousand gallons of cabernet. The two of us didn't get along. For a while we did, but I found out that the bastard couldn't be trusted to keep his word."

Bingo! Give a guy enough rope and he'll figure out a way to hang himself. "What do you mean by that?"

"You'd have to see my place to understand."

"I'm not in any hurry. Let's go."

Luciano glanced around. A guy in a sweatshirt and jeans was hosing down a tank about thirty feet from us. "Bear, that's one of the cellar rats I was telling you about." He yelled, "Carlos, I'm going to run home for a couple of minutes. Cover for me."

Carlos didn't raise his head. "Got your back, boss."

We walked to the parking lot and Luciano opened the passenger door of a brand new Toyota Tundra.

I said, "Nice truck. Cellar masters must be getting paid a lot better than CAL-OSHA inspectors."

He smiled. "I came into a few bucks and always wanted a new truck."

"Like winning the Lottery?"

Botarri didn't answer as he started the engine. "I'm taking you through the back way. That's a shortcut to my place."

We drove for a couple of minutes when I saw a bunch of guys pulling grape plants out of the ground. "What are those dudes doing?"

Botarri said, "Pulling out infected vines."

"Like they got the flu? I didn't know plants got sick?"

"All plants can get sick, but those vines over

there are really sick. We have to pull them out because they've got Phylloxera."

"Phil who?"

"Shit, I wasn't suppose to use the shortcut until they finished the job. If you talk to my boss, Martin St. James, don't tell him I drove you by the Bench-Land vineyard."

"Tell me about it. My boss is a pain in the ass too."

A couple of minutes later the truck popped onto the county road and after a couple of hundred feet, Botarri turned left into another vineyard.

"This is my place. Some of the vines here are over a hundred years old. See that building on the right?"

There was a rock and concrete barn-like building. It looked in pretty bad shape to me. "Yup, I see it."

"That's the old Botarri Winery and Brandy Distillery. My great-grandfather, Francesco Botarri, built the original winery in 1903, after he moved to Sonoma County from Lake Como, Italy."

"Hey, do you own all this?"

"That's the complicated part. I own the house and the half-acre the house sits on. A few years back I took out a big loan to restore the old Botarri Winery. Then the economy turned to crap and things didn't work out as I had planned. Before I could whistle 'Yankee Doodle', the Goddamn bank foreclosed. To pay off what I owed, the bank sold off the winery building and all of my vineyards to a rich bastard who lived in Portland, Oregon. Now the bastard wants to sell everything back to me."

"Hey, that should be good."

"I guess. He called me a few months ago and told me that he was in a financial pickle. If I could come up with two million cash, he'd sell me the vineyards and the old winery building. That might seem like a lot of money for this old place but back in the twenties, before prohibition, the Botarri Winery was one of the top labels in California. Finally, this was my chance to bring back the old family name. I talked to Paul Hellman and asked him to become my partner. I had worked with him for a few years and I was sure that with his reputation and connections, the bank would give us what I needed and then some."

"Hold on. Are you telling me that the guy that drowned at the St. James Winery was your business partner?"

"Sort of. That was my plan. I invited Hellman to come over and walk the vineyards. Then he checked out the old facility. Afterwards we came back to the house, sat down at my kitchen table, and decided to set up the partnership. Hellman agreed to do the winemaking and the business side of the operation— I'd take care of the cellar work and the vineyards. We even shook hands to seal the deal. A week later the bank told me they'd loan me the money. I called the man in Portland and agreed to his offer. Everything was set. Then out of the blue, Hellman, that double crossing son-of-a-bitch, backed out of the deal."

"How could the bastard do that? I mean he was your partner."

"Like a fool I didn't ask for a contract. No, I trusted Hellman and so did the bank. They gave us a loan commitment based on his word."

"Then what happened?"

"A month after we shook hands, the bank manager called Hellman to check on some bullshit detail and Hellman told him that he had changed his mind. He was backing out of our partnership. The bank manager called me and said that without the Hellman name, the loan commitment was off the table."

I choked back a grin. Yesterday, Pinky had told me he needed a man who had a reason to kill Paul Hellman and I just found him one, tied up with a pink bow, like a fancy birthday present. "Did you ever find out why he suddenly changed his mind?"

"Hell yes. After the bank manager called I drove to the winery and found Hellman working in the lab. I lost my temper and made a fool of myself. I broke some lab equipment and demanded to know why he backed out. The bastard said that when he informed the owner that he was leaving the winery, St. James pleaded with him to stay. Something about he couldn't afford to have him leave. Bear, between you and me, I think Hellman used me and our partnership deal to jack up his salary. He didn't give a damn that he screwed me out of my chance to restore my family name. Without Hellman my dream was dead."

Luciano's eyes turned darker than two pieces of coal, and at that second I was glad the chump wasn't pissed off at me.

I said, "So what happened then?"

"What could I do? Without the money from the bank my deal died quicker than a fish out of water. I still had my cellar master job at the St. James Winery, but the chance to have my own winery was gone."

"I'd like to talk to the bank manager that handled your loan request. Would that be all right with you?"

Luciano looked at me like I was trying to sell him a used car. "What the hell does talking with the bank have to do with your accident investigation?"

"Luciano, during my years with OSHA, I have found that no stone should ever be left unturned."

"I still don't understand what . . . shit, I've nothing to hide. His name is Eugene Burton. His office is at the Healdsburg branch of the Pacific Farm Credit."

SEVENTEEN

Bear-Healdsburg, California

I knew the boss told me to call him as soon as I left the winery, but the Pacific Farm Credit office was on the way back to my motel. I pulled my pickup into a parking space outside the building. After I unbuckled my seatbelt I called my motel room.

That scrawny kid answered.

I growled. "This is Bear. What the hell are you doing in my room?"

"Vacuuming the floor."

"Oh. Is Flo around?"

"Sorry, Florence is in a lounge chair by the river trying to catch a few rays from the sun. Can I give her a message?"

"Nope. I was just going to tell her that I'll be home in a couple of hours."

"I can do that."

"Okay, and kid—"

"The name's Ettamae!"

Jesus. That's all I needed, two smart-ass females biting at my butt twenty-four hours a day. "Right! Ettamae, I was going to ask if you could give me the name of a good place to eat tonight."

"If I was you I'd take Florence to Gordon's. They have pretty good grub, a great wine list, and there are a few tables set up on the deck so you can watch the river flow by while you eat in a perfect romantic setting."

"Do you think it'll be warm enough?"

"No problem. They've got a bunch of those cool heaters, and besides, it looks like we're in for some rain today. So it might not work out, but this could be your last chance to eat outside for the next couple of days."

"Thanks for the tip, kid."

"I've told you before, it's Ettamae!"

I dropped my cell into my jacket pocket and walked into the building. In front there was a counter and behind the counter there was a dozen of those stupid cubicles that make the workers think they have their own office. Looking over the tops of the cubicles I spotted a bunch of gray-haired old farts pushing papers from one side of their desk to the other.

A super-old broad behind the counter whispered, "May I help you?"

She was tiny and her face looked like one of those kitchen sponges that have been used too long. The best part of her was the big blob of blue-white hair that was piled on the top of her head like a giant spoonful of whipped cream.

I said, "Got a cold?"

She reached down, grabbed a tissue and blew her nose. "Woke up this morning with laryngitis."

"I heard that's going around these days. I need to talk with Eugene Burton."

Without looking up the old broad pushed a button. There was a little buzz and the gate in front of me opened. "He's in the last enclosure on your right."

I started to walk through and then stopped. "Thanks. Have you tried a cough drop?"

She flashed me her nasty face. "Are you a

doctor?"

"Hell no."

"Then don't go around telling sick people how to get well."

I hoped her cold was making her that way because if it wasn't, she'd be one tough broad to be around! I cruised past the counter and walked back to the last cubicle on the right. Burton had to be the oldest dude in a room where the average age looked to be around seventy. He'd combed over the last of his white hair across his bald, shiny head and had more bags under his eyes than a full luggage carrousel at the Reno airport.

I said, "Mr. Burton, my name is Bear Zabarte. I just left my old buddy Luciano Botarri and he told me that I should talk to you about a loan."

Burton grabbed a pad and a pen and said, "Sit down and you can give me the details."

"Before I get to that, I need to know if your loan commitments are firm. Botarri told me that you canceled his deal after Paul Hellman backed out. Is that true?"

Burton looked at me over the tops of his glasses the same way my sixth grade teacher, Mrs. Gardner, glared at me once she fingered me as the guy who had smeared Vaseline on the girl's bathroom doorknobs.

"Excuse me. Do I know you?"

"Nope. Like I told you when I got here my name is Bear Zabarte, and Luciano Botarri told me to stop by—"

"Mr. Zabarte, all information concerning loan requests for our Pacific Farm Credit clients are confidential. Now, if you'll excuse me, I have—"

I had started my day with only a couple of stale, miniature powered sugar donuts and crappy coffee, so this old fart was beginning to piss me off, but I leaned over and slapped a friendly smile on my puss. "Mr. Burton, let's try it this way. Forget what I said about Luciano Botarri. Let's talk about my need for a loan to build a winery. Okay?"

He nodded.

"Good. I own about fifty acres of vineyards in the middle of the Alexander Valley. Are you with me so far?"

The old dude grabbed a form from one of those little plastic shelves that all loan guys keep on their desk. "That's good. Fifty acres of grapes is a nice starting point for our discussion. What varietal or varietals are planted on the acreage?"

"Varietal?"

"Yes, the varietal. What kind of grapes are you growing on the property?"

Shit, he had me there. Then I remembered what wine Flo likes to drink. "Zinfandel, all the grapes are zinfandel."

The old dude scribbled some numbers. "That's excellent. Zinfandels are a very hot item in today's wine market. Now, how old are the vines?"

"How old are they? I don't know." I held my hand about three feet off the floor. "The last time I checked they stood about this high. Oh, I almost forgot. I hired a guy who knows all about grapes and he told me that some of the vines were sick with something."

"Was it leaf role virus?"

"I don't think that's what he called it."

Burton turned the form over and started to tap his fingernails on his desktop. "Mr. Zabarte, it strikes me that you are unusually ignorant concerning viticulture, but in today's world where every millionaire thinks he's a winemaker that's not unusual. What size of winery do you plan on your property?"

I recalled the broken down building on Botarri's spread. "I'm not sure but the building should be about fifty by a hundred feet."

Burton sighed. "Mr. Zabarte, an informed answer to my question would have indicated the size of the winery in cases of finished wine. Such as, 'Mr. Burton, we plan on producing fifteen thousand cases of zinfandel.' Either you are the most ignorant person I've ever dealt with in my fifty years of agricultural lending, or you're trying to pull some kind of a scam. Which is it?"

"I guess it's time I spill my guts." I stared at my feet for a second to let him think he'd nailed me. "The truth is me and my wife are getting a divorce."

"And what do your marital problems have to do with me and my position with Pacific Farm Credit?"

I whispered, "Remember my buddy, Botarri?"

He leaned forward and nodded. I figured he was rising to the bait. Now all I had to do was hook the old fart. I glanced around the room and then leaned closer so he'd think he was getting in on a big secret. "My lawyer told me that I have to hide a big wad of scratch from my wife."

Burton frowned, "How much?"

"Two hundred thousand."

"Wow."

"Now back to Botarri. He told me that he would sell me twenty-five percent of his winery operation for two hundred big ones. The deal sounded okay to me and to celebrate Botarri pulled out some white lightning he called grappa."

Burton smiled. "Mr. Zabarte, you need to go slow when your drink grappa. It hits hard and fast."

"You should tell that to Botarri. After he sucked

121

down close to half the bottle he let it slip that he had a loan commitment from you but you needed some guy named Hellman as the winemaker. Then Hellman died and with it your loan. Jesus, that was more than I needed to know. All I wanted to do was hide a bucket of cash from my wife's attorney, not piss it down a rat hole. Are you married?"

"Twice, and both were expensive divorces. I understand what you're going through."

I lowered my voice, "Okay, man to man, I've got a proposition for you and I'll make it worth your while," I whispered. "I'll give you an untraceable envelope with ten Benjamin's inside so there's no way for anyone to figure out where it came from."

"A thousand dollars! What do I have to do?"

"Just answer two simple questions, and Mr. Burton, you won't lose your job or anything because you won't have to say a word. All you'll have to do is blink your eyes once for yes and twice for no. Got it?"

"A grand is a steep price to pay for a couple of blinks."

"I know that, but it's a small price to pay to save me two hundred grand. Okay?"

The old dude nodded and sat back.

"First, you've got to write out your home address for me so I can mail you my . . . thank you notes."

Burton grabbed a slip of paper, scribbled something, and handed it to me.

"You ready?"

He blinked once.

"Good. Now, did you agree to loan Luciano Botarri the money he needed to start up his winery?"

One blink.

"Okay, after this question I'll be out of your hair quicker than my wife packed her bag. After Paul Hellman backed out did you cancel the loan?"

One blink.

"Mr. Burton, I appreciate all your help. I'll mail that envelope we discussed and I'll drop by in a few days just to be sure you received everything I told you I'd send. It has been a pleasure doing business with you."

EIGHTEEN

Pinky-Healdsburg, California

I had returned to my favorite wicker chair on the sunny side of the porch, and after a second glass of the house wine, dozed peacefully until a buzz from my cell snatched me from a blissful slumber.

"Boss, this is Bear."

"I recognize your voice, you dolt. Are you aware that you have pulled me away from a critical meeting?"

"Sorry, but you told me to call you as soon as I finished my winery inspection."

"Your interruption is no less than I expected. Give me a second." I took a sip of wine and for a moment I focused my attention on the delicate pink blossoms that covered a camellia bush a few feet away. "Go ahead, but be concise." Bear blathered on until I cried, "Stop. I've heard enough. I note that both you, and the police report, indicate there was a night watchman at the winery when Hellman was murdered. Your immediate assignment is to interview that man. His name is Mike Wilson."

"I'll do that first thing tomorrow. I promised Flo—"

"Bear, we have been through this before. I believe the phrase is, 'my way or the highway.'"

I listened to silence for a moment and allowed my slow-witted investigator enough time to consider his alternatives.

"Right, I'll interview the night watchman before I go back to my motel. Got his phone number?"

"It just happens I do. After you complete that task I have another assignment and this should take care of your concerns over leaving that woman of yours sitting around with nothing to do."

"Shoot."

"Martin St. James is married so he must have a wife. Assuming the two live together, I want you and Flo to visit her. You nose around, as you so crudely put it, and Flo will be there to give me a woman's take on their relationship. Find out everything you can about the pair. How long have they been married—do they have any children—are they a happy couple—that sort of thing."

"But boss, Flo is at the motel on the river, a good twenty minutes from where I am."

"Then I recommend you get yourself moving and pick her up. We have much work to do and precious little time left."

"She'll get pissed off."

"Frankly, I have never been able to figure out how you can tell the difference between normal and pissed off. Now shut up and listen to me. After I talk with my Sonoma County contact, I will call you and we will meet at the Downtown Pub in Healdsburg to tie up any loose ends."

"That reminds me, I think I found you a—"

"Tell me about it when we meet shortly."

"But Boss, this is—"

"Are you hard of hearing? I said later."

"Right. The Downtown Pub in Healdsburg."

"Now you are listening. Until then."

NINETEEN

Bear-Healdsburg, California

First thing I did was punch in Flo's cell number.

"Hello?"

"Babe, I just got a great idea."

"What time is it?"

"Why?"

"I fell asleep by the river in my bathing suit. Now it's cloudy, colder than a well digger's ass, and I'm freezing. What's your great idea?"

"I'm going to take you into Healdsburg so you can buy a new dress or something."

"Really?"

"Go take a hot shower and have a glass of wine. I'll be by in twenty minutes. I've got to interview a rent-a-cop, then we've got another little job, then we can go to dinner."

"We've got a little job? Am I really going shopping or are you scamming me?"

"You'll shop for stuff while I listen to the guard. After that, we'll drive to the St. James winery and talk to a broad."

"What broad?"

"The owner's wife."

"Humph," Flo was quiet for a second, meaning she was thinking. "It's about time I get to go to the fancy tourist town of Healdsburg."

"Flo, stop ragging at me. Are you going to get

dressed?"

"I'm hanging up now so I can shower."

Damn she can piss me off. I dialed the number Pinky gave me.

"Good afternoon, Mr. Wilson. My name is Bear Zabarte."

"Gaehhhh . . . Do you realize I got to bed at ten this morning. You can't be one of my friends 'cause they all know better than to call me while I'm sleeping. Who did you say you are?"

"Bear Zabarte."

"Don't know you. What the hell did you say you wanted?"

"I'm an investigator. I'm in the area and have a few questions to ask you concerning the Paul Hellman murder."

"I told the cops all I know. Good bye."

"I'll buy you a beer."

"Can't turn down an offer like that 'cept I don't drink before I eat breakfast. Buy me breakfast and we've got a deal."

I glanced at my watch. "I can do that."

"I'll meet you in thirty minutes at the Mountain Cafe. The joint's on Healdsburg Avenue, a couple miles north of the plaza."

"Make that forty-five minutes and we've got a deal. See you."

I grabbed my wallet. I was down to fifteen bucks. I'd get the waitress to write on the tab that the guard ate the breakfast so Pinky would have to pay me back.

Forty-five minutes later, I dropped Flo off at a dress shop across the street from the Healdsburg plaza. "Babe, I'll be back and pick you up right here in an hour."

"I only get an hour?"

"Hey, we can't afford to let you shop any longer than that."

A few minutes later I was sitting at a table inside the cafe when a bowling-ball-shaped dude in a guard's uniform walked in.

I said, "Mr. Wilson?"

"That's me." He sat down and giant slabs of his rear-end flopped over the edges of his chair. "I usually order the breakfast special but seeing that you're buying, I'd better check out the omelet menu."

"Mr. Wilson, I'm interested in your—"

"Hold on a minute, I need to order my breakfast first."

A female voice called out from the kitchen. "Want the usual, Mike?"

"Alice, my investigator friend here told me I could order anything on the menu. Bring me the Mountain Man omelet, and a couple of sides of bacon and sausage."

"But the Mountain Man comes with bacon and sausage."

"I know that."

"What kind of cheese do you want? You get your choice of two."

"Cheddar, and toss in some of that expensive French Brie."

"Okay. Thank God they're your arteries. Do you want extra toast and jam like usual?"

"You got it, Alice." He turned his head. "Okay Mr. Investigator, fire away."

"Tell me what happened the night of the murder at the winery."

"Not much to tell. While I was making my rounds, I noticed the top port of a tank had been left all the way open. I could see that wine was being moved from the tank, and they leave the top port open a little when they move wine from one place to another, but this time the top was completely open and that was unusual. So I climbed up the ladder to the catwalk and headed to the tank. That's when I spotted Hellman's tennis shoes."

"His shoes?"

"Yup. The poor bastard had been stuffed head first in that tank of wine and all I could see was the bottom of his shoes. So I grabbed his feet and pulled up. Hell, I didn't know how long he'd been stuck in there. It didn't take me long to figure out the poor soul was dead. That's when I saw the shadow out of the corner of my eye."

"Shadow?"

"I saw the shadow of a man on the wall about thirty feet from the tank that contained Hellman. Before I let go of Hellman's feet the shadow moved, so I figured out he was running away from me. I scrambled down the ladder, to chase after him, and tripped. That's why I didn't catch the murdering bastard red-handed.

"Why did you say the shadow of a man?"

The fat dude paused. "Cause females don't work at the winery after dark."

"Never?"

"Almost never. Once in a while the compliance clerk would work overtime when she got behind on her reports, but it couldn't have been her because she was fired a couple of months before Hellman was murdered. I've seen Florianna cruise around, but not often enough if you get my drift."

"You said you tripped. What did you trip over?"

"Hold on, this is the moment I've been waiting for." A waitress set down a plate piled high with bacon and sausage. The dude stoked a fistful of bacon into his mouth, snapped his teeth a couple of times and swallowed.

I said, "Miss, could you write on the tab that this breakfast is for Mike Wilson."

She nodded. "Now that's one of the dumbest thing I've been asked to do."

"Thanks." I set the tab on the table and said, "Now, what'd you trip over?"

"I tripped over a hose."

I'd seen hoses all over the floor when I was at the winery. "Why was the hose there?"

"You dragged me down here to ask me about a hose? What's to tell? I tripped over the damn thing. Lucky I didn't break something."

Shit, this dude could fall off a second story roof and wouldn't break a bone in his body. "What size of hose?"

He made a circle with his fingers and thumbs, "The kind they use all over the winery, one of those clear, plastic hoses. They're two, maybe three inches in diameter and around twenty to thirty feet . . . hey, what's this all about?"

"That's confidential."

"Then buzz off and let me eat my breakfast in peace."

Shit! Say something like Pinky would to keep this dork talking. "Mr. Wilson, please accept my apology. I am seeking information to help me understand what happened inside the winery the night of the murder. I cannot do that without your cooperation and I appreciate your assistance."

"Okay, apology accepted."

Jesus, it worked!

The waitress delivered a turkey platter covered with an omelet the size of a football. On each side of the eggs were hash-browned potatoes smothered with a river of great-smelling white gravy. Polishing off that mound of food was like finishing the Boston Marathon, but this dude looked like he could do that without breaking a sweat.

The guard's eyes widened and he started to shovel food into his mouth with the biggest spoon on the table. While chewing he said, "Now that I think about it, the hose was full of red wine. Are we done now?"

"One last question. You told me the hose was on the floor. Do you know why it was there?"

"Hoses are connected to a valve at the bottom of the tanks. Then they are laid on the concrete floor, and then connected to where the wine will end up."

"Do you remember where the hose was going?"

"Hey, you said the one before was your last question."

I was fed up with his smart-mouth answers. I leaned forward and growled, "I'm paying for that pile of food so answer my God-damn question."

Wilson blinked, like he knew he'd pushed me about as far as he should go. He picked up the side-order plate and offered me some bacon.

I grabbed a couple slices and said, "Thanks."

He downed a slug of coffee. "Let me think. The hose was attached to the tank where Hellman was found, went down the aisle, and then turned to the right. That would mean it was going to the bottling room. Oh, I forgot one more thing. The tank room has a video monitoring system but that night the system wasn't working."

I needed to check out who had access to the video system.

"No videos," I said. "That's a bad break. Thanks for the bacon and information. Sorry I called you so early. Enjoy the rest of your grub."

"I'll give it a try." He scooped up another pile of

eggs, bacon, sausage, potatoes, and cheese, and just before he dumped it into his mouth, he said, "Sorry I was a grouchy bastard when you called, and thanks for the Mountain Man."

"No problem."

I walked out of the café and climbed in my truck. I already knew that Flores was working in the bottling line the night of the murder. What bothered me was the guard told me that the hose ran from the tank where Hellman was murdered to the bottling line. I hated to piss Pinky off, but it was beginning to look like the kid sitting in jail could have been that shadowy figure the guard saw running away from the tank.

I drove back to the plaza and Flo was waiting for me at the dress shop, empty-handed.

"Didn't buy anything?"

"There was nothing in there under a hundred bucks, and that included a simple skirt."

"Hey, when we get back home I'll take you to the outlet mall. For a C-note you'll need a shopping cart to carry out all your stuff."

For some reason, Flo didn't seem to like my idea and she didn't say a word while I drove to the St. James winery. This time, when I reached the fork in the road, I took the right side and went up the hill to a really cool looking house.

Me and Flo got out and I pushed the doorbell a couple of times. I was about to give up, when the door opened a crack, and the face of a woman peeked through.

"Good afternoon, ma'am. My name is Harry Morgan from Western Casualty Insurance. The lady with me, Miss Maple, is my assistance. Is the owner of the winery in?"

"No, he isn't. I'm his wife, Nancy St. James.

132

What do you want?"

"As I stated, I'm from the insurance company. Before I turn over the settlement check, the head office requires I review the accident claim with the owner of the winery."

Her eye's blinked, like her ears didn't understand what they just heard. "What accident are you talking about?"

"The accident that killed your winemaker."

She gasped and started to close the door. "I'm sorry, but my husband is out of town—on an east coast promotional tour for the winery. You'll have to come back later."

"Perhaps you could tell me what happened. That might satisfy the head office."

Her bright red lips quivered. The broad was really trying to figure out what to do next when I sort of pushed on the door and me and Flo walked in. The broad was wearing a pair of shorts and an old tee shirt. Her hair was all frizzy like, but I think that was the way she wanted it to be. In her right hand she held a tumbler and what was inside the glass looked and smelled a lot like brandy.

When she pointed us in the direction of a couch I noticed she wasn't wearing a bra. As I passed her I forced my eyes up to her face and got real close. She had skin so white I could almost see through it, like a person that spends their days working inside an office, or throwing down shots in a bar. God knows I'd seen enough of that skin color tending bar at the Old Globe.

We sat down and Flo said, "Thank you for allowing us into your home. With your husband gone you must be very busy—you know, having to run the winery by yourself."

"Martin won't be gone that long and I'm not

involved with the winery. My husband and I met at college, U. C. Davis to be exact. Contrary to popular belief, not everyone who graduates from Davis goes into the wine business." She forced a smile. "I wouldn't know a grape vine from an orange tree. When Martin's out of town, Luciano runs everything."

The broad took a big breath. Her boobs jiggled a little and one nipple stuck out. Flo ground her elbow into my ribs. "Didn't you have a question, Mr. Morgan?"

"Huh? Oh yeah, who's Luciano?"

"He's our cellar master. Paul Hellman is our, oh excuse me he was our winemaker. Paul made all the decisions concerning the wine, but Luciano and his crew did all the work. Ever since Paul's death, Luciano has kept the place running. I don't know what Martin plans to do now that Paul's dead."

Flo said, "I'm sure your husband will find another winemaker."

"Yes, but not a big name. That would cost too much." Nancy was talking like she knew more about the winery business than she told us. "Right now, with all the replanting expenses, my husband doesn't see how we can afford to spend the amount of money it would take to get a winemaker with a great reputation."

Replanting expenses? What the hell is she talking about? I said, "Ma'am, I'm in the insurance game, could you explain what you mean by the replanting expenses?"

Nancy walked to the picture window and stared out. "You can't see the vineyard from here, but on the western border of our property, just above the creek, there's crew of men pulling out the cabernet vines in one of our vineyards."

"As I said, I'm just an insurance man and I still don't get it. Why would those dudes pull out a good grape bush?"

She smiled. "They're called vines. I don't remember why, but I do recall we've been forced to replant the vineyard and my dear husband is worried sick." Suddenly a light turned on in her dark eyes. "Hold on, I recall now. Martin told me we had to pull the vines because of Phylloxera."

There's that Phil Somebody again. Luciano told me that the Bench-Land vineyard was being replaced. Why didn't Nancy know the name of the vineyard?

Flo said, "Do you know how to spell that?"

"I think it's p-h-y-l-l-o-x-e-r-a."

Flo jotted that down and said, "Interesting. How long have you and Martin been married?"

She looked up, at the ceiling, like the answer was written in the sheet-rock. "Fourteen years."

Flo said, "I realize I'm imposing on your hospitality, but I need to use the bathroom. Could I use yours?"

"Of course. Through that door and down the hall."

As Flo jumped up she gave me a little head move, like she wanted me to do something. The only problem was I didn't have a clue what she wanted me to do. I said, "Are you okay, Miss Maple?"

"I'm fine, Mr. Morgan. While I'm gone, perhaps Mrs. St. James can show you the area where the grape vines are being removed."

Flo turned and sort of charged through the door leading to the hall. Man, she wasn't kidding. She really had to pee.

I still didn't know what Flo had in mind, but I jumped off the couch and got close to the no-bra

135

broad. "Mrs. St. James, I know you can't see the vineyard, but can you—"

She stared at me for a second. "I heard her." She raised her arm and pointed. "It's in that direction. Just over that hill." She kept her finger pointing but her eyes walked up and down me a couple of times.

After a while, she smiled, dropped her arm, and returned to the couch.

I took a big breath, to settle things down, and said, "Mrs. St. James, you have a great place here."

"Mr. Morgan, no Harry, life's too short for that kind of formality. Please call me Nancy. It's not often a big, strong man like you shows up and rings my bell. Would you care to join me in a glass of brandy?"

"No brandy for me, but if you've got a beer, that would be great."

She smiled, "I'll be right back."

Whew, that broad was coming on to me!

Flo walked in and said, "Where's Mrs. St. James?"

"Nancy's finding me a beer."

"So you're calling her Nancy already? Forget the beer, we don't have time to sit around and socialize. We have—"

Nancy walked in holding her glass of brandy and a bottle of beer. "Ah, Miss Maple. Could I get you a glass of water?"

Flo glanced at her watch. "I'm sorry, Mrs. St. James, but we're on a tight schedule. We appreciate your time, and please accept our condolences for the death of your winemaker, Paul Hellman."

"Mr. Morgan, did you tell me where you're from?"

"Ah, Dayton, Ohio. That's the head office of my insurance company."

"Welcome to the wine country. Are you staying

in the area?"

"Yup."

"Give me the phone number of your motel room. If I come up with anything, anything at all, I'll call you."

Flo gave Nancy her nasty look. "Mr. Morgan, we have to leave."

Nancy said, "Please, Miss Maple, I trust you have enough time to let your business associate refresh himself with a cold beer."

Before I could grab the bottle Flo looked at her watch. "Oh, Mr. Morgan, we're almost late for that appointment in Healdsburg."

Nancy said, "Oh! Who are you meeting with? I know everyone in town."

As Flo pushed me toward the door, she said, "We're not at liberty to disclose that information, correct, Mr. Morgan?"

Nancy ran up and pushed her bare boobs into my back. Wow!

I said, "I'm afraid Miss Maple's right. We can't hand out that information. And thanks for trying to give me a beer."

Nancy said, "Don't forget, Harry, I'm here day and night if you need anything."

We drove down the hill and as I turned back onto the county road, Flo said, "Sometimes you go out of your way to piss me off."

"Huh?"

"That no-bra under the thin tee shirt bit. If I didn't known better, I'd guess she knew we were coming. Hey, pull into that gas station. I've got to pee."

"I thought you did that five minutes ago."

"You're wrong. I'll explain when I get back."

While I waited for Flo, I tried to figure out what

the hell was going on between her and Nancy St. James. Finally, I decided that women were a whole bunch different than men and a dumb dude like me would go nuts trying to figure out every crazy move they made.

Flo opened the door and jumped in. "Okay. Right off I figured there was something about that woman and it's not PG rated."

"You mean the no-bra thing?"

"Hell no. It's just that she didn't know us at all and the next thing she does is shove her boobs at you. And don't tell me you didn't notice?"

"I saw a nipple, but I didn't—"

"That's when I decided to find out more about her."

"Huh?"

"Don't act stupid. That's why I went down the hall."

"I got it now. You nosed around. Find anything interesting?"

"Does a bird fly? First, Martin and Nancy sleep in separate bedrooms."

"Okay, but that's not—"

"Martin's bedroom is tiny, austere with a chair and single bed, nearly monastic."

"What's monastic mean?"

"The man lives a simple life, like a monk."

"Lives like a monk in the same house with that broad? That's weird."

"Nancy's bedroom is large, with a four poster bed. But that's not the X-rated part. Each of the posts are badly scuffed, as if something's been tied around them."

"Huh?"

"Wake up and smell the cheese enchiladas. Someone, my money's on Nancy St. James, ties their partner to the bed posts."

"Oh, like that bondage stuff?"

"And at the top of the four poster bed is a full length mirror."

"Wow! You got to watch all the kinky stuff."

"Bear, I need you to answer my next question honestly and don't worry, I'm not going to get mad. Did Nancy come on to you while I was gone?"

Shit. If I tell Flo the truth she'll get mad, and if I don't tell her she'll get mad. My Pop told me that when he was talking to my Mom, and if he couldn't figure out any other way, he'd tell her the truth. "I sort of thought she did, but it didn't make any sense to me. I mean you were in the other room and—"

"It makes sense to me. You're a keeper and women like her learn at an early age how to spot a keeper."

"Thanks, I think."

"And that bit about her calling you if she remembers anything, anything at all. My guess is she's a dominatrix and Martin's her slave."

"Hey, glad you got me out of there when you did. I'm not into that sort of thing."

Flo gave me a little kiss. "I know that. What about the rest of our visit with the queen of whips and chains?"

"When we first walked in she was sucking on a glass of brandy."

"I have found, in general, men don't need a reason to drink, but women do, and usually they drink to cover something up. It's possible that Nancy St. James drinks because she had something going on with Paul Hellman."

"Nancy and that fancy winemaker?"

"It could happen. That purple photo of the body showed he was a big, strong guy like you."

My cell buzzed and I pulled off the road. "What do you need, Boss?"

"Damn it, Bear, time is fleeting. Did you come up with anything from the night watchman or the winery owner's wife."

I said, "Hold on, Boss. Flo, give me that paper with the word you wrote down. Boss, we've got a couple of things that look weird. The winery owner's wife is sort of different. She's—"

Flo grabbed the cell out of my hand. "Pinky, I'm sure that woman is a dominatrix and she tried to seduce my man while she thought I was in the bathroom."

She handed my phone back and I heard Pinky yelling, "Flo, I don't care what Nancy St. James did to Bear—"

"Boss, that may happen to you everyday, but it was weird to me. Okay, the other thing, we figured out who Phil Something is. It's some kind of a bad sickness for grape plants. It's spelled p-h-y-l-l-o-x-e-r-a, and according to Luciano, it's in the Bench-Land vineyard."

Pinky said, "Phylloxera! The Bench-Land vineyard! Oh my God, that is disastrous news for fans of the St. James Winery. Did the owner tell you how pervasive the infection is?"

"I told you. We didn't talk to the owner, Martin. We talked to Nancy."

"Who is Nancy?"

"She's the Domino broad that Flo told you about. She told us a vineyard is being pulled out but she didn't tell us it's the Bench-Land vineyard and I think she knew."

"I am pleased that you found the time between your sexual encounters to discover the correct spelling for Phylloxera."

"Hey, I didn't have a sexual encounter. All I did was peek at her boobs."

Pinky said, "Did the woman disrobe while Flo was in the bathroom?"

"Nope. She had her tee shirt on the whole time."

"My boy, once we return to Carson City, I will make it my solemn duty to bring you up to speed on the lurid details of deviant sexual practices. Now, drive to the Downtown Pub, order a Berger Brown and wait for me. I will meet you there soon."

"But Boss, me and Flo are pooped. We want to go—"

The line went dead.

"Bear, it's starting to rain."

"Shit, there goes our dinner by the river."

TWENTY

Pinky-Santa Rosa, California

I arrived at the county complex that housed the Public Defender's office. After driving around a series of governmental structures for what felt like a lifetime, I finally discovered a parking place with a thirty-minute limit. Positive I would be meeting with someone who had ended up near the bottom of their class at law school, I should be able to obtain all their knowledge concerning the Flores case within that limited span of time. I parked, and dodged as many raindrops as I could until I eventually discovered the front door of the PD's office.

I entered. Immediately opposite me sat a young female behind a low counter. Her spiked hair with a green tinge didn't bother me as much as the large, stainless steel stud she had placed in the center of her tongue. The words she attempted to say were, may I help you, but what flowed past the stud were, "Meth I helth you?"

In a single sentence my already low expectations were caused to plummet further. "I would like to see the Public Defender."

"Do you hath an a apothemnth?"

"No."

"One momenth."

While she talked into her phone I glanced around the office. The carpet looked as if it had not

142

been vacuumed in a month. The tongue-studded receptionist's desk was covered with papers. Any attorney, even a Public Defender, who condoned this state of disrepair, should be drummed out of the legal profession. I considered reprimanding the female with the studded tongue, but decided that my criticism, however positively offered, would fall upon deaf ears.

"Mr. Neeley will be wthe you in a moment."

"Thank you."

I glanced back and remained verticle as the bench behind me looked to be covered with a thick layer of grime.

A moment later the door behind the receptionist opened and a man with no neck, a nearly square head and a truly bad haircut walked in. He was built along the lines of a football player, and I was positive the tweed jacket that covered his muscular frame had been purchased off the sale rack at J. C. Penney's.

He thrust his gnarled right hand toward me. "Good morning. My name is Freeman Neeley. You are lucky to catch me in and with a few moments before my next case. What can I do for you?"

I lowered my voice. "I require a private meeting concerning one of your clients."

The PD's charm-boy smile faded. "Would you be willing to divulge the name of that client?"

"What part of the word 'private' did you not understand?"

"Follow me to my office."

I trailed him through a door and down a dark hallway to a room no larger than an expanded broom closet. There was barely enough room for a desk and two chairs. The tiny floor space that remained was covered with stacks of paper rising up like stalagmites in a limestone cave. Neeley sat down behind his desk and gestured for me to sit on the small chair that backed against the wall.

"Mr. . . . ?"

"My name is J. Pinkus Delmont."

"Mr. Delmont, this is as close to a private meeting space as I can offer. Which of my clients are you concerned about?"

"Before I divulge the name, as the attorney of record for the afore-mentioned client, you must assure me that any discussion concerning your client will be covered under attorney-client privilege."

The Public Defender sat back. "Are you an attorney?"

I leaned forward. "Do you require a second admonition?"

There was a moment of silence while the PD mentally wrestled with my requirement. "Okay, from this point forward, whatever we discuss will be off-the-record."

"Mr. Neeley, not off-the-record—attorney-client privilege."

"Must I actually say the words?"

"Yes."

"Damn it, Delmont, I don't have time to play games."

We sat in silence for approximately thirty seconds before Neeley slammed his ample fist into his small, metal desk.

"Alright, from this moment on I will act as your attorney of record. Now what the hell did you do, rape a nun?"

"I, my good man, have done nothing. As I stated, I am here to discuss one of your clients."

Neeley's phone rang. He grabbed the handset and listened for a moment. " . . . Yes, I know I'm due in court. Call the clerk and tell him I ate a bad sprout sandwich. Don't interrupt me again."

"Mr. Neeley, I understand that it is not my place, but you need to replace that tongue-pierced woman who guards your gate."

Neeley stared at me. "You never answered my question. Are you an attorney?"

"Yes, but I do not practice in this state."

"What branch of law?"

"Much like yourself, I defend the indigent and downtrodden. Now that we have finally found ourselves on the same page, as the attorney of record for Enrique Flores, do I need to remind you that anything we discuss is—"

"Enrique? Right, what we say is covered by attorney-client privilege. Now what the hell—"

"Mr. Neeley, I am here to assist you and your client. A party has retained me to investigate the Hellman murder. My job is to find a second suspect for Hellman's murder, someone who also had the means, motive, and opportunity."

Neeley took a few seconds to tally up this new bit of information. Then he said, "Okay, what can I do?"

"I need to learn everything you know. What evidence the DA has against your client. And I need to interview your client to hear his side of what happened the night of Hellman's murder."

Neeley glanced at his watch. "I'm up against a time problem."

"Then we need to hurry. Have you visited the site of the murder?"

He hesitated. "Why?"

"Answer my question. Have you visited the murder site?"

"Are you questioning my competency?"

145

"Answer the question."

"No, I didn't visit the murder site. Mr. Delmont, I'm an attorney, not an investigator. My job is to give my clients the best legal defense I can. This office used to have an investigator, but he retired six months ago and the county can't find the money to hire a replacement."

"Then avail your client of my free investigative service."

He sat back, took a deep breath and said, "All right, what did you find?"

"One of my investigators visited the site. He walked the catwalk, looked in the tank in which the body was found. Frankly, he told me that Hellman would have been, to use his country homily, deaf-as-a-post, to fail to hear Enrique walk up behind him."

Suddenly, Neeley acted as if his underwear had ridden up. "As I told you, Mr. Delmont, my office does not have an investigator. There're only twenty-four hours in my day and I don't have enough time to look into every little detail."

"Is that why you recommended a plea bargain?"

"Yes. I suppose you're going to tell me that if you were Enrique's attorney you would have done more?"

The redness at the tips of Neeley's ears indicated that it was time I slowed down. "Mr. Neeley, I'm positive that, considering your lack of resources, you are doing the best job you can. This is your golden opportunity to bestow upon your client the results of my comprehensive investigation."

Neeley snorted and the color of his ears slowly ramped down to a normal pink. "Mr. Delmont, the DA's case against Enrique is solid as a rock. From my view the best I can do for him is to keep him out of the Green Room at San Quentin."

"We are all entitled to our opinions, Mr. Neeley."

Neeley glared at me for a second, and then he grabbed his phone and dialed. "Charlie, I'm stuck in the doctor's office . . . yes, my stomach is doing flip-flops . . . yes, the little sandwich shop by the freeway . . . another twenty minutes . . . thank you."

He turned to me. "Now that we both know where we stand, let's walk across the courtyard so you can talk to my client."

Neeley placed a second call. "I need to meet with Enrique Flores at once."

A moment later we entered the jail building. Neeley talked with a guard at the front desk and after the guard frisked me for weapons, we entered a small room reserved for attorneys and clients. Enrique was already there. Neeley said, "Enrique, this man is doing some investigative work concerning your murder charge. I'm not sure what good he can do, but we both need all the assistance we can get. Do you understand?"

"Yes."

Enrique stared at me, and it wasn't hard to spot the anger in his dark eyes.

Neeley said, "I want you to answer his questions just like you would with me. Remember, he's a friend and here to help you."

A touch, but not all of the resentment on his face faded. Enrique nodded.

Neeley turned to me. "He's all yours."

I pulled out the police report. "Enrique, let's go back to the night of the murder. Were you at the winery bottling wine?"

The young man glanced at Neeley, who gave him a reassuring nod. "Yes."

"According to the report you were working that

147

night to do a special bottling run. Is that normal for one person to run a bottling line?"

"No. During the day we have three or four people on the line when we do a full run, but once in a while, at night, the boss does a special run. When that happens I'm the only one who works. The boss pays me more money, so working alone was hard but worth it."

"Did you often run the line alone?"

"No. Just three times. The first time it happened was about a year and a half ago. Then about six months ago. The last time was the night of . . . " His voice trembled, as if he couldn't bring himself to say Paul Hellman's name.

"Do you know why there was a special bottling run?"

Enrique said, "No!"

I leaned forward, "Is it true that you planted marijuana on the St. James property, and that your illegal activity was discovered by Paul Hellman?"

He glanced at Neeley and again his attorney nodded.

"Yes."

"After Hellman found the marijuana, did he tell you he would call the Sheriff if he caught you planting marijuana again?"

"Yes."

"Did you plant the marijuana the police found near the winery the night of Hellman's murder?"

Enrique slumped in his chair. "Yes."

"And you knew that if the marijuana was discovered by Paul Hellman, jail could be a possibility?"

His response was a whisper. "Yes."

I paused, and then said, "Did you murder Paul Hellman?"

Enrique slammed his fists into the table. "No!" His voice cracked while his whole body shuddered. "Somebody has to listen to me! I was bottling wine!"

Neeley rose from his chair and placed his big arm around his client's shoulder. "Calm down."

Enrique started to cry.

It was then that the disparity in size between the two men hit me. I said, "Enrique, stand up."

When we both rose, I discovered that we stood eye to eye. Some of my detractors could call me short. I consider myself a perfect height for my weight and features. I might add that all of my ex-wives agreed with that assessment. But my height was not the question at the moment.

I said, "Neeley, any idiot can see that your client is too small to have committed the murder. The autopsy report indicated that Paul Hellman was over six feet tall and weighed 220 pounds. The police report stated Enrique killed Hellman and dumped him into the top of a tank of wine. Look at your client. He's about five-four and maybe weighs a hundred and thirty soaking wet. How could he pick up a two-hundred plus pound body and dump it in the top of a tank?"

Neeley stepped back and his eyes scanned his client's lack of physique as if for the first time. "I . . . I never considered Enrique's size. Hold on, the police report stated that Enrique snuck up behind Hellman while he was leaning over the tank full of cabernet, and he knocked out Hellman with the hammer."

I said, "Is that what your client told you?"

"Well . . . no."

"Is the hammer on the list of evidence provided by the DA?"

"No."

"So you accepted the police report over your

149

client's word?"

"Yes, I did . . . ah . . . you don't understand. I've been so busy."

"A final question, and this one is directed at you, Mr. Neeley. What was your final class ranking at your school of law?"

"Two hundred and thirty-fifth but that was out of three hundred and forty."

"I am not surprised. Your low class standing matches my expectations—an attorney who finds himself too busy for a client that faces a death penalty—an attorney who allows his front office receptionist to wear a stainless stud in her tongue— an attorney whose filing system consists of stacks of paper spread over the floor of his office. Congratulations, Mr. Neeley. You are the personification of the worst type of an attorney, one who becomes a Public Defender by default!!"

"You little bastard! Get your ass out of this room before I squeeze the life out of you with my bare hands!"

"Calm down, Mr. Neeley. I am leaving at once."

By the time I arrived at my car the rain had soaked my good jacket and there were two parking tickets on the windshield. I considered walking back to Neeley's office and turning them over to him, but decided that in this instance, discretion was the better part of valor. I tucked them into my coat pocket. I had plenty of time to send them to Charles.

Before I backed out of my expensive parking slot at the county complex I called Bear.

"Boss?"

I said, "Where are you?"

"Me and Flo pulled into a parking place on the plaza near the Downtown Pub and we're sitting here waiting for you to call."

"Good. I have completed my visit with the PD. Go in and order me a Berger Brown. I'll be there in a few minutes."

"Not good. That's why I'm sitting outside the joint here waiting for you to call. Don't go anywhere near that dive. It's not safe. How about we meet at that place where you sleep."

"That place, as you so crudely put it, is the finest Bed and Breakfast in Northern California. Give me one good reason why we cannot meet at the Pub per my instructions."

"Does being dead sound like a good enough reason? Like I told you, I'm in my truck and just before I got out I spotted that giant dude from Vegas, the one who walked into your office a couple of days ago. He's sitting in a black Cadillac near the Pub's front door and it looks to me like he's waiting for someone like you to show up."

"Oh my God! How did he find me?"

"Don't ask me. Did you FedEx the printouts back to your office like you promised?"

"Of course I did."

"Then there's more to this than the missing printouts—like the hanky-panky that was going on between you and his boss' wife."

"What I do in my spare time is none of your business if not total speculation on your part." But I feared my ignorant investigator had stumbled across the reason. "Sit tight. I'll call you back."

I keyed in Charles' office number, and after the standard clandestine routine with his gatekeeper he returned my call. "What's up?"

"Charles, I can't go into any details as to the reason why, but there is a man sitting in black Cadillac with a Nevada license plate outside the front door of the Downtown Pub. I fear the man has been sent from Vegas to kill me."

There was a perceptible intake of breath on the other end of the line. "Pinky, I don't know how you do it, but you manage to get yourself into the damnedest situations. I'll contact the Healdsburg Chief of Police. If what you say is true, and the man in the Cadillac has a concealed weapon on his person, they'll immediately place him under arrest. That should give you a day or two of breathing room, enough time to come up with my suspect, or return to Carson City with your tail between your legs. One final thought. I need to warn you that the moment you cross the Sonoma County line, any disagreement between you and the man from Vegas is your problem. Are we clear?"

My mouth had become so dry that I had trouble parting my lips. "Clear as a bell."

I hung up and called Bear. "I will meet you at the Red Rose B & B in a few minutes."

"Okay, Boss. By the way, yesterday I forgot to pick up the receipt for the breakfast that fat guard wolfed down. Will you call Lu and tell her it's okay to pay me back $13.65."

"My life hangs in the balance and you are asking me to clutter my head with a reimbursement concerning a breakfast check?"

"Thirteen bucks and change may not sound like much to a rich lawyer but—"

"My good man, your protestations are falling on deaf ears. Meet me at The Red Rose in five minutes."

"Hey, I was the one who called and told you to steer clear of the Downtown Pub. Boss, if I hadn't stopped you from walking in that dump your next address would be a cold slab of marble in the county morgue."

"Enough gibberish. Make haste to my B & B

and keep a low profile."

TWENTY-ONE

Pinky-Healdsburg, California

By the time Bear, Flo, and I met on the front porch of the Red Rose the rain had increased to a heavy downpour. However, the air temperature was a balmy sixty-seven degrees, a pleasant phenomenon caused by a storm front that had traveled across the Pacific from the Hawaiian Islands. As I directed, Bliss had served some glasses of the house red and immediately vacated the area.

To be honest, the house wine was borderline, but I was not about to spend good money on Flo, or her beer-swilling partner who could not discern a potable wine from rice vinegar. I said, "All right, give me a report of your investigative activities."

"Boss, is there anyway I could swap this red crap for a cold beer?"

"We don't have time for that. I need to wind up this California expedition and return to my office. Unlike you, I have important work to attend to. Potential clients languish in the Carson City jail as we speak—wretched souls who are dependent upon me to extract them from their present dire circumstances. Now get on with it. Have you come up with the name of a viable suspect?"

Bear scratched his hairy pate. "If I throw out that old dude at the farm credit joint, and the rent-a-guard, the only guy fits that bill is Luciano Botarri."

"Botarri?" While I had been pondering if Bliss

could find me a better cabernet, the name Bear spoke broke through. "Luciano Botarri? My boy, you are spot on. I met the cellar master during my visit to the winery, and like you, I consider him my prime suspect."

"Hey, I didn't tell you he was a prime suspect. He's just a guy I talked to at the winery. In fact, he doesn't seem like a killer to me, but you've ragged at me more than once that the guilty part was not my job. But one thing's for sure, Botarri sure didn't get along with Paul Hellman and—"

"I know all about that." I jumped up. "Give me a moment to call my local contact and give him Botarri's name. We could be back home by tomorrow." I walked to the far side of the porch, made the call, told the female who answered Charles' line that Padriag Murphy called and a moment later my cell rang. "Charles?"

"Pinky, you can't call me every hour. I'm a busy man and have—"

"I just left the Public Defenders office."

"So you met Freeman Neeley, my worthy opponent. What's your take on the man?"

"He ranked two-hundred and thirty-fifth in his class. Need I say more?"

Charles chuckled, "No. Pinky, I have an important meeting in a couple of—"

"Charles, have you ever met Enrique?"

"Of course. I observed him at the preliminary hearing. Why?"

"In my opinion, there is no way that a man of his physical stature could have lifted Hellman's body into that tank. He is just too small to have—"

"I've been through all that. The police surmised he hit Hellman with—"

"I know, he struck the victim in the head with a

155

hammer. Does the DA's office have the hammer in its possession?"

"No."

"So the police didn't find a hammer at the site of the murder?"

"No, but—"

"Did the autopsy indicate a blow from a hammer on Hellman's head?"

"The autopsy was inconclusive. The right half of his head was badly damaged when the coroner's team pulled the body out of the tank. They didn't notice the top porthole had sharp edges and—"

"Charles, spare me the gory details. Now I understand your reticence to prosecute the Mexican lad for Hellman's murder. In fact, if Freeman Neeley had one tenth of my ability he could convince a jury of zombies to acquit Enrique in seconds."

"Pinky, you've pulled me away from an important meeting." A touch of anger entered into my old schoolmate's tone. "Other than your unwarranted harassment, are you done?"

"No. I have completed the task that I was hired to do—to hand you a suspect who had motive, opportunity, and most importantly, the means, and the physical strength to dump Hellman's body into that tank."

I felt a tap on my shoulder. "Hold on a moment, Charles." I spun around and stared into the face of Flo. "Where did you come up with the unmitigated gall to interrupt me in the middle of an important call?"

"Pinky, Mr. Bliss, the owner of this fine B & B there told me you've got another phone call."

I glanced to my right. Bliss was standing on the porch and he held a wireless handset from his office. I demanded, "What is wrong with you people?

Can't you see I am in the middle—"

Flo said softly, "I talked to the man on the other end of that phone call. Trust me, you have two choices, grab that other phone and talk to him, or light your hair on fire."

A touch of fear reflected off Flo's face, something I had seldom detected. I lifted my cell, "Charles, one moment." I grabbed the handset from Bliss and barked, "What?"

A thick voice said, "Counselor, Antonio Macario here."

A tremor of terror caused my knees to buckle. I grabbed Bear's broad shoulder, and said, "Good afternoon, Mr. Macario. What can I do for you?"

"I have two items that require your immediate attention. First, it is my understanding that the Healdsburg police have detained an associate of mine. My associate has some extremely important printouts in his possession. I believe you are aware of the printouts I am talking about?"

I dropped my wine as the fingers that clutched the vessel gave way. The glass hit the porch and shattered along with my dream of a long and happy life. "I am not sure exactly what printouts you have in mind."

"I am going to give you a final chance, counselor. We are discussing the printouts you had delivered to your Carson City office a few days ago."

Why was he calling me? I thought his man had picked up the printouts at my office and returned to Las Vegas. And what was he doing in Healdsburg? I didn't have much time to contemplate the answers because I was talking with a man who snuffed out human beings with less emotion then he would have felt when he swatted a house fly. "Oh yes, I remember now, those printouts."

"Excellent. Counselor, it is imperative that you take possession of the printouts and destroy them immediately."

The picture was coming clearer. His thug had not returned to Vegas with the printouts and at the present time he was sitting in jail. But that did not answer the question of why the man came to Healdsburg. Tiny rivulets of cold sweat trickled down my back. "But Mr. Macario, your man is in custody and—"

"Counselor, that is why I need you to take charge of the situation. What you do, and how you do it, is in your hands. I believe we both understand that the printouts in question cannot be allowed to see the light of day. If that should happen, I cannot emphasize how sorry I would be concerning the potential fallout to you, all members of your family, and business associates."

He had left me no choice. Destroy the printouts or the four horsemen of the Apocalypse would descend upon my house. "Right! I will take care of that little problem as soon as we hang up."

"Outstanding. Now that brings me to the second item. Prior to this call I learned that you were representing my wife, Elena, in a minor domestic dispute. I am informing you that my wife has changed her mind. We have reconciled our differences and once again we are enjoying a complete immersion in the warm waters of marital bliss. It is vital . . . " Macario emphasized each word with a clipped staccato, " . . . for the well being of all concerned, that you return my wife's retainer, and destroy all records concerning Elena's little fling of madness. Counselor, have I made myself perfectly clear?"

Now I understood why his associate was in

Healdsburg and I owed my life to Bear's sharp eyesight. I grabbed Flo's near empty glass of wine and drained it in a futile attempt to clear the large lump in my throat. "Yes, sir, loud and clear." I hesitated, not sure if I could, or should speak first. "Mr. Macario, I assume you will contact your associate and let him know that his reason for coming to Healdsburg has been cancelled and he is to return to his home base?"

"I took care of that minor detail prior to this call, counselor. Now, I believe that concludes our—"

"Excuse me sir, but I have one more item. As a businessman, I am sure you will understand that I have incurred some unforeseen expenses unraveling this brief, but unfortunate chapter in our complicated lives."

I listened as silence was punctuated with heavy breathing. For a split second I considered the horrendous possibility that I had overstepped my bounds. "Counselor, I understand. Everyone has overhead. Once the previously mentioned items have been taken care of, you are more than welcome to send me a bill. However, to maintain the collegial atmosphere of our relationship, I would presume that the bill will be reasonable, and the definition of reasonable is left to my discretion."

"You have my promise."

A soft click informed me that our conversation was at an end. I felt a tingling sensation shoot from the top of my head to the tips of my toes—a joyful reminder that I was still alive.

I tossed the wireless phone to Bliss. "Bliss, remove yourself at once."

"Of course, Mr. Delmont."

As soon as Bliss left the porch I returned the cell to my ear. Charles was screaming, "Damn it,

Pinky. What the hell is going on? I'm a busy man and—"

"Charles, stop your blathering and listen. Do you recall the man in the Cadillac the Healdsburg police arrested?"

"Of course I do. That was only thirty minutes ago."

"Good. Now you can arrange to have him released and turned over to my custody."

"Are you nuts? Thirty minutes ago you told me he as going to kill you if—"

"I apologize. I made a mistake. Now can we get back to the reason I came to California—to find you a viable suspect for the Hellman murder?"

"Pinky, if I find you are screwing with me, I'll see that the Nevada bar hangs your ass to twist in the hot desert sun."

I waved my empty glass, to signal I required more wine. "Trust me, Charles, better men than you have tried and failed. Now listen to me. The name of your viable suspect is Luciano Botarri."

"Botarri? Are you kidding me?"

"Charles, Botarri is your man. He had a partnership with—"

"We already looked at him. I know all about his failed business deal with Hellman. Perhaps I haven't made myself clear. Giving me that name two days before I go to trial is a waste of my time. I need someone who was discovered holding a smoking gun."

"What you are demanding is tantamount to a suspect who has signed a confession."

"You could put it that way."

I paused. At this juncture I was damned if I moved forward and damned if I backed out. "Charles, you leave me no choice. I will find your killer with the proverbial smoking gun. Now, as soon as I hang up, call the Healdsburg police."

As I slipped my cell into my pocket, Bear said, "Boss, you don't look too good."

I downed the wine and forced a return of my stoic mask. "My good man, there is nothing to worry about."

"But what happens to me and you when that big bastard gets out of jail?"

"Nothing. In a moment, we will walk to the police station and I will talk to the local constabulary. Once they release the man to my custody, he will turn over the printouts you removed from Mr. Macario's safe and then scurry back to his lair in Las Vegas. As soon as I destroy the printouts we will have no more than forty-eight hours to complete our task here before we return back to the warm, beckoning arms of our hometown."

"So the dude's not going to kill you, or me, or Flo?"

"By now I would have thought that point was obvious. Let us move on. According to my last phone conversation with my Sonoma County contact, it seems we missed a major item concerning our viable suspect."

"What's that?"

I held out my glass and Bear filled it to the brim. "Our man, or woman, must be discovered holding a smoking gun."

Flo said, "Like you have to find someone who saw the suspect stuff Hellman into the tank? Fat chance of that happening."

"That or find someone who is willing to confess to the murder. Now, accompany me to the police department. After completing a few minor tasks, we will walk to the Pub where I will buy you all a glass

of Berger Brown in celebration of your excellent
vision."

TWENTY-TWO

Pinky-Healdsburg, California

Twenty minutes after we waved a fond farewell to the gentleman in the Cadillac, we stopped by a lawyer's office where I paid a young lady twenty dollars to shred the toxic documents.

I said, "Now we deserve a frosty glass of Berger Brown."

Bear said, "Beer? I thought you hated beer."

"There is a world of difference between what they brew at the local Pub and that liquid trash you toss down your gullet."

I found a table and the three of us sat down. Arianna immediately appeared at my side and she gave my shoulder a gentle, but clearly sensuous squeeze. "Hi, cutie. What can I get you?"

Bear ceased to breathe, and once his eyes completed their initial scan of her body, his gaze settled on her taut nipples that pressed against a pale blue gossamer fabric. When Flo tracked his eyes to their eventual destination she buried her right elbow into his ribs.

I said, "Arianna, this is Bear and Flo. Bear just resolved a major problem of mine and I have brought him to the home of the best brewery on the west coast, if not all of America. Three Berger Browns if you please."

Flo thrust her hand up. "I'd rather have a glass of red wine."

Arianna said, "Whatever. The wine they serve here is crap, but you're the customer and if that's what you want, so be it."

Flo stared at her for a second, "Okay, I'll make you a deal. Bring me a shot glass of the beer. If I don't like it, I'll trade it in for a red wine."

"You've got it."

She walked away from our table and Bear, mouth open, watched her hips gyrate under her rose-colored harem pants. I said, "My boy, close you mouth or bugs will fly in."

Bear said, "Wow! That babe is something else."

I noticed Flo kick her leg under the table. Bear cried, "Hey, that hurt."

Flo said, "Keep your mind on business and that won't happen again."

Bear said, "Right. Boss, do you know her?"

"Yes, we met the day I arrived in Healdsburg. Now let us get down to work. To make this a legitimate business meeting, go over your visit with the guard and Botarri. Did you learn anything that seemed out of place?"

"A couple of things. When Botarri drove me to his place he took a short cut through the back part of the St. James vineyard and he let slip something he shouldn't have."

"What was that?"

"Just after we passed a bunch of guys pulling out those grape plants he said—"

"They are called grape vines, not plants."

"Boss, do you want me to tell you what I saw or sit there and burn my ass?"

Perhaps spending a full day with Flo has made my ursine friend a bit touchy. God knows I would be contemplating suicide. "Please continue."

"I asked Botarri why anyone would pull out

those old plants and he said it was because of Phil something."

"That is when you learned about the Bench-Land vineyard's Phylloxera infection."

"Yup, but the minute Botarri said, Phil something, his face got all screwed up, like he just smashed his thumb in the car door. He begged me to clam up about the plants being pulled out."

"Interesting. Anything else?"

"The rent-a-guard told me there was a hose connected to the tank of cabernet where Hellman drowned and that hose ran to the bottling room where Enrique worked."

I said, "Another interesting observation. Enrique told me that he ran the bottling line alone three times, and the night of the murder was the third occasion. My good man, Enrique is not the killer, but the fact that he worked alone could be an important piece in this puzzle. Anything else?"

"Yeah. The old dude at the farm bank told me that Phil something was really bad for grape plants and if you had it you were up shit creek without a paddle."

I had heard that Phylloxera was a dreadful infection for grape vines, but I was not sure what replacing the vines would cost a winery. A phone call to my old friend at my favorite zinfandel winery could clear up the mystery. "I believe it is time that we put our heads together and attack this enigma. It seems to me that we have a thousand-piece jigsaw puzzle but no idea of the big picture. To resolve this dilemma I think we need to get together and brain-storm, a modus operandi if you wish, that—"

Arianna arrived with our glasses. "Here's your order. Pinky, it's funny how things work out sometimes. Remember? A couple of days ago you

165

asked me if I had a twin sister and I told you yes? Well, she called me last night in a panic and asked me for help. Imagine, my big time, uptight, college-grad sister, asking her dumb beer-selling sister for help."

Not the least interested in her familial problems, I forced myself to say, "Sorry to hear that. What was her difficulty?"

"She's in New York and her purse was stolen. Her airline tickets, credit cards, all her cash, gone."

"What did she expect you to do?"

"Wire her five hundred bucks so she could continue with the winery promotion tour. She needs something to tide her over until replacement cards arrive."

"And did you accommodate her request?"

"Are you kidding? Can't send her what I don't have."

"Arianna!" A deep, male voice barked from the bar. "You've got other customers waiting for their orders."

"Whoops. Bye."

As Bear watched Arianna walk away, Flo said, "I still don't know why you're picking up the tab, but thanks."

"A small token of my appreciation. Do you like it?"

Flo took a tentative sip. "It's not as bad as I thought it would be, but your girlfriend left before I had time to tell her that I wanted a full glass."

Bear took a giant gulp, wiped his paw across his mouth and let out a fifty-decibel belch. "Boss, did you say that super broad has a twin?"

"Hard to imagine that amount of femininity could be duplicated, but true. I met her sister, Florianna, the day I went to the winery, and she's their Club Cabernet coordinator."

"Let me see if I have this straight. The beer—babe's twin works at the winery, but she's stuck back east because somebody copped her purse?"

"That is my understanding, but my good man, are your verbal ramblings heading in any particular direction, or are . . . " Suddenly, the answer to our problem formed in my mind. . . . "Bear, that beer-babe, as you called her, has presented us with a foolproof plan."

Bear furtively glanced at Flo. "Boss, she's not my beer-babe. As my grandma used to say, you shouldn't sit there and call a pot black."

"Spare me your grandmother's twisted homilies. My God, this plan is perfect."

Bear said, "Hey, there's no such thing as a perfect plan. Something always happens and screws things up. Remember Fresno? If we'd followed your plan, we'd both be six feet under, not drinking some pretty good beer in Healdsburg. Besides, me and Flo are tired of this assignment. We've had it with this place—too many redwood trees—too many green hills, and way too much rain. We're ready to head back home, to our dry, dusty, sandy apartment."

Flo said, "He's right. I was ready to pack up this morning and go home. How will your plan change my mind, at least for a couple of days?"

I ignored Flo's question and said, "My boy, as the titular head of this organization setting the direction is my responsibility."

"I don't know what that means, but Boss, stop talking and listen. Maybe more money will help keep us both happy. How about a bonus? Something that will help me and Flo want to stick around."

I said, "A bonus? I do not recall any discussion of an additional benefit for you and your woman."

Bear slammed his glass on the table, jumped up, and started toward the pub exit.

I demanded, "Where are you going?"

"Come on, Flo. Let's head back to the motel. We've got to pack up. Me and Flo have done everything you wanted. I did the OSHA bit in Modesto. I checked out the murder site at the St James Winery with Botarri. I sat there and watched that fat guard eat a giant breakfast. I even threw in a stop with that old dude at the farm credit joint. We talked to Martin's wife. That's it. We're done. We're going home."

"Sit down and give me a moment." Damn, for an ignorant clod he knew what button to push. "All right. Stick around for two more days and I will pay you an additional five thousand dollars as long as the suspect we turn over meets the criteria as set by my Sonoma County contact."

"Boss, it's not that I don't trust you, but I don't have a clue what you just said. Give me something I can understand so I know you aren't screwing me."

"My boy, you are testing my patience."

Flo said, "Try again, but this time cut the legal crap and use simple English."

"I will pay you an additional five thousand dollars when my Sonoma County contact accepts our suspect."

Bear said, "Watch my lips, Boss. I still don't—"

"And you can monitor the phone call when I give him the name to be sure he accepts the suspect."

"And the five grand goes directly to me and Flo."

I sighed, "In fact, I will tell Lu to make out two checks. Each one for twenty-five hundred dollars."

Flo smiled. "That's something I can understand. Okay, now that we have a good financial reason to continue, does your epiphany come up with a way to get me into the winery."

I emptied my glass and signaled Arianna for refills. "Why is that necessary?"

Flo said, "Remember when you sent us to the Yosemite View Winery in Modesto?"

I nodded.

"Okay. While Bear cruised around the joint following that OSHA guy, the winery manager escorted me to his office where he showed me how he tracks all sorts of winery information on his computer. I thought the dork just wanted to get a closer peek at my assets, but he showed me the actual computer program that helps him fill out all the Federal and state forms that he has to file. You don't know this but every month a winery has to file all kinds of paper work that shows how many tons of grapes they've crushed—how many gallons of wine they've got stored in tanks and barrels—the different kinds of wine they're storing, like cabernet, or zinfandel, and how much wine they've got bottled. When the manager had to go to the can, because I sort of accidentally dumped some coffee down his shirt, I dropped the computer program disk into my purse."

"My good woman, are you confessing to me that you committed a blatant felony while working under my direction?"

"Yes I am."

I sighed. "Do you still have the program disk?"

Bear emptied his beer. "She does and the brains how to use it."

Arianna served us three more glasses of Berger Brown and tossed her blonde curls as she left. Bear, who up till now had been rendered speechless by the winsome female, said, "Boss, I don't see how she'll get Flo into the . . . hold on, I get it now. The beer-twin is going to walk Flo into the St. James Winery by pretending to be her winery-twin sister."

For once my simple investigator showed a flash of brilliance. "I am glad you appreciate my plan."

"Once Flo is inside, she'll dig into the nitty-gritty of the winery. You give my babe enough time and this puzzle will turn out to be a piece of cake."

"And perhaps she will come up with the name of the murderer."

Bear shook his head. "Flo's good with a computer, but she can't make a fancy purse out of a pig's ass."

I considered correcting him, but that would be like trying to stop water leaking through a strainer. "Walk me through your understanding of my plan."

"First, the winery-twin has to stay back east. So somebody, like a rich lawyer I know, will hand over five Benjamins to the beer-twin so she can wire the cash to her sister."

"You have it so far."

"Tomorrow morning, me and Flo will pick up the beer-babe and we'll go to the St. James Winery. Everybody there will think the beer-babe is her twin so they'll let us in. I'll take my OSHA badge along so I can hang around in case something blows up."

I said, "My boy, there may be a few wrinkles to iron out, but you have to admit my brilliant strategy should work."

Bear pushed his chair back and stood up. "Okay. Call me once you're sure the winery-twin will stay on the east side of the Rockies."

I said, "Hold on. I did not say this meeting was concluded."

"Boss, it's getting late. If we're going make our dinner reservations we've got to get our butts in gear and get back to the river. "

Bear turned and as I watched my man walk out of the pub, someone with a deep voice that was heavily laced with stale garlic whispered into my ear. "Don't look back. Just stand up and walk with me to the door left of the bar. Don't make any funny moves 'cause I got a shiv up my right sleeve. You need to know I've stabbed a couple of dudes before, and both times my shyster worked out one of those self-defense things with the DA."

TWENTY-THREE

Pinky-Healdsburg, California

I glanced at the Pub entrance and the happy couple was long gone. I said, "Stay calm. I will do what you requested."

As we passed the bar I could see in the mirror that my assailant was Thor, the bearded, muscle-bound, bartender. The ruffian pushed me through the door left of the bar and I found myself in a tiny office. The aroma of stale beer filled the air. The walls were lined with cases of beer and wine. Thor closed the door and moved the knife blade back and forth close to my nose. I could not take my eyes off the blade—about six inches long and it looked sharp—very sharp indeed.

Thor said, "Okay, you little bastard. Just what makes you think you can waltz into town and take bread out of my mouth?" He lowered the knife and began to slice tiny curls of nail off his left index finger.

"Mr. Thor, I do not believe we have been properly introduced. My name is J. Pinkus Delmont. My friends, and I hope to include you in that group, call me Pinky."

Thor stopped his grooming ritual and slammed the point of his knife a good two inches into the desktop. "Stop all the Pinky bullshit. That's all I hear—Pinky this—Pinky that. If you want to keep breathing, don't say that name again. I don't know what your game is but Arianna works for me. Every shift my broad puts in here at the Pub, the beer sales jump more than twenty percent."

I should have known. In the world of true love money trumps everything. "Mr. Thor, like you I am a successful businessman so I can sympathize with your situation. My intentions are honorable. I propose a deal. I desire to rent the services of Arianna for two days."

He grabbed the knife handle, ripped it out of the desktop and stuck the tip of the blade on my Adams apple. "Hey, watch your mouth. I'm not a pimp."

I could feel the point of the blade, less than an inch from opening the blood supply to my brain. "I apologize if I left that impression. Now, let us get to the reason for this discussion. I am scouting the area for a major movie studio and I want to use Arianna as a stand-in for my female star."

"You mean my babe looks like your movie star?"

He closed his eyes and I assumed he was trying to match his waitress' face with one of the big named actors.

He said, "Hey, I'll bet it's—"

"Their contractual agreements would not allow me to tell you even if you gave me the correct name. Now, let us get down to the deal. What is it going to cost the studio for two days of Arianna's time?"

Thor stood there. Here was his big chance to stick it to the man and I could see that although he had dreamed of this moment, he was uncomfortable with the actual implementation. "How much do you think I can get away with?"

This was almost too easy. "I would start off at five hundred."

"Wow! For each day?"

"You can always come down."

He poked his finger into my chest. "Okay, Pinky, how about five hundred a day?"

"I fear that is a touch high. Would you settle for two hundred?"

"Okay, I'll take it."

"Mr. Thor, you might consider coming back with a number above two hundred. Perhaps two hundred and fifty. Of course that would include letting Arianna off an hour early this afternoon so she and I can shop for some appropriate clothing."

He plunged the knife blade back into the desk top, this time three inches deep. "Okay, how about two fifty."

"Give me a moment to consider your bid. Is that your final offer?"

"Yup."

I stuck my hand out. "You have a deal. Mr. Thor, between you, me, and the gatepost, you drive a very hard bargain. Now, if you will excuse me, I have to return to my B & B. Please inform Arianna I will pick her up at four for the shopping tour."

While I walked across the plaza, I inhaled the fresh, clean air, and felt very much alive when suddenly, as if a bolt of lightening struck me, my life or death commitment to Macario thundered through my head. I pulled out my cell and called my office.

"Lu."

"Yes."

"I need you to take all the paper records concerning the Elena Macario divorce from my files and shred them. Then go into our computer data base and delete everything concerning Elena Macario."

"Do you want me to pull the card with her address and phone number from your personal address file?"

"Yes, but before you do that, make up a final bill for five hundred, no, make that twenty-five thousand dollars, no, too high, make it ten thousand. That amount should meet the reasonable agreement. Stipulate that the bill is for legal advice."

"Do you want me to indicate the billable hours?"

"No. Just show the ten thousand total. Mail the completed bill to Antonio Macario at the identical location I have in my file for Elena Macario. Once you have addressed the envelope, remove that woman's card from my file, take the damn thing outside, place that pariah on the sidewalk, sprinkle some lighter fluid over the paper, and burn it!"

TWENTY-FOUR

Bear-Rio Nido, California

The rain was coming down so hard I could barely see through my windshield as we pulled up to our cabin. Before I opened the door I heard a hand pounding on Flo's side of the pickup. She opened the door and the kid was standing there in the rain.

"Flo, remember you said you'd teach me how to paint my toenails?"

Flo said, "Right. We're a little late but I'm sure we can do it."

"Yippee."

We walked into our cabin and inside of three minutes, Flo was prancing around the room on her bare feet with her toes standing at attention. She'd stuck little hunks of white cotton between her toenails, and the skinny kid sat on the bed and laughed herself silly.

I popped a beer and said, "What's so damned funny?"

Flo said, "I'm just going to paint my toenails. In five minutes I'll be ready to start on Ettamae's first pedicure. My plan is to show her how important it is to be a well groomed woman at all times."

Except for the endless bucks she cost me, I didn't have a thing against Flo and her suitcase full of little bottles of beauty stuff. In fact, I liked her looking good, but she usually wore shoes so painting her toes seemed like a big waste of scratch. I drained the can, popped a second one, and said, "Oh, I get it now. You're going to teach the kid that all she has to do is paint her toes and that'll make her a woman."

Flo glared at me and shook her head.

The kid, kind of like she didn't hear what I'd said, jumped off the bed and waved two little bottles of nail polish in Flo's face. "Florence, this one is called 'Jam and Jelly'. The other is 'Pinking of You'. Which one do you think I should try?"

"Make it the 'Jam and Jelly'. That way, tomorrow morning you can ask your grandpa if he wants 'Jam and Jelly' on his toast and he'll think you're talking about real jam but you'll be talking about your toes."

They both giggled again just like Flo told the funniest joke in the world.

"Flo, we're fifteen minutes from our dinner reservations at Gordon's." I chugged down the beer and pulled a third one out of the tiny refrigerator. "Kid, I think you're going to have to finish your toes later."

The skinny one came right up to me, like she was going to pop me one. "I've told you this before, my name's Ettamae, just like your name is Bear. I would appreciate it if you would show me some respect and call me by my given name."

I had to give it to the kid. She was one tough, little broad.

Ettamae walked back to Flo and said, "Don't worry, Florence, we'll have plenty of time to do my toes tomorrow."

I said, "We might not stay for the whole reservation. We could be done with our work tomorrow afternoon."

Flo said, "That'll be the day. Don't worry, that

little Napoleon will find some way to get himself into a pickle and you'll have to rush in and rescue him."

"Listen, Flo, I've worked hard all day and I came up with a damn good suspect for the murdered winemaker. I think you'd—"

Flo flashed me her nasty stare and held her finger to her lips. "We need to hold off on discussing the details of your investigation."

The kid headed toward the door. "Based on the conversation I think I've overstayed my welcome, so I'll leave you two to get ready for dinner. Bear, don't forget, you've paid for three more nights and those nights are not refundable. If you complete your work early, you might consider spending a few days relaxing by the river."

I listened to the raindrops pepper the metal roof of the cabin. "Sure, kid. After breakfast, I'll go down to the beach and soak up some of that liquid sun that's falling out of the sky."

The kid shook her head. "Florence, your boyfriend suffers from a lack of optimism. See you in the morning at the breakfast spread and I can promise you that tomorrow we'll have something better than those boxes of powdered sugar donuts."

Once the kid cleared the door I said, "Why should I watch what I say around the kid?"

"That child is only ten years old and she's heard enough about death in her short life, first her mother and father, then her grandmother. Ettamae puts on a good front but what that little girl needs is love, not you going into the grisly details about a man drowning in a tank of cabernet sauvignon. And that brings up another thing. Do what she told you to do, call her Ettamae, or get ready to sleep by yourself on the floor tonight."

"Hey, I was just giving the kid a hard time."

Flo slipped her sweatshirt over her head and the sight of her knockers bumping together stopped me from breathing while she stretched her arms to the ceiling.

"Bear, it's up to you. The bed or the floor?"

"Okay. From now on I'll call her Ettamae, but if I forget once or twice, don't get pissed off at me."

Flo pulled me to her and I damn near drowned in her skin. "Come here, big guy, I knew I could count on you. Now, how long did you say before our dinner reservation?"

I glanced at the clock radio on the bed stand. Hell, right then I didn't care if I ever ate again, but she had asked and I knew Flo would get pissed off if I lied. "Inside ten minutes."

Flo pushed me away and put her sweatshirt back on. "I'm starved. Let's eat."

We drove a couple of miles downriver to Gordon's and just like the kid—whoops, Ettamae—had told me, the food was damn good and they had a nice selection of those little half bottles of wine so Flo didn't get soused. We ate indoors because of the heavy rain and after we returned to the motel, I stood on the porch for a second and watched the river.

"Are you coming to bed?"

"Be right there." I took a last look at the river. "Babe, it may be my imagination, but the water looks like it's coming up fast."

"Bear, get in here now. I'm interested in something else rising and the Russian River has nothing to do with it."

Oh boy!

179

TWENTY-FIVE

Bear-Monte Rio, California

I woke to a weird, buzzing noise that sort of sounded familiar. I glanced at the clock radio on the little stand by the bed. It was seven-fifteen. I lay there for a second trying to get my head together.

Then that sound happened again.

Flo snorted. "Answer the damn cell phone. I'm trying to sleep."

"Oh." My mouth was as dry as the desert sand at noon. I grabbed the phone and staggered to the bathroom. "Hello?"

"Tempus fugit, my boy. Tempus fugit. I'm not paying you that exorbitant salary to sleep the day away."

"Slow down, Boss. My brain's not working yet. What's going on?"

"My boy, your brain functions at less than normal speed twenty-four hours a day."

"Boss, where are you?"

"What has that—"

"Is it raining where you are? On the river it's been coming down like cats and dogs since—"

"Is that rain I hear?"

"Nope, I'm peeing. What do you want?"

"I definitely do not want to sit here and listen while you empty your bladder."

"Sorry, Boss. But you woke me up and I didn't

have a chance to—"

"Be quiet and listen to me. I'm going to FAX the police and autopsy reports to you at the motel office. You can read the gruesome details while you eat breakfast. That may help you develop your thought process for Flo's visit to the St. James Winery."

"What! Me and Flo are heading to the winery this morning? When I left yesterday things were still up in the—"

"As I said, Tempus fugit. By the way, you left the Pub before I could give you Arianna's address."

"Just a minute." I grabbed a pencil and paper and scribbled down numbers and a street name. "Where exactly is that?"

"Just outside the quaint village of Geyserville, north of Healdsburg. Take the Geyserville off ramp and head east. By the way, I purchased her a rather sharp woman's business suit so she will look like her sister."

"Boss, I can understand you'd have the broad's address, but it's interesting that you know where she lives. Does that means you've been to her place—"

The line went dead.

Flo was back to sawing logs. I sat down on the edge of the bed and said, "Babe, we have to get going."

"Uhummm."

"It's time to get up and grab some breakfast."

She pulled a pillow over her head.

"Pinky's set everything up. We're going to the winery today."

Flo groaned from under the pillow. "Let me sleep."

"Babe, remember the deal we made with Pinky—the five thousand bonus—we each get twenty-five hundred."

She threw off the pillow and jumped up like she just stuck her finger into an electrical socket. "Twenty-five hundred. It's about time. I told you the last time, when we went to Needles, that was the last time I was working for free."

"But Pinky's paying you a grand to help me on this trip."

"Nowhere near enough for my ability. What exactly am I looking for this time?"

"Start by using that computer program you clipped in Modesto to find out what's going on at the winery. Like you did when you found that hidden file with the cooked Brady Blackstone books. Hell, I don't know what or how you do anything with a computer. I'm just a stupid bartender."

Flo walked into the bathroom, turned on the shower, and called, "I'll consider his proposal."

"Shit, this ain't a proposal. We told Pinky you'd do—" The shower door slammed and Flo turned the water up to high.

Twenty minutes later we were standing in the motel office eyeballing Ettamae's latest morning spread.

She said, "What do you think, Florence? Does the present breakfast selection look better than yesterday?"

The over-ripe bananas were leftover from yesterday and by now they'd gone past making banana-nut bread. The apples still looked green, but the kid had added a full pitcher of orange juice that had a real orange color, a dozen hard-boiled eggs, a stack of ham slices cut real thick, and a giant mound of good-looking French bread.

I gave the kid a pat on the head. "Ettamae, you've done it. This is a professional breakfast spread."

Ettamae said, "Thank you Bear. I appreciate the compliment."

Flo said, "Ettamae, it rained hard all night long and it's still going strong. Does it come down like this all the time?"

"Not all the time, but don't figure on spending the day outside unless you plan on turning into a prune."

I said, "The weather's not a problem, Babe. Remember, we've got work to do. We're going to the winery and you need to—"

Ettamae said, "Going to a winery? Sounds like fun."

Flo glanced out the window at the gray, wet morning. "I'm not going anywhere until I figure out this weather. Ettamae, any chance this storm could clear up soon so I could catch a few more rays."

The kid shook her head. "Florence, like I said, this rain is not going to stop. According to the TV news, the storm front has stalled off the coast and Grandpa thinks we need to be on guard for a little flooding."

Flo leaned forward and gave the kid a worried look. "Would you define a little flooding for me?"

The kid kind of scrunched her eyes. "It depends. I'd bet a couple of the stairs to your cabin might end up under water by nightfall, but don't worry, I'll keep an eye on your things if you have to go to the winery with your man."

Flo stopped chewing her hard boiled egg and set her fork down. "Ettamae, one lesson you need to learn right now. I make all the decisions concerning if, and when, I join Bear while he conducts the business activities. Now that we've cleared that up, did you say that it's possible we won't be able to drive to our cabin?"

Ollie poked his head into the room. "Folks, I just received a bunch of stuff on our FAX machine. Does this belong to you?"

I jumped up and grabbed the paperwork from him. "Thanks."

Ollie said, "And don't worry about the cabin. We go through a little flooding like this every ten years or so. Ettamae and I can handle everything."

After a couple sandwiches of ham and boiled eggs, I was fuller than a tick in springtime. I said, "Okay. Babe, once you finish your coffee, we'll head to the winery."

Ettamae said, "Have fun."

I said, "This is work. We don't have fun while we work."

Flo snorted, "You can say that again."

Flo's nasty remark really burned me, but I clammed up and listened to the windshield wipers as we drove through the vineyards on the way to Healdsburg. Finally I couldn't hold it back. "What do you mean, you don't have fun working with me? You get to lie in the sun around motel pools. You eat out every night at fancy restaurants. You even find time to do your toenails."

"What about that motel in Eureka—no pool. Or the motel in Needles where it was so damn hot that you could cook a three-minute egg in two minutes on the deck by the swimming pool. But I will say this, life with you is a lot more exciting than living by myself in east L.A."

I think she just told me she was sorry for being nasty, or maybe she didn't. With Flo I was never sure about anything.

Flo said, "Again, what exactly are we looking for at the winery?"

"I don't know. Just dig through the winery

records. Find something that's out of whack. You know, the usual junk."

"Humph!" She started to read the papers Pinky had faxed to their motel. "Wow! According to the cops report, Enrique is a dead man walking . . . Holy cow! I'm glad I didn't see this picture of the purple winemaker before I ate breakfast." Flo turned the picture of the purple dude over and sat back. I could tell she was thinking about something. "Is Pinky the only one that's talked to the winery-twin?"

"Yup."

"That alone worries me. You keep telling me that Pinky's a giant when he gets inside a courtroom but all I've ever seen is an undersized blowhard."

"Cool it, babe. He's not the greatest boss I've had, but working for him beats the crap out of mopping up barf in a bar."

Flo shook her head. "Bear Zabarte, if I hear that line one more time, I'll make sure the following ends up on your tombstone—Working For Pinky Delmont Is Better Than Mopping Up Barf."

TWENTY-SIX

Bear-Healdsburg, California

With Flo following the road signs and numbers, we found Arianna's place around 8:45. The joint was about what I expected—a little, not-to-bad, frame house painted white. A few rose bushes hung around the front porch and there were a couple of fruit trees stuck in the middle of the six-inch high lawn. Outside the garage sat an old VW bug parked next to an even older, green John Deere tractor.

Before I got out of the truck, Arianna popped out the front door of the house. She was wearing a fancy kind of business suit and the broad sparkled like a million bucks. She started to the driver's side of the truck and I heard Flo mumble, "Over my dead body."

Flo jumped out her side and yelled, "This way, Arianna. I've saved the seat nearest the window for you."

They got in, and before I started the engine, the smell of warm peach pie filled the crowded cab, you know, that kick-ass smell of sugary peaches and cinnamon.

Looking straight ahead, Flo said, "Interesting perfume."

Arianna said, "Thanks. I like it too."

Flo said, "Bear tells me you work full-time at the Downtown Pub."

"Yeah. But today and tomorrow, I'm working for Pinky. He bought me this expensive suit yesterday. Do you like it?"

Flo said, "Yes, it's very smart."

The cab got real quiet as I tried to figure why Flo thought the clothes Arianna wore were smarter than what she'd had on yesterday at the Pub. I thought duds were just something you wore to keep from getting cold in the winter, not dumb or smart.

Arianna asked, "Bear, when I say something do I sound different?"

"Different than what? You look different but sort of sound the same to me. Why?"

"Pinky told me I had to look, and act, and talk like my sister. That's really hard because she's stuck up and a real pain to be around. But that's not what's bothering me. I have to get past Luciano."

Flo said, "Tell me what you're going to say to him."

Arianna sat up straight, stuck out her chin, and said, "Luciano, this woman's name is Florence. I hired her to clean up the office backlog. Now, if you'll excuse us, I'm sure we all have a lot of work to do."

She looked at me and Flo. "What do you think?"

Flo said, "You sounded a lot different to me."

I said, "But you sounded like you're really pissed off at Luciano for some reason. Did you two have something going on in the past?"

Her chin dropped. "You're right, but that was a long time ago."

By now I should know better than to trust one of Pinky's great plans but as Grandma said, in for a penny, in for a C-note. "Beer-babe, were not playing games here. A dude was murdered at the winery and I think there's a good chance the killer's still there. Tell us what happened between you and Luciano."

187

Flo said, "I don't agree. Their previous relationship should remain between Arianna and her God."

"Babe, not when something could hang our asses out to dry. That killer might not stop at one murder. Spill it."

Arianna said, "It was the Senior Prom. Me and my sister were always the prettiest girls in school and I was the most popular. Florianna was, well she was as pretty as I was, but not as friendly. The only guys that ever asked her out thought they were talking to me."

Flo said, "If you were truly identical, how could the boys tell the difference?"

"I always wore a few colorful ribbons in my hair and Florianna wore dark, dull ones. One day, a month before the prom, she took one of my ribbons out of my side of the dresser drawer and wore it to school. Luciano, he was the star quarterback on the football team and my dream prom date, picked that day to ask me to the prom, but because of the colorful ribbon, he asked my sister to the prom by mistake."

"Sounds to me like you should be pissed at your sister, not Luciano."

Flo put her arm around Arianna. "Just what I'd expect from a man. Bear, shut up and let her finish the story."

I said, "Did you go to the prom?"

"I did but it was with one of the dweebs who talked about math all night. From that night Luciano and my sister were an item. Me and my sister continued to live in the same house, but never really talked again, if you know what I mean. In fact, we've never really been close since then. She went on to college. I tried the local JC for a while but nothing interested me. I got a job at the Pub and have been working there ever since."

We pulled into the winery property. When I reached the fork in the road I hung a left and drove down the hill to the main building. Pinky's car was parked near the door. Flo said, "Did Pinky tell you that he was going to be here?"

"No, he didn't."

That really bugged me. Pinky was enough of a problem when I knew where he was and what he was doing. Our plan didn't include him being at the winery while Flo did her thing. If everything clicked just right, Flo could come up with some juicy evidence, but with Pinky butting in, it seemed to me that the boss could blow our caper sky high.

TWENTY-SEVEN

Pinky-Healdsburg, California

I was reading the paper and sipping my second cup of coffee at the B & B, when the cell buzzed.

"Yes?"

"Mr. Delmont, my name is Martin St. James. I've just returned from a trip back east. My Club Cabernet coordinator has informed me that you dropped by the winery during my absence. Are you still in the area?"

"Yes, my business lasted a bit longer than anticipated."

"Outstanding! Now that I've returned to the winery I trust you'll give me the opportunity to personally escort you through my facility."

"Mr. St. James—"

"Please, Mr. Delmont, call me Martin. You have purchased the maximum allotment of my finest wine for nearly twenty years. That alone should qualify you as a friend."

"Martin, call me Pinky, and we have a deal."

He laughed. It sounded a touch forced but in the competitive world of wine a forced laugh is better than no laugh at all. "Pinky, can you come by this morning?"

I glanced at my watch. It showed 8:20. "I'll be there in fifteen minutes."

"I'll meet you at the main building. See you

soon."

When I drove up to the main building, a tall and handsome man with silver hair waved at my car.

"Pinky, I'm Martin St. James. Welcome to my winery."

"Thank you."

"Is there anything you would especially like to see first?"

"No. Lead on and I will follow in the master's foot steps."

"Please, you make me feel important. I do very little here."

This was the perfect opportunity for me to slip in the obvious question. "Come to think of it, there is one place I would love to visit, your Bench-Land vineyard, the hallowed home of your world famous cabernet grapes."

He hesitated and his right thumb twitched twice. "I'm sorry but time constraints preclude a visit to the vineyard. However, I will pour you some tastes of the latest bottling."

"More than I could ask for."

We entered the winery and wandered about for a few minutes. Having toured many wineries I arranged an excited expression to my face to veil my boredom. The mask remained until surprise took over when I spotted Bear walking up an aisle of tanks. Martin said something about the cabernets being pumped into a tank before bottling but all I could think of was Bear standing there with his OSHA tag around his neck. Then the door opened and Florianna walked in. Or was it Arianna? Anger roiled in my stomach because if the woman standing before me was Arianna, she was not following my plan. But what if it was the real Florianna? I tucked myself between Luciano and a tank and prayed that either way the female did not spot me.

After Arianna, or Florianna, complained about her long airline flight, and left the tank room, the next thing I heard was Bear's voice. "Hey, Luciano, is there a can around here? I've got to pee."

"Head back to the door we came in and turn right."

I called to Bear, "Just a minute, young man. I also need to use the facility."

"It's a free country, dude. Do whatever turns you on."

In a moment the two of us were standing together in a tiny room with a sink, a toilet, and most importantly, away from Martin St. James and Luciano.

"Boss, you'd better throw some water on your face. You don't look so good."

"My boy, I am in excellent shape. Why would you insinuate otherwise?"

"Cause your stupid idea of swapping twins damn near blew up in our face. Now clam up and let me bring you up to date."

Bear rattled on about leaving Flo in the office. Then I explained my newfound relationship with Martin St. James.

He said, "Wow. I now pronounce you husband and winery owner. I hope you have a happy life together."

"Stop your tomfoolery. I plan on using our new rapport to find out if the owner has something to hide besides the fatal infection of his Bench-Land vineyard."

Bear said, "Did you pick up the eye contact between Martin and Florianna? I'd bet my next paycheck there's something going on between them. Kind of interesting that they were both gone and then showed up on the same day. I'd give my right nut to see if they took the same plane? Hell, for all we know they could have shacked up at a local motel. Hold on, I've got an idea." Bear pulled out his cell.

I said, "While you are making the call I will flush the toilet in case Luciano's listening."

"Get real. Do you think that dude has nothing better to do with his time than to plant his ear on the door to listen to a couple of guys pee? . . . Flo, what's Arianna doing? . . . I've got a job for her, something that could be important."

Bear talked to Arianna while I scrubbed my hands pink with soap in a futile attempt to banish the germs that lurked in all public facilities. "Bear, I am still the leader of this expedition. Explain Arianna's important job."

"I told her to call around to all the motels in the county. Once she finds the person that runs the joint, I told her to kind of hem and haw, like she was embarrassed or something. Then tell them she spent a couple of days with a dude with silver hair. Now here's the punch line: She's going to say that she accidentally left a diamond ring in their room. She can't leave her name of course, but if they find the ring they're to call her and she'll give them a thousand bucks reward for the ring and their silence. Got it? It's just a little fishing trip, but there's a chance we'll find out if the winery boss is diddling the winery-twin."

I paused. His idea had merit but my hesitation would let him know that I had some reservations. "I approve, but in the future pass your ideas by me first."

Bear dropped his cell into his pocket. "Right. Now, I've got to get back to Luciano. Are you going to unzip and do something?"

193

"No. In fact, I find it impossible to urinate in front of other men."

"I don't have that problem and I've got to pee really bad."

"And?"

"Boss, it's crowded in here and if you don't clear out right now I might get some on your new shoes."

My skin crawled at the unsavory concept. "I'll wait for you outside."

Moments later we found Luciano standing by a tank covered with a layer of ice. He said to me, "I think I've seen you before. Have we met?"

"I fear you are mistaken. Now, I would appreciate it if you could call Martin and tell him I'm ready for my tasting."

Luciano made the call and then he said, "The boss will meet you by the main building door in a couple of minutes."

While Bear steered Luciano toward the bottling room I briskly walked back to the office that was situated by the main entrance. I opened the door a crack and peeked in. Flo was hunched over a computer keyboard and Arianna was sitting at a desk with an open directory and a phone to her ear. "Flo?"

She jumped up. "Jesus, Pinky. Give a gal some warning and knock next time. What the hell do you want?"

"I thought I needed to warn you that I am meeting Martin St. James outside this office in a couple of minutes."

"I can't afford to leave now. If he tries to come in rattle the doorknob. Arianna and I will hide in the broom closet."

"I will do as you suggested. By the way, please inform Bear that I will call him later this evening to set up a strategy session for our final assault tomorrow."

Flo looked up. "You know something I don't know?"

"No. As you should know by now, I always conduct an internal brainstorm before making my final arguments to the jury."

"I hate to break this to you, but we're in Healdsburg, not Carson City, and we're trying to find a murderer, not spring one of your guilty clients out of jail."

"I know where I am." I wanted to close with, 'you witch', but Flo's computer expertise was proving valuable. "I was attempting to explain the preferred investigative methods in a simple way so a neophyte, such as yourself, would comprehend the steps required. Bear and I will put our heads together, so to speak, and go over all the important information we've collected prior to our final assault tomorrow."

"Humph! So I'm not invited." Flo swept her hand across the desk and a large stack of paper tumbled toward the wastebasket. "I guess we won't be needing these documents I discovered digging through the St. James computer files?"

I hesitated. I wanted to spend as little time as possible close to Bear's woman, but it was within the realm of reason that she had come up with some vital data. "Flo, I apologize. With the twins running around the winery the importance of your task slipped my mind. Have you discovered anything interesting?"

"It depends. The records concerning your favorite wine, the Bench-Land cabernet, are screwed up. I can't track the grape to the bottle."

I did not have any idea what she was blathering about. When she stopped talking I said, "My dear, we could not possibly meet tonight without an integral and valuable member of my investigative team being present. You are invited."

"Whoopee, now spare me your line of crap and clear out. I've got work to do."

I closed the office door and a moment later, my newest best friend, Martin, fresh smile painted on his lips, joined me. "Pinky, I hope you are ready for the tasting of your life."

"I am. By the way, is there a chance that I will be able to purchase a few more cases of the Bench-Land cab? I was told by the club coordinator that everything was sold out."

He laughed, but once again, his expression of joy was not genuine. "Of course you can. As I told you, I checked my sales records. My God, Pinky, after my top restaurant accounts, you are my best customer and have been for years. I can't ignore that sort of loyalty! After the tasting we'll return to the warehouse where I am sure I can come up with two or three cases for you."

"Thank you for your generosity. I was concerned that with Paul Hellman gone . . . "

"Not to worry. Forget all those stories you hear about outstanding winemakers. Great wines are grown in the vineyard. The greatest winemaker in the world cannot make a silk purse out of a sow's ear."

That comment is about what I would expect from a winery owner who was committed to selling his wine, crafted by Paul Hellman, or not. "Martin, as a true neophyte, I appreciate all of your expert opinions concerning the art of winemaking."

TWENTY-EIGHT

Bear-Healdsburg, California

Arianna opened the winery door and the three of us barged in.

Luciano was leaning back on his chair, drinking a cup of coffee, and reading a magazine.

I yelled, "Luciano, I told you before, leaning back like that is a safety hazard. Put all four legs of that chair on the ground or I'll write you a safety hazard citation."

He dropped the magazine, jumped up and spilled some coffee on his hand. "Don't write me up, Bear. I won't do that again." Then he caught sight of Arianna. "Florianna, I thought you were—"

Arianna stuck her chin out and her voice was colder than a penguin's balls. "That's obvious, Luciano. You thought I was back east so you could sit around while the work piled up. Just about what I expect from you. This is Florence, a woman I hired to clean up some of the compliance paperwork backlog. While she is here you are to leave her alone. In fact, the compliance office is off limits to you for the rest of the day."

Deep down, the beer-babe was more like her twin sister that she knew. I said, "Excuse me, ma'am, I'm from Cal-OSHA and I need to check things out with Luciano in the tank room. Will that be okay with you?"

Arianna waved her hand, like she was the new

queen on the block. "Cal-OSHA man, whatever your name is, remove that two-timing bastard from my sight."

Before Luciano could figure out what she had just called him, I hustled the dude through the tank room door.

I said, "Wow, that bitch is almost as cold as these tanks."

"Tell me about it. She's been after my ass ever since we . . . Bear, why are you back? Have we got a new safety problem?"

"You mean besides you leaning back in that chair? Not really. My boss told me I had to take another look at the tank where the accident took place."

He grabbed my arm and pulled me down a row of tanks. "Like I told you before, the death wasn't an accident. The winemaker was—"

Pinky and another dude suddenly appeared at the end of the row. I heard the new dude say, "As I told you Pinky, all of our cabs are pumped into one of these tanks before bottling. Ah, here's my cellar master, Luciano. He will continue on as your guide and after he's answered all your questions, he'll give me a call and I will personally conduct your tasting."

Luciano gave my boss a long, hard look, like he thought he recognized his face and figured Pinky was trying to pull something, but he wasn't sure what.

The silver-haired dude next to Pinky stuck his hand out in my direction and said, "And you are?"

"Bear Zabarte. I'm from Cal-OSHA." I stuck the ID that hung around my neck in his direction.

He said, "I'm Martin St. James. Pinky, I'll leave you in good hands with Luciano. Due to the blizzard conditions on the east coast the winegrowers association cancelled the rest of the eastern promotional tour. I'm a little jet-lagged so I'll go to my house now and unpack. If you'll excuse me."

I glanced at my boss and his eyes were the size of dinner plates. As far as we knew Florianna was on the same tour. If she flew back with her boss, she could show up any minute, and we'd have twin business-suited broads wandering around the winery. Another example of why I needed to have my head examined for going along with one of Pinky's dumb-shit ideas.

I grabbed my cell and looked at the screen. "Excuse me, I just got buzzed. I have a call from the main office in Sacramento."

I stepped a few feet away and dialed Flo's cell.

"Yes!"

"Babe, somehow bad weather back east got everything screwed up. The real Florianna could show up any minute."

"I'm up to my elbows in paperwork here . . . what do you mean by the real Florianna?"

"The evil twin."

"No shit."

"Tell Arianna and be ready to make a quick exit."

"We can't leave yet. The books and records in this office are a real mess but I've found a couple of hot items that need further investigation. Give me a few more hours and—"

The door to the bottling room opened and Florianna, at least she looked like the real Florianna, moved toward our little group. The tank room was at least two hundred feet from the office where I left Flo and Arianna. The babe standing in front of the group was wearing the same kind of fancy suit we had put on Arianna and it was the same gray color. I whispered into my cell. "Babe, is our Florianna still in the office with you?"

"Of course she's here. Why?"

"Has she still got on the gray suit?"

"Of course she does."

"Then we're up shit creek."

Flo said, "What's going on?"

"Can't talk now, the broad's too close."

The real Florianna whispered something in Martin St. James' ear. She didn't seem to notice Pinky tucked behind Luciano. Then Florianna caught Luciano's eye. "Luciano, because of the flight change I had to switch planes in Chicago and Denver. I'm exhausted and I'm going home. First thing tomorrow morning we'll go through everything that's happened over the last few days. Good-bye." She turned and walked through the door.

I whispered to Flo, "We're in luck, she's pooped from her flight and going home. All you have to do is keep Arianna in the office until the winery-twin drives off."

"Okay, but what about Luciano? He's seen the real Florianna and thinks she's gone home. What do I do if he comes into the office?"

"I got it, Arianna could tell him she's not tired anymore."

"If you can't come up with a better solution than—"

"Hold on, Arianna told Luciano he couldn't go into the office so you should be safe."

"Good. Now leave me alone. I've got important work to do."

I looked up and Luciano was headed in my direction. "Me too."

When he got close I stuck my hand out and said, "Luciano, it's been great. I wish all the winery dudes were like you. Some of the guys I have to deal with are real pains in the ass. I'll tell my boss that I checked the tank and I'll send you the results in a couple of weeks. Just need to check out a couple of past investigations that should be on file in your office. The broad in there can find what I need."

"I don't know. She's new here."

"I'll take my chances. Give me your cell number. If I need your help I'll call."

I beat it back to the office, opened the door a crack and said, "Flo?"

"This place is busier than the post office on income tax day. What the hell do you want?"

"Wondering how Arianna's doing."

Arianna looked up. "So far, I've struck out. Just finished the tenth call. I guessed that you were looking for romantic places so I concentrated on those. I have about eight places left to call."

"Hang in there. How's it going with you, Flo?"

"I can tell you this much, there's something wrong with the inventories of the wines. According to that guy in Modesto I should be able to track every bottle of wine back to the grapes hanging on the vine."

"So?"

"The records for the 2009 and 2010 vintages of Bench-Land cabernet are missing."

"Isn't that the same wine the boss goes gaga over?"

"Yes. And they've lost about two thousand gallons of bulk red wine."

"Maybe they're going to make some of those little boxes of wine you buy at the grocery store?"

"Not likely. These guys don't make—"

Arianna jumped up and talked real loud. "Yes, we checked out this morning. Thank you. And when you find the diamond ring, be sure to call me." She slammed the phone down. "That was the Bodega Bay Spa. You know, the one that advertizes on TV—romantic rooms with champagne and a private beach. My sister and Martin spent the last three days there. Frankly, I'm embarrassed. Florianna's been jumping in bed with Martin St. James, a married man who's old enough to be her father. I know Thor's not rich but at least he's not married and he doesn't need to take Viagra." She gave a big sob and her face started to blubber up.

Flo got up and put her arm around Arianna's shoulder. "That's okay. They're all bastards."

I said, "Hey, what about me?"

Flo gave me a cold stare. "I guess I could exclude the present company."

I wasn't sure exactly what Flo meant but it sounded okay, so I said, "Flo, have you found enough stuff so we can wrap up and clear out of here?"

"I think I have enough on my flash drive to figure out what's going on. You're right, we need to get out before Luciano gets wise."

I peeked around the office door to check the area. Luciano was nowhere in sight so me and Flo and Arianna skedaddled into my truck. Twenty-five minutes later, after we dropped Arianna off at her place, my cell rang.

I pulled out my cell and Flo grabbed it. "Give it to me. It's still against the law to talk and drive in California." She said, "Hello," listened for a couple of seconds, then cried, "Stop the truck."

I pulled over and Flo stuck the cell next to my ear so both of us could hear. "Ettamae, I didn't get it all the last time, tell me again."

I heard the kid's voice, and she was crying. "Florence, we need you and Bear right now. The water is still coming up so Grandpa Ollie went into

202

your cabin to take out your suitcases. While he was inside, a tree floated down the river, hit the stairway, and took it out. Grandpa's stuck at your cabin door and there's about a five-foot drop into the water. Every minute the water's getting higher and moving faster. Grandpa Ollie can't see a thing. I don't know what to do."

I yelled, "Run your skinny butt up the hill to the motel office, grab a strong rope, the longest one you can find, and wait for me."

"You don't understand. The river's gone wild. I'm afraid any second the cabin will break loose and Grandpa will die."

"Listen to me. Flo will call 911 to get the Sheriff heading your direction so stop worrying. We'll be there inside of five minutes and I'll figure out a way to get your Grandpa out of the cabin."

She screamed, "But what happens if you don't get here in time?"

I slammed my foot on the gas pedal. "Kid, your job is to run up that hill, get that rope, and wait for me. My job is to get there in time to save your Grandpa. Trust me, Kid, I'll get there."

TWENTY-NINE

Bear-Rio Nido, California

Flo grabbed my arm so hard I damn near drove off the road right into a ditch full of water. She said, "What's going to happen to that sweet little girl if you don't make it?"

Then she started to sniff and snort, like she does before she goes on one of her crying jags.

I'm pretty sure Flo knows that I lose it when she cries. I peeled her fingers off my arm and said, "Babe, stop your blubbering. We'll be there inside five minutes."

Her tears stopped real fast and she said, "You didn't answer my question. What's going to happen to Ettamae?"

I think we both knew the answer so I didn't say a thing.

I glanced through the window to look at the sky, and it was getting darker and darker.

I said, "What time is it?"

"Ten after four. Why?"

"We'll get there in time, but I can't see in the dark. My bet is we don't have much more than a half hour of light."

Flo started to whimper again. She wasn't sniffing and snorting like a minute ago, and this time those were real tears trickling down her cheeks.

Out of the gloom I spotted the neon sign of

Chapman's River Resort shining through the rain and I cranked the wheel a hard left. The Kid, as wet and soggy as one of my old bar rags, stood in the middle of the parking lot with a big coil of rope over her skinny shoulder. I rolled down my window and yelled, "Flo get out and wait for the Sheriff. Kid, climb in. Me and you will head down the hill and save your grandpa."

The Kid jumped inside. The rope looked strong enough to do the job, whatever that job was going to be. I gunned the engine and once the hood of the truck peeked over the crest of the hill, I slammed on the brakes. Shit! The water had come up five or six feet since me and Flo had left that morning. The picture through the truck's windshield was like one of those summer disaster movies where all the cities and towns next to the ocean were under water because a weird alien from outer space figured out a way to make the oceans rise.

This morning, before we left, our cabin looked no different than the day we checked in—a building set between a rock outcropping and a grove of giant redwoods—a covered porch with a stairway that led to a nice beach stretching for a couple of hundred feet—fancy lounge chairs sitting on the beach and tucked under redwood trees—an old brick Bar-B-Queue across from our cabin where I'd grilled a steak a couple of nights ago. I thought I'd seen a lot of bad shit in my day, but nothing was this bad. The beach, the fancy chairs, the brick Bar-B-Queue, were now under five to six feet of water, or down the river, but from what I could see, they were all long gone.

I jumped out of the truck and that's when the noise coming from the flooding river hit me. Flo loved sleeping in the cabin, with the window wide open, so she could hear the sound of trickling water. But now,

205

that trickle had changed into a loud, spooky roar, sort of like a dozen out-of-control eighteen-wheelers shooting down the steep Grapevine North of Bakersfield.

I squinted through the rain and picked out the cabin. I wanted to see the rock outcropping and the steps that led up to the porch but there were no rocks, no steps, in fact most of the covered porch was gone, only the wooden cabin was still standing. Just inside the front door of our room stood Grandpa Ollie. He was yelling something but I couldn't hear him with all the noise from the river. He swished his white cane up and down and back and forth toward the empty space that used to be a wooden porch, like he hoped that if he poked around long enough there'd be a place to step.

I yelled as loud as I could. "Ollie, it's Bear. Stay where you are."

He must have heard me because he looked in my direction and yelled back. "Bear, I can't find the porch with my cane."

"That's because it's gone. Give me a minute. I'll figure something out."

Ollie stopped waving his cane. "Don't do anything foolish on my account. Just make sure Ettamae's safe."

"Hey old man, stay cool. I'll get you out of there." Actually I didn't have a clue what I was going to do next and I think Ollie knew it.

He waved his white cane again and yelled, "Ettamae, whatever you do when you grow up, be sure to make your old grandpa proud."

The Kid said, "Bear, don't just stand there with your mouth hanging open, do something!"

Every second it was getting darker. Between the sun setting and the steady rain, if I didn't get off my

206

ass and try something fast, even if it didn't work, the chance of Ollie breathing something other than water was down to a few minutes. "How much rope did you bring?"

"I don't know."

"You take one end, I'll take the other. Walk uphill and pull it as tight as you can."

The Kid ran up the hill. I figured the distance between me and her was about thirty-five feet. I glanced at the distance between me and the cabin and it was about the same. I might not reach the cabin, but for the Kid, and her grandpa, it was worth the try.

I yelled, "Get back in the truck." I slipped the gear shit into reverse, popped the clutch, and once the gears kicked in I gave the steering wheel a hard crank. The truck spun, and just like that the rear end was pointed at the cabin.

The Kid pounded her fists on the dash. "Wow! That was cool. Can you do that again?"

"Maybe after I figure out how to save your Grandpa."

I slowly backed down the hill and said, "Kid, jump out. You watch my rear wheels and yell when they are under about six inches of water. Got it?"

"Got it."

I slowly backed up and the Kid cried, "Stop!"

I grabbed the rope and hooked a loop on the trailer hitch. Then took off my belt and threaded the rope through the belt loops round my waist and tied it tight. Finally, I looped my belt through the rope wrapped around my waist. Now all Ollie had to do was grab my belt and hold on.

"Kid, this is the plan. I'm going to wade through the water to the cabin. If we're lucky I'll be able to walk all the way. Once I get there, I'll tell your grandpa to jump down. I'll grab him, and using the rope, I'll pull both of us back to dry land."

"Okay, but what happens if the water's too deep to walk to the cabin? Or the current's so strong that you can't pull yourself back. What are you going to do then?"

Shit, the Kid had me there. I thought for a second and said, "I know you're just a little snot-nosed kid, but did you ever drive a truck like mine?"

She gulped. "You mean a full-size pick up?"

"Yup."

"Last year Grandpa let me drive his little Toyota pick-up around the Safeway parking lot in Guerneville, but it was real hard for me to push the clutch all the way to the floor with my short legs. Why?"

"Here's the chance for you to give a real truck a try. I'm going to leave the engine running. If me and your grandpa end up being pulled away by the current, or if it's too deep for me to get my footing, all you'll have to do is push the clutch pedal down, throw the gear shift into first gear and pop the clutch. That way the truck will drag both of us out of the water."

The Kid stood up real tall. "I can do that. I'm a year older and a lot stronger then the last time I tried to drive Grandpa's Toyota."

"Okay. Let's go."

The cabin was about thirty feet away. I glanced back at the rear tires on the truck and the water was up to nine inches. Damn, up three inches in five minutes. I checked the sky. Giant raindrops smacked my face. I guessed we had five to ten minutes of daylight left. I walked into the moving water. The first five steps were okay but then, about ten feet from the cabin, when the water got above my waist, I stepped in a hole and lost my footing. The current grabbed me, took me under, and spun me around. Before I could do anything the river slammed my right knee into the rock outcropping that bordered the steps next to the cabin. I fought to get my head up and after spitting out a bucket of muddy water I grabbed a mouth-full of dry air. The rope was tight and I was floating a good fifteen feet away from the cabin. I grabbed the rope with both hands and worked against the current. It was like trying to pull me through a giant bowl of cooked oatmeal. Finally, as I was about to call to the Kid to pop the clutch, I gained a couple of inches, then a foot, then two feet, and finally I was able to stand up.

The kid yelled, "Bear, your pants are torn and your knee is bleeding. Are you okay?"

I knew if I even looked at my knee, Ollie would never get out of that cabin. I said, "My knee's okay. I'm going to try again."

I started back toward the cabin, but this time I tested each step before I put my weight down. The water was about chest high and the current was trying real hard to push me away from the cabin when I grabbed hold of a white trim board near the front of the little building. "Ollie, are you still there?"

"Bless you, Bear. Where are you?"

I stopped to think for a second and that's when I realized how cold I was. "Near the front side of the cabin. Have you got a belt on?"

"Yes, why?"

"That's good. Go inside the cabin. There's an extra belt in my suitcase. Take it and loop it through your belt. Ollie, I know you're blind, and I don't want to scare you, but you'd better get your ass in gear. It's almost dark and if it gets any darker we'll both be blind."

"I understand. I'll do my best."

While I waited for the old dude to rummage through my suitcase, my fingers were getting stiffer and holding onto the one by six trim board was getting tougher. A couple of times the current surged and caught me and I had to fight like the devil to hold onto the cabin. My teeth started to chatter and it was getting darker. If Ollie didn't find my belt real soon I'd have to give up and . . .

"Bear, I found your belt. What do I do next?"

"Stand at the door and stick your cane to the right . . . I see it. Now a little further . . . okay, stop and hold it there. Ollie, I know you can't see, but move your right foot around to see if any porch is left. If there is all you have to do is follow your cane down and to the right and I'll be waiting for you."

Over the increasing roar I heard Ollie say, "I've already checked and there's still about two feet of the porch on my right."

"Is it enough to get down on your hands and knees and crawl?"

"My chances have got to be better than standing here waiting to drown."

Through the rain and gloom, I saw Ollie's hand, then his arm. "Ollie, I can see your arm. Keep crawling, you're almost there."

I felt the cabin gave a shudder, like it was about to go.

Ollie yelled, "The river's about to take the cabin. Whatever you have in mind you'd better do it fast."

I knew that, but I was afraid to make the next move. I had to grab Ollie, but against the wild current I knew I couldn't hold him. Then it hit me, stop fighting the current and let it do the work. I let my self float toward the cabin. In a second my left leg ended up next to Ollie's hand. "Okay, now reach out and grab my leg and find the belt loop."

I watched his fingers walked up my leg and bump into the belt. "Bear, I have it."

"Okay, now open the buckle and connect it to the belt you've looped through your belt, remember, the one you got out of my suitcase."

"I get it now, I have a belt around my waist and the one I got out of your room is looped through. Now I'll loop the one you just gave me through that. Bear, are you positive all these belt buckles will hold?"

No I wasn't, but I had reached the point that if I didn't get out of the water pretty soon both of us were going to die. "Ollie, all we can do is hope."

I looked over my shoulder to be sure the rope was still attached to the truck. No much to go on but at least we had a fighting chance. "Ollie, are you ready?"

"I am."

"And you have secured the belt buckles?"

"I think so."

"I hope you're right because those leather connections are the only things guaranteeing you'll end up on the right side of the grass tomorrow morning. Now lean out as far as you can so I can grab hold of your belt."

I reached out and felt his belt but the water was so cold my hands were damn near frozen. I took my right hand out of the water and stuck my fingers into my mouth. After a couple of seconds I bit down, felt a sharp pain, so I punched my hand back into the water and grabbed the belt again. I closed my fingers around the leather and yelled, "Ollie, say a short prayer for both of us and roll off the porch."

The shock of Ollie's weight hit me first, then the current, and ripped my hold off his belt. Ollie started to float away then he stopped, held by the looped belts. We were in deep shit. My fingers were numb. There was no way I could pull me and Ollie against the current and I knew the belt buckles wouldn't hold much longer. I screamed at the top of my lungs, "Kid, this is it. Pop the clutch."

I don't know how long it took for the Kid to do her thing, maybe no more than twenty seconds, but when an old man's life depended on a couple strips of connected cowhide and cheap metal buckles, twenty seconds felt like twenty minutes.

Suddenly the rope around my waist jerked so hard that me and Ollie popped up and skidded on top of the water, like a couple of salmon being pulled up a fish ladder. Then the rope went slack and the current took us again. Ollie shot back, feet first, into the rock outcropping. I heard him scream just as the rope started a steady pull and dragged me and Ollie out of our watery grave. For a couple of seconds, both of us just lay there, in a few inches of water. My teeth were chattering from the cold and my knee hurt like hell but I was still breathing air. Ollie was lying on his back. I heard him whimper that both of his legs hurt real bad.

The Kid ran towards me. "Bear, do you recall when I told Florence you lacked optimism? Guess what, I was wrong. You're loaded with optimism." She planted a big kiss on my cheek. "In fact, you're my hero."

"K-K-Kid, we were both goners and then you popped that clutch. G-Guess that makes you my hero." My knee was killing me, my fingers wouldn't move, and I had to find a way to get warm. "M-me and your Grandpa tha-thank you. Ca-Can you find me a blanket or something?"

"Bear, you can call me Kid if you want. In fact, I think it's kind of endearing." She ran over to Ollie, lifted his head and gently kissed him on his forehead.

About that time, Flo appeared at my side followed by an ambulance. The red lights flashing on the roof of the ambulance lit up the side of the cabin as the wooden building broke up and slipped into the raging current.

Flo said, "Bear, are you okay?"

I couldn't stop shivering but me and Ollie were alive. "I-I-I've been better. Help me walk up the hill to the office. I-I'm freezing."

"Hold it right there, bud," said one of the ambulance dudes. "You could bleed out if we don't close that big gash below your right knee."

I said, "What about Ollie?"

"The old guy has a compound fracture of his left leg and his right ankle's broken. My guess is he has multiple fractures and those fractures at his age could be slow to heal."

Flo said, "Let's can the idle chatter, my man's freezing. Slap a bandage on his knee and get the man a blanket. He'll get his knee stitched up as soon as we get to the Healdsburg Hospital."

The ambulance dude said, "Sorry, lady, we're not going to Healdsburg."

Flo demanded, "First, get my man that blanket."

The dude walked to the ambulance, grabbed a blanket and handed it to Flo. She wrapped it around my shoulders and said, "Now, where are you taking Ollie?"

"To the nearest emergency center in Santa Rosa."

Flo said, "Not on my watch, buster. He goes to the Healdsburg Hospital or I'll call the Sheriff and ask for a different ambulance service."

"But ma'am, Santa Rosa is—"

"What is there about the simple word,

213

Healdsburg, that you don't understand?"

I could see the ambulance dude was doing what he thought was right, but he'd never bumped into a woman like Flo before. I said, "Du-Dude, give up and take Ollie to Healdsburg Hospital before we both die out here."

The ambulance dude shook his head. "Right, Healdsburg it is."

Flo said, "Thank you. We'll be directly behind you."

The ambulance dude slapped a big bandage on my knee but I was so cold I didn't feel a thing. I climbed in the truck, turned the heater on high, and yelled to Flo to get in.

She said, "Slide over, I'm going to drive."

"Nope, my knee is okay."

I fired up the engine and the ambulance dude tapped on my window. "Hold on, you forgot the kid."

Ettamae yelled, "Mister, my name is Ettamae and I'd appreciate you addressing me that way in the future. Now, open the back door, I'm riding with my Grandpa in the ambulance."

Just like Flo, that Kid was a real firecracker.

The ambulance dude threw up his hands and let Ettamae in the back with her grandpa. With red lights flashing we followed the ambulance. About a mile down the road, Flo said, "If you're going to be macho about your knee, hand me your cell phone. I need to make some important calls."

I reached into my pocket and my phone wasn't there. "Babe, it was in my pocket when I went into the river to get Ollie. It's probably half way to Hawaii by now. Can't you use your phone?"

"I can, but how do I know that Pinky will pick up the monthly charges now that my cell has become your business cell?"

214

Boy, she was a pistol. "Babe, nobody can guarantee what Pinkly will do so you'd better wait 'til we talk to him."

"This can't wait." Flo pulled out her cell from her purse and a notebook. "I'm writing down the time and date, and when we reach the hospital I want you to initial my note. Pinky will have the specific time and day your cell went into the river so he should have no problem picking up all my cell phone expenses."

Deep inside her gut, Flo had to know that pigs would fly before Pinky would pay her cell phone charges, but what the hell, I'd scribble my initials on a scrap of paper if that would keep my Babe happy. "Why are these calls so important that you can't wait?"

"Just drive and listen." She keyed in a number. "Willow, it's Flo . . . No, things are not so good here . . . I'll give you a detailed account later. First, I have an important legal question for you. Bear and I know a little girl. She's ten years old and her only living relative, her grandfather, has just been injured . . . he's alive but both legs are broken and according to the paramedic at the scene . . . right. Now, this is my question. While the grandfather recovers from his injuries, can we legally take the child with us when we return to Carson City? . . . Right, the grandfather would move to Carson City as soon as he can travel . . . Thank you, Willow. I knew I could count on you. Bye."

I said, "What the hell are you talking about. We're not taking that kid with us. Where would she—"

"Hush." Flo keyed in a second number. "Lu, it's Flo. We've run into a little bump in the road. An elderly man, the grandfather of a young friend, just

215

broke both his legs in a tragic accident. Lu, I understand this subject might be hard for you to discuss, but before your father passed on, he lived in an assisted living facility. Number one question, would you recommend that facility for . . . excellent, and the name of the place . . . Carson Valley View, just south of town on the west side of the highway . . . yes, I know the area well. Bear and I will check out the place as soon as we return . . . Thank you, Lu. I knew I could count on you . . . how soon 'til we're back? I don't know. You'll have to ask the northern Nevada Napoleon. Bye."

I said, "Babe, I think you've—"

"There you go, thinking again. Just follow those red lights on top of the ambulance and I'll take care of the items that need to be resolved."

She keyed in another number. "Harry? It's Flo . . . and it's good to talk with you too. Now, I've had a hell of a day and I need your help listing a business . . . yes, it's a motel/resort on the Russian River. The name is Chapman's Riverside Resort in Rio Nido, and the owner, Ollie Chapman, just became incapacitated due to an unfortunate accident. . . . No, other than a ten-year-old granddaughter, the owner has no relatives . . . asking price? I don't have a clue. Check out some comparables and let me know what you think. Harry, the owner is a sweetheart, blind as a bat, and now he's stuck in a hospital with two broken legs. Don't let anyone, and that includes you, try to take advantage of Ollie's situation . . .hell no, I'm not sweet on him, like I told you, he's old enough to have a ten-year-old granddaughter . . . okay, but I'm going to monitor this deal from start to finish, so don't you or any of your friends try to pull anything shady. You can contact Ollie through me . . . that's what I said. You're going to have to go through me on this one . . . Thank you, Harry. I knew I could count on you."

I yelled, "Babe, have you lost your marbles? You can't ask some dude to sell Ollie's resort without talking to him first."

She ignored me and keyed in another number.

"Mr. Bliss, my name is Florence Sunderland. I am an associate of Mr. Delmont's . . . yes, that Mr. Delmont. An unforeseen situation has come up and I'll require a two bedroom suite for . . . no, I'm sure two nights will cover our needs . . . you have a suite available? Excellent. First, we must stop by the Healdsburg Hospital and we'll arrive at the Red Rose B & B in an hour or so . . . I'm sorry, I missed that . . . a credit card number? At present I'm riding in a pick-up truck rushing two injured men to the Healdsburg Hospital. We will discuss the details of our stay once we check in . . . what do you mean you require a credit card number to hold a room. I don't think you understand. As Mr. Delmont's associate, our bill will be combined with his bill . . . fine, I have no problem with you checking with Mr. Delmont to be sure the billing arrangement is acceptable with him, but first you should know the reason that we've been forced to seek immediate shelter at this late hour.

Our former place of residence, one of the top resorts in Sonoma County, was swept into the Pacific Ocean by the record-breaking flood on the Russian River. That disaster, coupled with the heroic efforts of one man, the man who is seeking shelter at the Red Rose B & B, is the reason for my call today. Mr. Bliss, I would hate to consider what an unscrupulous person could do with the tale of how the proprietor of a popular B & B turned away Bear Zabarte, the son of a Basque sheepherder—a man who is a national

217

hero—the man who risked his life to save another human being—a living icon who was just informed there was no room for him at the Red Rose B & B because of a disagreement over a credit card number . . . yes, Mr. Bliss, I understand your concern about booking unscrupulous persons . . . and don't forget the local newspapers, the Bay-Area television stations, even CNN, once they discover that you refused to allow Mr. Zabarte, a man who braved certain death . . . of course I understand there are two sides to every story . . . those same news organizations could be informed that after Mr. Zabarte's dramatic river rescue, The Red Rose B & B opened up its heart and assisted Mr. Zabarte, the wounded hero, through his time of adversity . . . excellent! I'm gratified that you discovered the generosity in your soul and found Mr. Zabarte a dry, warm bed during this wet and stormy night . . . to be sure there's no misunderstanding, we will require the two room suite we discussed earlier . . . thank you, and as I stated, we will arrive inside of two hours. Thank you, Mr. Bliss. I knew I could count on you."

THIRTY

Pinky-Healdsburg, California

I had called Bear's cell for the third time and had been transferred to his voice mailbox each time. The last time, I left the following message. "Damn it, Bear, turn on your phone and call me immediately or you are fired." To say I was angry would be an understatement. I was not paying that plodding dolt an outlandish salary to ignore my calls, or to disappear off the face of the earth for hours on end.

On a hunch, I called Lu.

"Law Office of J. Pincus Delmont."

I never tired of hearing my efficient secretary voice that greeting. "Lu, this is Pinky. I have been attempting to reach Bear and—"

"He's either on his way, or he should have reached the Healdsburg Hospital by now."

"Hospital? What? Slow down and explain yourself." I slumped into a chair. With Bear heading to a hospital the possibility of clearing Ben's nephew from the murder charge grew dimmer by the minute. I demanded, "What is wrong with him?"

"Flo called me and told me that—"

"Cease your babbling and give me Flo's cell number."

She did. I keyed in Flo's number.

"Hello?"

"Flo, Pinky here. I need to—"

"Who gave you my private cell number?"

"Flo, that is not why I called you. It is imperative that—"

"How did you get my number? Tell me that first or get off my line."

"Lu gave me the number. Now stop interrupting and answer my question. What happened to Bear?"

"It's a long story. He destroyed his knee rescuing the owner of our motel from drowning in the flood. As we speak, Bear is in the emergency room undergoing treatment along with the owner of the motel that has a broken leg and a broken ankle. That's not all. Our cabin, plus our suitcases with all of our clothes, was swept away by the raging river. At present, I am sitting in the waiting room with motel owner's ten-year-old granddaughter. As soon as Bear gets patched up we'll check in at the Red Rose B & B. Of course the term checking in is a touch silly because we don't have any clothes, or a tooth brush, or—"

"Flo, I have heard enough. While you wait for the doctor to complete Bear's medical needs, call Bliss and inform him that you will require toothbrushes and tooth paste for three. He is a rodent-like creature, but the man should solve your immediate dental hygiene problems. As for your clothing, I will contact Arianna. She remains on my payroll for one more day and I am positive she would love to assist you in resolving your clothing requirements." I glanced at my watch. "The moment you are settled in your room, and assuming Bear is up to the journey, walk across the hall and knock on my door."

An hour later, as I sat in my room reading a book, Flo called my cell. "Pinky, there's been a change in your plan. You need to knock on our door.

Bear is okay but I think he'd feel more comfortable with his leg stretched out on the couch in our sitting room."

I hesitated. How did they end up with a two-bedroom suite with a sitting room? And was I ready to abdicate my position as the leader of this investigation to that woman?

"Pinky, it's now or never. Walk across the hall or our strategy session will be over before it starts. And bring me a bottle of wine. After this day I could use a taste of something red."

Angered at Flo's brash mouth, but resigned to the fact that time was running out on Enrique, I snapped off the lights and stormed toward the door. Suddenly, I recalled her command for a bottle of wine. I considered ignoring her demand—the only wine I had in my room was what I had purchased from Martin—an extremely limited and very expensive cabernet—but for the next twenty-four hours, with Bear's unknown physical condition I needed Flo on my side. In the dark, I reached down, opened a case box and extracted a single bottle.

A moment later I knocked on the door and Flo stood there. "Come in."

She grabbed the bottle out of my hand and disappeared through a door.

Sitting on the couch, with a thick wrap of bandage around his right knee, was my investigator. "My boy, how bad is your injury?"

"Not too bad, Boss. The doc threw in a couple of stitches and it doesn't hurt much when I walk."

Flo's voice shot in from the adjoining room. "Don't listen to him. The doctor told me he was very lucky. Had his leg hit the rock an inch higher, he would have sheared off his kneecap. And it wasn't just a couple of stitches. The doc closed the wound

221

with thirty-one. Pinky, Bear's injury happened while he was working for you and that entitles him to file a Workers' comp case. I'll check California's law on that subject first thing tomorrow morn—"

A door opened next to the couch and a thin child, possibly a female, entered the sitting room. She held a blanket around her body with her left hand and she waved her other hand in my direction. "Hi, my name is Ettamae. And you are?"

"J. Pinkus Delmont." I turned toward Bear. "Who is this creature and what is she doing here?"

Flo, a full glass of red wine in her hand, said, "Remember? I told you about the blind motel owner that Bear saved from drowning. Ettamae is the granddaughter of that man."

"Does anyone, other than myself, note that my question concerning her appearance in your sitting room remains unanswered?"

Bear said, "Boss, it's just temporary. Her grandpa's in the hospital with two broken legs. Tomorrow the doc will tell us what—"

Flo interrupted, "And Bear forgot to add that Ettamae will remain in our custody until her grandfather is physically able to take care of her."

Bear jumped off the couch onto his good leg. He seemed as surprised as I was over Flo's statement. "Babe, I know how much you bonded with the Kid, but—"

I interrupted, "Did I hear you correctly? You two are being paid a princely sum to investigate a murder. Not baby-sit a child."

The urchin known as Ettamae spun around, tossed a corner of her blanket over her shoulder, and said, "Once again, from the tone of this conversation, I detect it is time for me to return to my room and watch TV. It was a pleasure to meet you, Mr.

Delmont. Good night."

All eyes watched the tiny female leave the room. Once the door closed we all started to talk at once.

"She can't be expected to. . . "

"But the Kid doesn't . . . "

"You cannot hope to raise an underage child . . ."

Eventually I cried out, "Cease the babble!"

Flo took a gulp of her wine, held onto the mouthful for a moment, and then swallowed. Her expression was one of surprise. She looked at her glass and then back at me. "Pinky, tell me the name of your 'world's greatest' cabernet again."

I said, "Do not attempt to change the subject. We have one day before Enrique's trial starts and that child's future has nothing to do with—"

Flo walked out of the room.

I stomped my foot and demanded, "Bear, do something to bring that woman under control."

From the adjacent room Flo yelled, "Pinky, Bear has no control over me and if you haven't figured that out by now you are a lot dumber than I thought."

A moment later she returned holding an opened bottle of wine. She turned the label toward her and said, "Damn it, I asked you for the name."

I sighed, "St. James Winery—Bench-Land Cabernet Sauvignon—Vintage 2007 or 2008. Now can we move on?"

"Not yet. You recited everything except for the year. This bottle's a 2010. Pinky, I buy all my red wine at Costco. It comes in a cardboard box, the equivalent of four bottles, and each box costs me sixteen bucks. Between you and me, my Costco red tastes better than this crap. How much did you pay for this plonk?"

I reached out and grabbed the bottle from her.

The witch was correct. The bottle was labeled as St. James Winery, Bench-Land Cabernet Sauvignon—Vintage 2010.

"Pinky, you haven't answered me. How much did this bottle cost you?"

I ignored her taunt, lifted the bottle to my lips and allowed a tiny amount of the wine to trickle onto my tongue. Then I pursed my lips and slowly drew some air over the liquid—to release the flavors and bouquet that remain locked inside the tannins of a new vintage world-class cabernet. To my horror, my palate detected a wine infused with the flavor of dried prunes, an undesirable tang that completely overwhelmed the expected essence of black berry, cassis, and tobacco. Also, the structure of the wine was soft and flabby, lacked acid, and the tannin required so the young cabernet could age for at least a decade. The wine in this bottle had come from over-ripe grapes grown in the hot central valley of California, not the St. James Bench-Land vineyard located in the perfect climate of the Alexander Valley in Sonoma County.

"My God, Flo, you are correct. This wine is Fresno plonk."

"You still haven't answered my cost question."

"Each bottle cost me one hundred and twenty-five dollars and that includes my ten percent case discount."

Flo said, "Did you buy this bottle at the winery?"

"I did. Before I left the winery Martin St. James sold me two cases of the 2007 and one case of the 2008 vintage. When I arrived this afternoon I had Bliss carry the sealed cases to my room for safe keeping."

Bear said, "If the cases were all sealed where did this bottle come from?"

I explained to her that I had opened one of the cases in the dark prior to crossing the hall.

Flo said, "Do you think there are anymore mislabeled bottles in that open case?"

"We need to check."

Flo said, "Bear, lay your head back and close your eyes. Pinky and I'll take care of checking the wine bottles."

I said, "I agree. We will return in a moment."

We walked across the hall and as I opened my door, Flo said, "Pinky, get used to the fact that you're working with me tonight. Bear nearly lost his kneecap and came close to losing more than that while saving Ollie's life. My man's exhausted and I will not allow you to talk with him again until tomorrow morning."

I did not get along with Flo in her previous incarnation, and this new personification, an even more assertive one was truly appalling. As we stepped into my room, Flo made a beeline to the open case and started to pull the bottles out of the cardboard case box.

"2010, 2010, 2010. Pinky, they're all the same year. In fact, the label on the case shows 2010. What year does the label show on the other cases?" She ran to the window, where the other two cases rested on the floor. "These are both 2007." Flo looked up. "Somehow, Martin got mixed up and sold you a case of the 2010 instead of the 2008." For a moment the woman stopped moving around my room and remained static long enough to cry, "That's it!"

"What is it?"

She said, "When I was going through the records in the compliance office I discovered a gap in the records of the 2009 and 2010 Bench-Land cab."

"Bring me up to speed."

"Remember, when you walked into the office, I told you some of the records for your favorite wine, the Bench-Land cabernet, were screwed up? For some reason I couldn't track the grapes to the bottle."

"That seems a long time ago, Flo. Remind me what you mean by tracking the grapes to the bottle?"

Flo gave me a quizzical glance, sat down and placed her dirty shoes on my bedspread. "You don't have a clue what I'm talking about do you?"

Her shoes had sullied my sleeping chamber. I masked my anger with a warm smile and controlled the urge to grab her arm and leg and fling the female into the hall. "I understand what I need to, my dear. Now, provide me with your conclusion concerning your inability to follow, as you put it, the 2010 Bench-Land grapes to the bottle."

"Okay. Federal law requires each winery, to file various forms on each wine they make. Those forms track the grapes, down to the pound, from the winery that crushed the grapes, to the winery that bottled the wine. A good example would be the St. James Winery 2008 Bench-Land Cabernet Sauvignon. They had the forms that prove they picked, crushed, fermented, and bottled that wine. In a second example, and this one I'm making up, in September of 2010, The Yosemite View Winery picks, crushes, and ferments a central valley cabernet. The St. James Winery buys the cabernet from The Yosemite View Winery, ships it north, and bottles it under the St. James label. With me so far?"

Maintaining my friendly demeanor, I said, "I understand. In the first example, St. James had control of the product from vineyard to bottled wine. In the second, another winery did all the work and St. James bottled the cabernet under their label."

"Right. Now let's run through some dollar

numbers for the 2010 Bench-Land cabernet."

"Go ahead. I am ready."

"I don't think you are, but I'm moving on anyway. When a winery crushes a ton of grapes they'll end up with around 120 gallons of finished wine. So in my little scenario, let's say we pick twenty tons of grapes from the St. James Winery, Bench-Land, Cabernet Sauvignon vineyard."

"Right."

"Those twenty tons of grapes will give the St. James Winery approximately two thousand-four hundred gallons of finished wine. That amount, once bottled, will produce . . ." The woman seemed to be calculating the math on my bedspread with her fingernail. ". . . About eighteen hundred cases. Now we get to the interesting part. You paid one hundred and twenty bucks per bottle, or fourteen hundred and forty a case. Hang with me Pinky for one last calculation. Eighteen hundred cases times fourteen-hundred and forty dollars a case amounts to a whopping two-million, six-hundred-thousand bucks."

My ears perked up. Now we were talking real money. "Could you go over that grape to the bottle part again."

"No. Stick with me. Let's say St. James Winery purchases twenty-four hundred gallons of central valley cabernet from The Yosemite View Winery at ten bucks a gallon. St. James would be out of pocket twenty-four thousand dollars. Once the central valley cabernet was safely bottled under the St. James, Bench-Land Cabernet Sauvignon label, St. James could clear a profit of more than two and a half million."

I said, "I see. And if St. James could sell their mislabeled cabernet where no one knew anything about wine they might get away with the switch. My dear, we are on the right track but we are still missing some pieces to the puzzle."

Flo jumped up, finally removing her soiled shoes from my bed. I made a mental note to tell Bliss to change the bedding.

She said, "Try this on for size. What if Paul Hellman wandered through the tank room the night of the bottling session? Hellman knew the winery didn't have any 2010 Bench-Land cabernet."

"And the murderer spotted Hellman. My God, we've come up with the motive of why Hellman was murdered."

"So the poor bastard was murdered because he was in the wrong place at the wrong time."

I nodded, "The ultimate case of bad luck. However, our luck changed the moment I pulled that bottle out of the case."

"Bear once told me that occasionally, solving one of these murder cases took more luck than brains."

For once, Bear's view of the cosmos was correct, but I would never let Flo know that I agreed with my old bartender's conclusion. "It is now time for you to quietly return to your suite. If Bear is asleep on the couch, so be it. I will take the bottle of plonk off your hands to continue working on the mystery of how Martin St. James planned on selling his mislabeled wine for fifteen-hundred dollars a case."

"I thought you told me that you paid fourteen hundred and forty a case."

"You forgot my ten percent case discount."

"Okay, where do we go from here?"

"As stated, we will sleep on the problem and I will come up with plan in the morning. Good night."

A few moments later, alone in my room, sipping the plonk, I detected a delicate knock on my door.

Fully expecting to see the overly endowed Flo

standing there, perhaps in her flimsy nightgown, I was momentarily taken aback when I faced the ferret-like features of Mr. Bliss.

I glanced at my watch, to inform him that I was tracking every minute. "What now?"

"Sorry to bother you, Mr. Delmont, but I have a question concerning my agreement to lodge the three guests in our most expensive suite across the hall."

"Mr. Bliss, you have five seconds to explain to me why you have interrupted my privacy. One . . . two . . . three . . ."

"Mr. Delmont, that woman across the hall, a Mrs. Sonderlund I believe, informed me that she and the gentleman, a Mr. Zabarte, were your colleagues, and as such, their lodgings were to be combined with your final bill. Mrs. Sonderlund refused to provide me with a credit card number, so I'm sure you can understand my concern that—"

"Mr. Bliss, at present, my personal well-being is the only item I care to discuss. I am positive that the State of California has lodging regulations concerning scam artists, and other nefarious types who skip out in the dark prior to settling their lodging bill. Good day to you."

"But Mr. Delmont, I—"

I started to close the door, and then opened it again. "Mr. Bliss, I just recalled an important item. I require a complete change of bedding before I use my bed tonight. Now, remove your obnoxious person from my threshold!"

I slammed the door in his face. A moment later, I pondered his innkeeper's tale of woe. According to him, Flo had attempted to stick me with her bill. Obviously, the woman thrives on chaos, and in the future, I would need to scrutinize her every move. Conversely, I could not ignore the fact that her antics were a never-ending source of surprise and entertainment to me.

I poured myself a full class of wine. The over-ripe taste was appalling, but I trusted the high alcohol, the direct result of the extreme sugar content of the central valley grapes, would kick-start my brain.

I grabbed my cell and dialed Arianna's number.

"Hello."

"My dear, I have a favor to ask. Two of my staff and a tall, skinny, ten year-old female lost all their clothes in the flooding river. Is there anything you can do to help them out?"

"Got it covered. I'll call my buddy that owns the 'Everything Store'."

"But it is so late I am sure the store is closed."

"Like I said, the owner's a bud. He'll open the place up, give me what they need, and they can pay him tomorrow."

"And when I pick you up for dinner, you can hand me the clothing and I will turn the items over to my staff. How long will you need?"

"No more than an hour and I'll be in town so I'll meet you at the restaurant."

"Fine, I will call the establishment and move our dinner reservations out to 9:30. Arianna, after our sumptuous repast, do you see our relationship expanding into something more?"

"Pinky, more than you can imagine."

THIRTY-ONE

Bear-Healdsburg, California

I woke up and rolled out of bed and tried to stand. "Ouch!"

Flo groaned and said, "Be careful. The doctor told me that your knee would hurt."

"Hell, he should have told me."

Flo sat up, her beautiful boobs jostled around like two volleyballs trapped in her old sweatshirt.

I said, "Flo, I hate it when you wear something to bed. I want to feel you, not an old sweat-shirt."

"I put it on so you'd get some needed sleep. We both know how amorous you get every time you crawl into bed. How's your knee feel now?"

"Not bad. Hurts a little, but not bad."

I heard a knock on the bedroom door. For a second, I couldn't remember anything that happened after I pulled Ollie out of the river. I looked at Flo. "Who's that?"

Flo said, "It's Ettamae, you fool, Get your naked butt back under the covers. What do you want, Ettamae?"

The Kid yelled, "Three things. I'm so hungry I could suck a raw egg. I have to get to the hospital so I can visit with Grandpa. Finally, somebody left a bag of clothes for us. My jeans fit and my t-shirt looks cool. I hope you're both decent because I'm coming in."

I jumped for the bed and made it under the sheet as the Kid marched through the door. "Morning Flo, Bear. It's time to get up and greet the morning. For the first time in days there's no rain and the sun is shining. I saw some red tulips outside my window. It must be springtime."

"Kid, one day without rain doesn't count as springtime. By the way, you're way too cheery for me. Now clear out so we can get dressed."

"What'll I do 'til then?"

Flo said, "Go across the hall and pound on Pinky's door."

"Kid, she's only teasing. You do that and he'll get pissed off. You see, Pinky's my boss and—"

Flo poked her sharp elbow into my side. "Bear, in the future, within the hearing distance of Ettamae's innocent ears, I insist you stop using that foul language."

"What did I say?"

Flo said, "Pissed off. And your list of banned words will include shit, asshole, horse pucky, and—"

"Florence," the Kid interrupted. "I've heard all those words and more that were a lot worse. I'll leave now so you can get dressed. By the way, Bear, do you normally sleep naked?"

"Why?"

"Because I caught a flash of your bare butt when you jumped for the sheets."

Flo buried her elbow into my ribs and said, "See. I told you times have changed."

The Kid said, "Bear, I've got a little poem for you that my grandpa taught me. 'A polar bear sleeps in his little bear skin, and he sleeps very well I am told. Last night I slept in my little bare skin, and I got a heck of a cold.' Since grandpa told me that, I wear pajamas every night."

I laughed. "That's a good one. Now clear out."

After we were alone, Flo said, "And that's another thing, if you wore pajamas you could get up, go to the bathroom, wander around the apartment, and not shock the neighbors."

"Babe, I'm okay with the Kid staying with us for a few days, but I'm not changing into a monk. She takes me as I am, or she goes."

"Goes? Where can she go? Until Ollie gets back on his feet, Ettamae has nowhere to go. She's forced to live with us."

I knew Flo was right about the Kid, but every once in a while I hankered to go back to the days before I met Flo in LA. The days when I lived by myself. My refrigerator was always full of beer, cheese and salami. I could let go a big, juicy fart and no one would yell at me. I'd eat all my meals off a TV tray and never miss a Red Sox game, or any other program on ESPN. In the summer I'd spend my days checking out the babes by the pool, and my nights playing three-card poker. Now Flo's telling me I've got to change my life again, but this time it's for a ten-year-old kid. "Babe, I'll do my best, but I can't guarantee I won't screw up and stay pissed-off the rest of my life."

"I'll accept that. It took Bess Truman, the president's wife, thirty years to get him to say manure instead of cow shit. I can see that you're trying to change and that's the best a woman could hope for."

Ten minutes later, decked out in duds, we walked down the stairs and the Kid's eyes almost popped out at the beautiful dining room. There was a big oak table surrounded by fancy, high-back chairs with red velvet seats. Along one wall there was a long oak table with a fancy cream-colored marble top. The marble was loaded with food for our breakfast. There were bowls of fresh fruit—peaches, nectarines, and apricots—three kinds of melon, raspberries, strawberries, cherries and grapes. Next to the fruit were fried eggs, scrambled eggs, and poached eggs. Next to the eggs were link sausages, thick fried bacon, sliced ham, two kinds of potatoes, three kinds of juice, four kinds of bread, blueberry muffins, little coffee cakes, and my all-time favorite, hot, fresh-baked cornbread.

The Kid, loading her plate up with fruit, jabbed me with her elbow. "Bear, I did my best with the breakfast spread at Grandpa's place but this joint must have found the pot of gold at the end of the rainbow."

That made me think about what Flo called our two-bedroom suite. The suite had more than two bedrooms. Our bedroom had a fancy canopy over the bed and a bathroom with a claw foot tub. There was a smaller, second bedroom for the Kid that Flo told me included her own bathroom. In between the two bedrooms there was a big, third room, Flo called it the sitting room. It was large enough to fit in a couch, four chairs, a cool writing desk with paper and four pens. On the south wall there was a big screen TV. Everywhere I looked, the furniture, the wallpaper, the carpets, the breakfast spread, all screamed big bucks. I hoped Flo knew what she doing when she booked us in here.

Flo said, "Ettamae, you're right about the pot of gold. Add that gold to our five hundred a night two-bedroom suite and they can afford this kind of a spread."

When she said five hundred a night I almost choked on a little sausage. Jesus, I wonder if Flo knows I don't have a thousand clams.

The Kid said, "Florence, it's a lot of money, but from what I can see, it's worth every penny. I guess Grandpa should have built his resort in Healdsburg."

A dude with a mouse face pushed his head over my shoulder, and said, "Mr. Zabarte, my name is Mr. Bliss, the proprietor of this establishment. When you get a moment, we need to discuss the bill for your two night stay at my fine establishment."

Five hundred a night, two nights. My God, Flo did lose her marbles. I said, "Sorry, but we don't have time right now. Got to drop the kid off at the hospital, then have a quick pow-wow with Pinky. After the meeting, we've got to head to the winery to finger a murderer. Right Flo?"

The dude gulped, sort of like he'd just choked down a small frog. "I am sorry. I didn't get all that. Who's Pinky? And just how does one finger a murderer?"

About that time Pinky waltzed into the dining room. The mousey dude darted away and saved me from inventing a few more lies. While the dude bent Pinky's ear, I tried to figure out where I was going to come up with a grand. I glanced at the Boss and he was smiling. Don't get me wrong. There's nothing wrong with smiling, but when Pinky cracks a big one, I start thinking about catching the next bus heading out of town.

Pinky grabbed a cup off the sideboard and said, "Mr. Bliss, I note that all the other guests have completed their breakfast. Bring the three of us some fresh coffee and vacate the dining area. I will require complete privacy for the next hour."

The mouse dude said, "Whatever you need, Mr. Delmont."

A woman carried in two full pots of coffee and Bliss closed the big, sliding oak doors.

"Boss, you need to grab some of this grub. It's great."

He glanced at the sideboard and shook his head. "My boy, I am totally . . . ah . . . I guess you could say I remain satiated from last nights delights."

Flo gave him a long look, and said, "Are you talking about your dinner with Arianna or something that happened later?"

Pinky flashed his super-cold glare at Flo.

"Boss, I loved the way you took care of that mousey dude. That was very cool."

"Thank you, and now . . . " Pinky spotted Ettamae who was sitting behind Flo. "One moment, I thought all the guests had finished their breakfast?"

Flo said, "Remember, this is Ettamae, the granddaughter of Ollie Chapman, the motel owner that Bear pulled out of the river yesterday?"

The Kid walked over to Pinky, waited until he shook her hand, and said, "Technically, the pick up truck pulled my grandpa and Bear out of the river."

"The Kid's right. But if she hadn't stuck the truck into first gear, and popped the clutch, me and her grandpa would be shark feed from here to Japan."

Pinky said, "Enough of this blather. We have work to do." He turned his head toward the oak door and whispered. "Mr. Bliss . . . "

The sliding door popped open. "Yes, Mr. Delmont."

"Normally, your propensity to scrutinize every conversation I have is a disagreeable attribute, but at this moment your annoying habit came in handy. Drive my ward to the Healdsburg Hospital."

"Your ward? Does that mean you accept responsibility for—"

"Mr. Bliss, my statement, drive my ward to the

Healdsburg Hospital means nothing beyond transporting this young woman to your local house of healing."

Flo gave the Kid a peck on her cheek and said, "Don't worry, we'll stop by and pick you up soon."

Ettamae gave us a wave, and with Mr. Bliss at her side, walked out of the dining room.

Pinky closed the sliding door and said, "Now, let us get to work. Bear, last night, after you casually dozed off, Flo and I had an interesting discussion. Flo, while I pour us some coffee, bring him up to date on how we think someone substituted the expensive cabernet grapes with some cheap wine grown in the central valley."

I chewed on my breakfast while Flo went through a long story she called the big wine switch, but once she said that more than a two million clams would end up in someone's pocket, I sat up and listened with both ears. "Are you telling me that all anyone has to do is switch some wine labels and they can walk away with more than two million?"

Flo said, "Not everyone, very few wineries are in the position to pull it off."

"Name one."

Flo said, "St. James Winery and the owner, Martin St. James."

Pinky said, "Personally, my money is on Luciano."

I jumped in. "Don't forget Florianna."

Flo said, "Or what about a combination of the three."

"Okay, Boss, what's next."

He sat back and stared on his coffee, like he was laying out the perfect plan to steal all the gold out of Fort Knox, but I knew that was Pinky's way of telling me he didn't know what to do next.

Flo said, "Okay, we're pretty sure Paul Hellman was killed because he walked into the tank room the night Enrique was doing the bottling run. Let's go over it again. Who was at the winery the night of the murder?"

I said, "Luciano, and don't forget the owner lives a couple of hundred feet up the hill, so Martin was as good as in the tank room. We don't know where Florianna was, and short of asking her, I don't see how we can find out. And we can't forget Martin's wife."

Pinky said, "That is correct. According to another winery owner I talked with they have been called the golden couple."

"And she lives in the house up the hill, so she's a suspect too, Boss."

Pinky said, "Also correct."

Flo said, "So were looking at one of these four, Martin, Luciano, Florianna, or Nancy St. James."

We all sat there for a second, then Pinky said, "I will visit Florianna and question her concerning her whereabouts during the time of the murder. You and Flo go the winery, and look for hard evidence that some wine labels have been switched and the wine was sold to someone. After I complete my interview with Florianna, I will join you at the winery. I need to taste a bottle of the 2008 to make sure that vintage was actually made from Bench-Land vineyard grapes. Then I will taste a 2009 and then a 2010 vintage to be sure they are not a Bench-Land Cabernet."

I said, "How will you know that?"

Pinky shook his head, like he was tired of explaining things to the dumbest guy in the world. "Any man with half a tongue could, and would, pick up the difference. Once I have tasted the wine, and

238

you have discovered, and copied the evidence, we take everything to my Sonoma contact. He will release Enrique from jail and we will return home to Carson City. Do we all agreed on our final plan of attack?"

Flo said, "Not quite. Before we leave, you need to tell us if you and Arianna did the deed last night?"

Pinky's mouth opened and closed for a second, like he was doing an imitation of a fish out of water. I've known Pinky for years and never once, in a court, in a bar, anywhere, have I seen him working this hard for his next word.

Finally, he said, "My relationship with Arianna has little to do with this investigation, or our final assault to discover the real murderer."

Flo smiled, "I think it does. Pinky, would you be willing to risk a small wager to find out?"

"What do you have in mind?"

"You pick up the bill for our five hundred a night, two-bedroom suite?"

"And what are you willing to put up?"

"On the off chance that Willow asks Team Zabarte if anything untoward happened during your visit in Healdsburg, whatever went on between you and Arianna will vanish from our memory."

Pinky stopped, like he was trying to figure the odds of Willow asking that question. Pinky and Willow are a funny pair. Flo tells me that they still love each other. Hell, I don't think Pinky ever actually loved anyone but himself, but Flo could have a point. They still go out to dinner, and they never tell anybody what they did after. Anyway, I guess Pinky figured the chances of Willow finding out must be pretty good because he said, "What is your proposition?"

"It's simple enough. If you can you prove to me

that the woman you jumped into bed with last night was Arianna, you win. If not, you lose."

"My good woman, you are on."

They shook hands. I knew Flo was looking for a way to stick Pinky with our bill, but I was pretty sure Pinky had never been so drunk that he didn't know the name of the broad he crawled into bed with.

Pinky put his hands behind his back and started to pace around the dining table, like he does in court when he's got the prosecutor on the run. "Without question I slept with Arianna last night. What sort of fool do you take me for? After a grand dinner at . . ." Suddenly Pinky's feet stopped and his eyes got as big as silver dollars. "Oh my God. Flo, you could be right. Those two are identical twins—when they were children they dressed alike—talk alike—even acted alike. Remember, Arianna told us the story how she and her sister fooled their mother and father at their tenth birthday party? How do we know they are not doing the same today?"

Flo jumped in. "And how about that bit when Florianna tricked Luciano into asking her to the prom. Those two could be working together. And what about that tale Arianna told us that she and her sister haven't talked for years. Remember when Arianna asked you to send five hundred bucks to her sister? If I had a sister I hated, the only thing I'd send her would be a box full of warm dog shit. "

Pinky, his face a little pale, picked up a cup and saucer and the cup was filled with hot coffee.

I said, "Flo, remember the rules you laid down with the Kid? We can't say shit anymore."

The boss worked to hold the cup steady, but his hands shook so bad that little waves of coffee bounced over the edge and onto the saucer.

She snapped back. "She's not here, is she?"

Pinky stared at the cup and didn't say a word for a good fifteen seconds, a new record for my motor-mouthed Boss. Finally he set the cup down, and slowly walked out of the dining room.

I said, "Flo, you don't really think it's possible that Pinky jumped between the sheets with that cold broad, Florianna?"

"No, but you've got to admit that it was fun knocking your shrimp-like boss down a peg or two."

"I guess, but one way or another, you've stuck him with our bill."

Flo grinned. "Right."

Her evil smile reminded me of Debbie the dodge ball queen, a little broad I went to fifth grade with at the Starr Road School. When the weather was good we'd play dodge ball everyday at school. That's when I really got to know that broad. She was my age, not that big, but she could take a guy's legs out with one throw. Every recess I was real happy to find out that me and Debbie ended up on the same team. A few minutes ago, I watched Flo take Pinky's legs out with a single throw, just like Debbie did day after day. And just like those dodge-ball games at the Starr Road School, I was sure-as-hell happy that me and Flo were on the same team. We finished our coffee, brushed our teeth with new toothbrushes sitting in our bathrooms, and started for the winery.

We hadn't gone a block and I was about to turn left when Flo said, "Hold on, what about Ettamae? We can't leave her at the hospital all day. What's she going to do after she talks with her grandpa for an hour?"

"What do you want me to do? Take her to the winery and listen to her talk to me all day? That's the dumbest thing you—"

"I'll keep her in the office with me."

"That won't work. We could run into Martin, or his wife. Besides, it's dangerous. I'm damn sure one of those dudes, Martin, his wife, Luciano, or Florianna, actually murdered that winemaker."

"Okay, we'll stay in the office and find the evidence. After I finish we'll wait in the office while you and Pinky wander around trying to figure out who the bad guys are."

"But Flo—"

"No buts. You're going to stop at that hospital and pick up Ettamae or you can say adios to the rest of our sex life."

Would she really do that to me? I glanced over and her eyes were sparking like a couple bolts of lighting. I was pissed off, but she held all the cards and we both knew that. I knew that whatever I did, or said, I had to be careful or Flo would get even. She wasn't the easiest person to live with, but snuggling up to her good parts usually made a bad day turn good. Flo had just taken Pinky's legs out and I was smart enough to see that this was not the day to play dodge ball with her. "Okay, I get it, it's your way or the highway. I'll stop at the hospital and pick the Kid up, but she's your problem for the rest of the day."

"Just pick up the child. I'm getting home-sick for Carson City."

"I know, but we can't go home until we find the real murderer."

"I understand that. Now pick her up."

THIRTY-TWO

Pinky-Healdsburg, California

I sat down in my room and gathered myself. The unmitigated gall of that woman. To threaten my future relationship with Willow—my favorite ex-wife—was beyond the pale. I pulled out my cell to call Arianna. I was fully aware that she was quite a bit younger than I, and that she worked for a man capable of violence, but we had connected during the past few days in a way that belied our age and pedigree differences. I felt obliged to give her the opportunity to . . . to do what? To tell me that it was she, and not her sister with me last night? I was struggling with a way to broach the subject when my cell buzzed.

"Boss?"

"What?"

"Flo just came up with a great way to fix your problem with your twin babes."

I sighed. "Go ahead, but I reserve the right to ignore any solution hatched by that woman."

"Boss, don't say anymore. I'm handing her the phone."

"I do not have time to talk with—"

"Pinky? All you have to do is come up with a reason for her to wear a little bandage on her finger. Then you could tell—"

"Excellent idea, Flo. I should chop the tip of

Arianna's little finger off and then render first aid. But why stop with a finger? I could sever her hand, or perhaps her whole arm."

"You can be such a pain in the butt." The line went dead.

I started to key in Arianna's number and stopped. Perhaps Bear's witch was on to something. Something as simple as a bandage on her finger! But how?

I finished keying in Arianna's number.

"Pinky? I've been waiting all morning for you to call. Are you mad at me or something?"

"Mad? No my dear. This has been an extremely busy morning. How are you?"

"I miss you. When will I see you again?"

"Soon. We need to return to the winery, with you dressed as your sister."

"But last night you told me we'd go shopping today at those expensive shops on the plaza."

A man will say most anything in the heat of the moment. And what was this never-ending desire by all females to shop for clothing? I have the finest wardrobe in northern Nevada, but spend little of my valuable time acquiring clothes. Once a month, my personal haberdasher comes to my office, takes the required measurements for a new suit, drops off new dress shirts, selected ties, and the finest Italian leather shoes. Perhaps my longing for companionship had clouded my desire for a permanent relationship. "We will do that my dear, but first things first. Can you be ready in thirty minutes?"

She hesitated, conceivably smarting over the change in her plan to use my credit card to shop for new frocks. "Give me an hour."

"As you wish."

I returned my cell to my pocket and pondered

the possibility that I had misread Arianna. She had told me that she hadn't spoken with her twin for years. I found it hard to believe that twins could live in a small area with one supermarket and that they had not bumped into each other in the checkout line. Had Arianna lied about her sister? That question was easy to resolve.

I called her again.

"Hello"

"Arianna, sorry to bother you, but I need to talk with your sister. Do you have her telephone number?"

"Pinky, I was about to jump in the shower. Can't—"

"My dear, I am pushed for time. Her number please."

"It's 707-4 . . . "

My heart sank. Visions of a possible summer wedding at the Carson City Courthouse faded from my future. "Thank you for the information."

"I'll see you in forty-five minutes."

"My dear, something unexpected has come up. I will call you later."

"Don't say that."

"What?"

"I'll call you later. That means you are giving me the kiss-off." Her voice rose close to a scream. "I can't handle more rejection. Pinky, we don't have to go shopping. You come over right now and we can—"

"Good bye." I hit the disconnect button and keyed in the number Arianna gave to me.

"St. James Winery, Florianna here." This voice had the same pitch as her sister but her tone was more strident.

"Good morning. My name is J. Pinkus Delmont. I am interested in—"

"Mr. Delmont. I recall your name. I believe you are one of our charter Club Cabernet members. What can I do for you?"

"I dialed what I thought was your home number. Are you at the winery?"

"During working hours I call-forward all my personal calls to my business number. Who gave you my personal number?"

"Your sister from the Downtown Pub. We were talking about wine and she mentioned that you worked at the St. James Winery. She also informed me that you are identical twins so if I wave at you in town you should not get upset with me because I think I am waving at Arianna."

"I understand. That's happened to both of us since we were little children. Now, what can I do for you?"

"I envy you two. I was an only child and can merely guess at the bonds between identical twins."

"We are still very close, although not as close as we were when we grew up." I heard a low chuckle. "What I mean by that is we seldom wear the same clothing, that sort of thing, but we do get together on a regular basis. Now, if you don't mind, I'm trying to catch up the paper work that piled up during my recent absences."

"I would love to stop by and discuss my future allotments."

"Mr. Delmont, I can take care of that over the phone. Give me the spelling of—"

"I would rather discuss my wine requirements in person."

"Fine. Do you know where the winery is located?"

Excellent, she does not remember me. "Yes. My B & B provided me with a map of the Alexander

Valley."

"Fine. Once you reach the winery entrance, drive to the main building and walk in. I'll make sure the gate is open and the main building door is unlocked."

"Thank you. I look forward to meeting you."

"The pleasure will be mine."

She hung up and I immediately dialed the Arroyo Verde Winery.

"Bill? This is Pinky."

"Hello again. Are you in the market to purchase more of my finest zinfandel?"

"Ah . . . yes, but this time my questions concern vineyards."

"You're in luck. My vineyard manager is with me now. Care to join us?"

Bill's place was about three miles south of St. James. "Thank you. I will be there in few minutes."

Ten minutes later, after Bill introduced me to Angelo Nobili, we sat down. Bill poured a full glass of zin for each of us.

Bill said, "Angelo, my friend here has a few questions about vineyards."

I said, "Thank you. Angelo, I am interested in a quick overview concerning Phylloxera."

"Mio Dio." Angelo made the sign of the cross on his chest and downed his glass of wine. "Phylloxera is the name of a tiny bug that eats the roots of grape vines. Once you get the bug in your vineyard, it's curtains."

I said, "What can you do?"

"Nothing. Rip out the vines, sterilize the ground, and then replant."

"I have heard of a winery where they are replanting a vineyard, and I believe that Phylloxera remains in the ground. Are they crazy, or ignorant?"

247

"I can't say. You see Phylloxera eats the roots of vinifera grapes. That's the type of grape vine that produces the great wines, like cabernet sauvignon, or chardonnay, or zinfandel. A hundred years ago, a university scientist discovered that the Phylloxera bugs didn't like to eat the roots of grape vines native to America. So grape growers figured out how to graft vinifera stock to the resistant American roots."

I took a sip of wine. It was early in the day but the zin was excellent. I wanted to ask Bill for more information concerning the wine, but duty called. "My good man, if grafting solved the problem then why are vines still infected with Phylloxera?"

He smiled the smile of a man who had seen much in his life. "One of the resistant root stocks, called AXR1, turned out to be less than resistant. Over the past thirty years, almost all of the vines planted in Alexander Valley used AXR1 root stock."

"Ah-ha, are you telling me that the operative word here is resistant."

Angelo nodded. "Exactly. Today you can beat Phylloxera, but you might run out of money first. It will cost around forty to fifty grand an acre to replant. Take a ten-acre parcel. Replanting costs will run around four to five hundred thousand and that's cash out of your pocket. But there's more to this tale of woe. You also have to figure in the loss of your crop from the vines you pulled out. Those ten acres should produce around fifty tons of grapes. At a price of $2500 a ton, the loss of income to a winery would exceed a half a million over a five-year period.

My mind spun as Angelo's tale crept toward the million-dollar mark. "Bill, assuming Angelo's numbers are correct, could that kind of a financial hit sink a winery your size?"

"It sure could. Now tell me why all the

questions. Last time we talked you didn't have any friends with vineyards."

I considered my alternatives. I either told these men the truth, or I would never get Enrique released. "Bill, Angelo—I am going to disclose some important information and ask that everything I say to you will be held in strictest confidence."

Bill topped off our glasses and we lifted then high. Together, Bill and Angelo said, "The zinfandel guarantees our fidelity."

We emptied our glasses.

I said, "The Bench-Land vineyard at the St. James Winery is being ripped out as we speak."

Bill sat back. "My God. If you're correct, Martin St. James will lose everything. But there's more going on here than some sick grape vines. Give us the whole scoop."

In for a penny, in for a pound. "I have been hired to find out who murdered Paul Hellman, and trust me, it is not the Mexican kid sitting in jail."

Angelo said, "Then who did it?"

"At this point I am not sure, but I do know I am getting closer." I glanced at my watch. "I must be going. Thank you for the wine and the information."

"You're welcome."

This time Bill let me off without requiring me to buy more wine. Perhaps his inventory was running low.

I returned to my car with the knowledge that Martin St. James was about to hit the bread line, but no closer to finding the real murderer. Before I started the car my cell buzzed.

"Yes?"

"Ben Hamilton here. The trial starts in two days. Do you have any news concerning Enrique?"

"My number one investigator, and I, have

249

narrowed the field to three, no, four possibilities. My investigator has just now arrived at the winery and I will join him momentarily."

"Pinky, we both know I've paid you a large amount of money with no guarantee of success, but now I have reached total desperation. I'm going to sweeten the pot. Get my nephew out by tomorrow, before the trial begins, and I'll give you an additional check for one hundred thousand dollars."

"Ben, I thank you for your vote of confidence. Now, if you will excuse me, I have work to do."

"And I will not impede you. Good bye."

THIRTY-THREE

Bear-Alexander Valley, California

I pulled the pickup into an empty slot by the door. Parked on the other side of me was Luciano's truck. Next to the truck was a yellow Mercedes SLK 350. Pretty nice car, but for fifty big ones I'd need to get a lot more out of a car than 'pretty nice'. Me and Flo and the Kid got out and walked in the door.

Luciano sat on the other side of the reception room, reading a Playboy, and he was leaning on the back legs of his chair. He looked up, saw me, and all four chair legs hit the floor. "Bear, don't write me up. You told me that's an unsafe way to sit and I promise I'll never do that again." Then his I-just-got-caught-with-my-hand-in-the-cookie-jar look vanished. "Hold on, I thought you'd finished your inspection and went back to your office in Sacramento."

For the first time, Luciano seemed to notice Flo and the Kid. He eyed Flo up and down a couple of times. "Hey, who does the babe belong to? And what about the kid?"

I flashed him the evil eye. "Don't ever call my wife a babe again. I know she's a knockout, but I'm the only guy that can call Flo a babe. The kid? She's my daughter, Ettamae. They've always wanted to see what I do when I make one of my inspections and I didn't think you'd mind if I showed them your winery. I told them that except for the way you sit on

251

your chair, and that little accident where the winemaker fell in that tank and died, this place has a perfect safety record."

"Bear, I keep telling you that death wasn't an accident."

"I don't think your opinion will lower the non-compliance fine we're about to give to the winery, but you have the right to disagree with me. Now, Flo wants to look through the office first."

"Sure. Poke around the place. Can I get anyone some coffee?"

The Kid piped up. "I could handle a cup."

Luciano looked at her and smiled. "Cream and sugar?"

"Nope. I take it straight up, like my Scotch."

I said, "She's kidding about the booze." I never knew what the Kid was going to do or say next, a real sign she'd been hanging around Flo way too long. "But she'd kill for a hot cup of coffee."

Luciano headed to a counter where there was one of those coffee makers. He poured the Kid a cup, and said, "Got to head out to the warehouse and move some pallets around. We're shipping some wine to a distributor and the truck will be here in a couple hours. Bye."

After the door closed, the Kid said, "Bear, if that guy's the sharpest man around this joint, then this winery's in trouble."

Flo said, "You're right, Ettamae, the winery's in trouble, but not because of him. Bear, let's get moving. We don't have time to fool around. I've been thinking, if Pinky's right about that 2010 vintage, then all we have to do is figure out who in this world has a ton of money and an unsophisticated wine palate."

While the girls talked on, like they do most of

the hours I'm awake, I steered them into the compliance office. I said, "I've heard those Muslim dudes don't drink very much and those guys that run around in robes sell us a pot full of oil so they must be rolling in dough."

Flo said, "Hold on. Luciano said something when we came in . . . that's it, he's getting ready to ship some wine out today."

She jumped toward a file cabinet and that jump sort of caused her boobs to bounce, and when Flo bounces, wow, she really bounces!

She said, "All we have to do is find the shipping paperwork." She planted a big kiss on my cheek. "You did it, big guy. Somewhere in one of these office files we'll find some shipping invoices."

"I don't get it."

"There's going to be some documentation here showing that Martin shipped that phony cabernet far, far away from Sonoma County."

She opened the top drawer of a big filing cabinet. "Ettamae, don't just sit there drinking coffee, get over here and help me look through these file cabinets."

"Sure; what are we looking for?"

"Any paper with the word 'shipping'. You take the bottom drawer."

"Okay."

Flo stopped and stared at me. "And what about you. Are you just going to stand there?"

"I'm waiting for Pinky to show up."

"And while you wait you can start on that file cabinet on the other side of the desk."

"Sure," I said, and I did what she wanted me to do, but I didn't like it. Flo was better with all this kind of stuff; besides, maybe Luciano would let me read his Playboy if he had to work. I glanced at Flo. I

253

could tell she wasn't going to fall for a dumb excuse so I pulled the top drawer of the file cabinet. The drawer was filled with hanging files that float on those little metal tracks. All the files had pretty pink colored tabs sticking up. In front was one labeled Corks, then Foils, then Labels, then Shipping, then Payroll, then . . . hold on, didn't that tab say Shipping?

"Babe, what did you say we were looking for?"

"Anything to do with shipping."

"I've got file here that says—"

Flo jumped over, grabbed the file, and pushed me away. I'm a big dude, but when Flo wants something fast, you learn to get out of her way or wish you had. She opened the Shipping folder on the desk and started through the stack of paper. The top form showed 10 cases of wine shipped to Chicago, 25 cases to New York, 8 to Charlotte, 50 to Los Angeles, and on, and on.

About fifty pages into the pile, Flo said, "Here it is. Far East Wine Brokers. Ship: Three (3) pallets (224 cases) of 2010 Bench-Land Cabernet Sauvignon. Special instructions at the bottom say the wine to be to be delivered to The Port of San Francisco, dock number nine, for shipment on the Hake Maru. Destination: Jeddah, Saudi Arabia via Tokyo."

She laid the form on the desk and kept working her way down through more, and more paper. A minute later, she pulled out another form. "Here it is! A faxed order from The Far East Wine Brokers. Amount: 224 cases of St. James 2010 Bench-Land Cabernet Sauvignon. Cost: $1000.00 per case. Payment due on delivery to dock. A typed note at the bottom reads, Paid in full with a Cashiers Check from the Bank of Riyadh for an easy two hundred and twenty-four thousand bucks."

I snatched the paper out of Flo's hand. At the very bottom there was a scribble, or an initial, but I couldn't figure out who it was because who ever signed it must have learned their writing from a doctor.

I said, "Jesus, and I thought my handwriting was bad."

Flo said, "If we could figure out who wrote that scrawl we'd know who killed Hellman. I know a handwriting expert that might help us. Ettamae, make me a copy of both while I try to figure out how to use that FAX machine over there."

"Got it."

I looked around. There were two desks but no phones. I said, "Flo, give me your cell phone. I have to call Pinky and tell him we've found the smoking gun."

She said, "I'll take care of that and I'll remind that little pipsqueak that he owes us—"

The office door opened and Martin St. James walked in.

He looked at us, Flo standing by the FAX machine, the Kid by the copy machine, and me, just standing there. "Who are you and what the hell are . . . hold on, I recognize you, and you're that OSHA inspector." His eyes zeroed in on my chest. "Where's the identification badge you had hanging around your neck."

I slapped my hand against my hip. "Golly gee, I must of left it back at the motel. Mr. St. James, this is my wife, Flo, and my daughter, Ettamae. They wanted to come with me today because—"

"Little girl, what are you doing at the copy machine?"

"Nothing. Just copying something I was drawing. I was bored out of my skull. Pop thinks I want to come along on these stupid trips, but—"

Martin's expression told me he wasn't sure what was going on, but he said, "Okay, but don't make too many copies. Those ink cartridges cost me a fortune." He forgot the Kid and turned to me. "If I recall, your name was Zabarte."

"Right."

"I understand by state law, OSHA has access to my place of business at any time, but coming today, without any identification, and with your family in tow, far exceeds the law. Why are you here?"

He had me there. I was about to plead the fifth when the Kid piped up. "Daddy promised me that after he found the inspection forms he was looking for, he would take us to that movie guy's winery. I know you can't swim in the pool in the winter, but you can see his cool Oscars and all kinds of movie stuff."

I said, "That's right. In fact, I really don't need that form after all. Okay, let's pack up and head out."

"Mr. Zabarte, I am going to report this curious invasion to your supervisor. Before you leave, I want you give me his telephone number."

"Hey, don't be such a hard-ass. All I wanted to do was give my wife and kid a day in the country. I know I stretched the regulations a little but—"

"No buts. Give me the number."

"Her name is Mrs. Olsen and her number is 916 555-3232." I grabbed a blank piece of paper. "Here, I'll write it down for you."

He looked down his nose and said, "Thank you. Now, leave the winery at once."

For a second, it looked like we were going to get away.

The Kid handed Flo the forms. "Mom, I want to keep these drawings."

Flo said, "Good idea. We'll use those little magnets and stick them on the refrigerator when we get home."

Flo stuffed the forms in her purse and we were heading to the door when it opened.

Florianna stood there and said, "Martin, I'm sorry but I have to go home because . . ." Then she saw me, and Flo, and the Kid. "Who are these people, and what are they doing in the compliance office?"

Martin said, "That was my question. But Mr. Zabarte has cleared the air to my satisfaction and they are leaving. Florianna, you have my permission to go home. I was about to run up the hill for my lunch."

"Martin, hold on, I've seen this guy before." She stared at me, and said, "In the tank room— yesterday—Luciano told me he was an inspector from OSHA."

Martin smiled. "That's right. Mr. Zabarte brought his family to the winery today to recover a lost form. Good bye, my dear, and have a nice lunch."

Flo and the Kid made their way past Martin, when Florianna said, "One more thing. I just talked to a man with the name of Delmont. He will stop by soon to go over his Club Cabernet allotment. I told him that I could take care of any changes over the phone but he insisted on coming to the winery."

I fell in behind Flo and tried to push her and the Kid out of the office but Florianna blocked the way.

Martin said, "That's interesting. Yesterday, Mr. Delmont purchased three cases of our Bench-Land cabernet. I wonder . . . Florianna, before you leave it is imperative we verify the inventory to be sure I actually handed over two cases of the 2007 and one of the 2008. The records are hanging on the wall adjacent to the pallets of wine."

257

"I'm sorry, Martin, but I don't have time for that right now. The moment I hung up from Mr. Delmont's call, I received a call from my sister. That's why I have to go home. She isn't feeling well and asked me to stop by. You know how it is with my sister, I never know if she's truly ill, or if she stopped taking her Lithium. You can check out the inventory after you meet with Mr. Delmont."

"That's not possible. The case count of those wines must be completed immediately."

"Martin, what's wrong with you? I don't understand. Making a little mistake concerning a case of wine is not a matter of life or death. My sister's well being comes first."

"I'm sorry but verifying that inventory is a matter of life or death."

Florianna frowned, "What do you mean, life or death?"

"My dear, we've had some wonderful weekends together during the past year, so please remember that I offered you the option to leave." Martin closed his fist and with a quick backhand, he caught the beautiful Florianna flush on her jaw. She dropped to the floor like a sack of wet sand as Flo screamed. Watching him knock out that broad stopped me for a second and before I could do anything Martin had reached into his back pocket and pulled out a revolver that looked like an old Smith and Wesson 357 Magnum.

Martin pointed the gun at the three of us and yelled, "All of you, move away from the door."

We all backed up and then Martin said, "Mrs. Zabarte, dump the contents of your purse on the floor."

"Why?"

"Flo," I said, "Don't argue with a dude when he's

holding a gun."

My babe shrugged her shoulders, turned her purse over and shook. All sorts of junk fell out. Martin kicked her cell phone and stomped it with his heel.

"Now," he said, pointing the revolver at me. "You're next. Set your cell phone on the desk."

I lifted my arms up and turned slowly so he could see I wasn't packing anything but a wallet. "Don't have one. I used to but it fell in the Russian River."

"Take out your wallet and keys, drop them to the floor and turn around."

I did.

"Okay, you're clean. Now, kid, you get over here." Ettamae stared at me. She looked like she was going to cry.

Martin was about fifteen feet away and there was a big metal desk between us. I didn't have a clue what to do next, but I knew I wasn't going to let him touch Ettamae. I said, "Kid, stay where you are."

Martin stared at me for a second, like we were doing one of those Mexican standoff things. Then he said, "There's more than one way to skin a cat. Mrs. Zabarte, take the child by the hand, walk into the closet, and close the door behind you."

The bastard was crazy but I knew he wasn't dumb. Every time I'd move a step closer, he'd move away, keeping the same distance and the desk between us. I didn't know what I was doing but I had to try something. "Martin, what happens to them after they go into the closet?"

"Nothing. I can't say the same for you, but you have my promise they will be safe."

That was pure bullshit. He couldn't let anyone get away from here. "Martin, give your self up. I

259

work for the best defense lawyer in northern Nevada. By last count he has twenty-four acquittals out of twenty-four murder trials. That's a one hundred percent acquittal rate. Hell, he's so good he even got me off. Think of it, twenty-four out of—"

"Shut up." He turned the gun barrel in my direction. "Mrs. Zabarte, you and the child go into the closet or I will shoot your husband. Based on the stopping power of my weapon, a shot in his spinal column may not kill him, but I can guarantee he will never walk again."

"Don't listen to him, Flo."

Flo cried, "Don't shoot him. Ettamae and I will do anything you say." They stepped in and Flo closed the door.

Martin, with his eyes on me, moved to the closet. "Mr. Zabarte, I now have my gun aimed at the closet. If you move a muscle, or they open the door, I'll shoot them."

I watched him slip the key into the door lock and heard a loud click. At least, for a couple of minutes, Flo and the Kid were safe.

He pulled a cell out of his pocket and pushed a button. "I'm going to need some help. Come to the tank room immediately."

Then he waved the gun in the direction of Florianna. "Pick her up and carry her to the tank room."

"I'm not one of your slaves, find somebody else to do your grunt work."

Martin aimed down, toward Florianna's head, and he pulled the trigger. Tiny pieces of splintered floorboard exploded near her face. The shot missed her face by an inch. My ears rung and eyes watered from the smoke that filled the air.

Flo pounded her fists on the closet door. "Bear,

are you okay?"

"I'm fine." But I really wasn't.

"Woman, get away from that door or the next bullet comes your way!" yelled Martin

Florianna moaned. I was damn sure that after I carried Florianna to the tank room, Martin was going to kill us. Then he'd come back to the office and kill Flo and the Kid. I had to come up with something fast.

Martin said, "I'm not the best shot in the world, but at this range, I'm deadly. Mr. Zabarte, it's time to stop being the hero and do exactly what I say or I won't miss her the next time."

I lifted the beautiful broad off the floor. She was lighter than I thought she'd be. As I held her close I picked up the same peach-pie perfume her sister wore. After we got to the tank room, maybe Pinky would arrive, go to the office, hear Flo and the Kid pounding on the closet door, call the Sheriff, and save my ass. But at that point I was pretty sure I was blowing smoke. Betting on Pinky to save my sorry butt had the same chance as the tooth fairy leaving a quarter under my pillow.

Martin opened the heavy door to the tank room. I walked in. The room was as cold as a slab of marble. Standing about twenty feet away, between rows of tall, stainless steel tanks, was Martin's wife, Nancy. Shit, I'd guessed wrong again.

She said, "Martin, what's going on. Every time I leave you to clean up a problem, you make it worse. And just what do you plan on doing with those two?"

"Florianna knows too much about the label switch. The guy? He just ended up being in the wrong place at the wrong time."

"I see. Was he . . ." She stepped closer. "Hold on, I've met this man before. His name is Morgan from some insurance company as I recall."

Martin said, "He told me his name was Zabarte."

"Morgan or Zabarte. My dear, incompetent husband, that guy, as you called him, is not here by coincidence. Are there more?"

"Yes. I locked a woman and a kid in the compliance office closet."

"And why did you do that?"

"I don't know. I just panicked."

"Martin, this is the same lack of initiative that has stunted our married life. It's as if you have never learned how to be a man. And what were you planning to do with all of them?"

"I have an idea but I wanted to run it past you first. That's why I called for help."

Nancy turned toward me. "Is the woman in the closet the same woman you had with you when you visited me in my home?"

"Yes, but the kid doesn't have a clue what's going on. She's only ten years old and her grandfather's in the—"

About that time Florianna woke up. She opened one eye, looked up at me, and screamed, "Put me down!"

I set her feet on the floor and whispered, "Cool it, I'm a friend."

Nancy said, "Martin, did you ever consider that we could have offered Paul a piece of the action? I could have lived with that. St. James would still have its star winemaker and I would still have Paul to help me get through the night. Do you ever consider me before you act? There were all sorts of options you could have tried, but no, that giant Neanderthal brain of yours compelled you to bash another human being over the head!"

262

While the bitch ranted on, I glanced around. Behind me, to my right, was a heavy-duty light switch. I didn't know what went on or off, but if I was lucky, and I could get to the switch before Martin could squeeze off a shot, maybe, just maybe, all the lights would go off. To my left, about twenty feet away, there was a pegboard mounted on the wall. On the hooks hung all sorts of stainless fittings, ring-things, valve things, and all sorts of shiny, heavy stuff.

Nancy kept on grinding her husband down. "I'm not sure you remember this simple fact, but in a couple of days Paul's killer goes on trial. If I can hold a cover over this latest mess of yours, and once that Mexican kid's convicted, we'll get away with everything. But you need to remember who's running this show. If it wasn't for me, we'd be broke. Who thought up the label switch scheme? Huh? What have you contributed to our cash flow problems? Nothing! You crushed the skull of one of the world's great winemakers and dumped his body in a tank full of wine. Martin, you killed one of the few men I allowed in my bed, and for that, I'll never forgive you. One final bit of bookkeeping. Paul's body contaminated the wine we were bottling so I had to spend an additional twenty-seven thousand dollars for more cabernet. Martin St. James, you are more trouble than you are worth!"

While Nancy's mouth pounded at Martin, I gave Florianna a wink and nodded my head to my right. She looked over and saw the light switch. I was pretty sure she figured out what I had in mind.

The way Nancy was yelling at Martin, I was starting to feel sorry for the bastard. "And that's another thing. I understood you fooled around with other women, but I thought you knew better than to

263

screw one of the employees. There's a line my father taught me that goes something like this, 'Smart men know they shouldn't get their bread where they get their honey.'"

Martin said, "What's good for the goose is good for the gander."

"My relationship with Paul Hellman is not part of this discussion."

Martin said, "Are you telling me that Paul Hellman wasn't an employee?"

The door to the tank room popped open and Pinky walked in. "Ah, Martin, if it would not be too much bother, I would love another taste of the 2008 vintage and then one of the 2009." Pinky's mouth stopped flapping when he spotted me, then Florianna, then the gun pointed at his head. "I seem to have interrupted an important meeting. If you will excuse me, I will take you up on your generous offer the next time I venture back to Sonoma County."

Martin waved the weapon at Pinky. "Step in and close the door, Mr. Delmont."

My brain raced back as fast as it could move—trying to figure out if Martin could connect the dots that showed me and Pinky worked together.

I said, "Martin, how many people did it take to do the dirty deed? There's you, and Nancy. Tell me, is this shrimpy dude part of your gang?"

For a second Martin looked confused. Then Nancy, obviously the brains of the family, said, "Don't listen to that fool."

Martin said, "Mr. Delmont, why did you say you are here today?"

Pinky glanced at me. My eyes pleaded with him to think before he answered Martin's question. Then he said, "I came here, at your invitation, to taste some of your award winning 2008 Bench-Land."

Stop right there, I thought. Taste the damn wine, clam up, and get your ass into your car. But in my gut I knew that the idea of my boss knowing when to shut up hadn't been invented yet.

THIRTY-FOUR

Pinky-Alexander Valley, California

The Delmont/Zabarte plan had seemed so simple at the time of its inception. Each team had a task. Bear and Flo were to seek the documents, the hard evidence, that connected the label switch to Hellman's murder.

My task was more difficult, but my palate was up for the occasion. Taste the 2009 vintage. If that wine matched the 2010 central valley plonk, I would have discovered the true motive for Hellman's murder.

Once the evidence was turned over to Charles, then I would call Ben and collect my rather large bonus.

Considering what had transpired since Ben and I had first talked in Healdsburg's plaza, a cool six hundred thousand dollars was not bad for a week's vacation in the wine country.

I parked my vehicle near Bear's truck and entered the winery. The reception area was empty. I called, "Hello, Florianna, it's me, Mr. Delmont! I'm here at your invitation to taste the new vintages of the Bench-Land cab!"

I heard nothing but silence, so I opened the door to the compliance office and stuck my head in. A file and its contents covered the floor between two desks but the room was empty of people. I closed the door and headed to the tank room, opened the door and immediately spotted Martin. "My good man, if it would not be too much bother, I—" My vision suddenly expanded to include, Bear, Florianna, and to my horror, Martin's hand that held a gun pointed directly at me.

Frankly, I was appalled. For years, I had spent thousands of dollars at this man's winery and as one of his best customers I had come to expect better treatment. I said, "Martin, lower your weapon. You have nothing to fear from me. I am a lover of great cabernet who seeks a taste of life's magical wonders. I love your wine. If I had room in my cellar, I would purchase every bottle you produced. That's why I am here today. To kneel at the feet of the master." I glanced at my watch. "However, my good man, time has flown by. I must leave or I will be late for an appointment with a client."

Martin said, "Before you leave, tell me what sort of clients are you talking about?"

"My full name is J. Pinkus Delmont. I am an honest, diligent, hardworking, yet thoroughly humble attorney."

Martin glanced at Bear and back at me. "What type of law do you practice?"

"I defend the downtrodden, the poor, the oppressed."

Martin said, "Have you ever defended a murderer?"

I smiled. "My good man, you have stumbled across my specialty. At last count, I was twenty-four out of—"

"Twenty-four." Interrupted Martin. "I believe that equates to a one hundred percent acquittal rate." Martin's eyes shifted to Bear. "Am I correct Mr. Zabarte?"

Martin approached me and pressed the barrel of his weapon into my forehead. "Delmont, remove your cell phone from your pocket and drop it on the floor."

"My good man, my cell phone is a delicate instrument filled with intricate electronics."

"Drop it or I'll shoot you where you stand."

I did as he commanded. The plastic case bounced a few times on the hard concrete floor and a piece of the corner broke off.

"Now back away. "

Again I did as ordered.

Martin raised his heel and stomped down. I watched helplessly as my costly cell phone shattered into innumerable pieces.

"Now, Mr. Delmont, put your hands behind your head and walk over to meet my wife, Nancy."

THIRTY-FIVE

Bear-Alexander Valley, California

Pinky faced a steel ladder. Martin's revolver was jammed in his back. The boss looked like he was going to throw in the towel but he bucked up long enough to say, "Martin, I'm sure we can work out some sort of an accommodation. If it's money you require, I can arrange a transfer of any sum you desire to a Swiss bank. Once that simple task has been completed, we can—"

"Shut up."

Nancy walked over and patted Pinky's shoulder. "Hold on, Martin, this is the exact situation I talked about earlier. Did you offer Paul a cut when we did the label switch last year? No, you did not. One thing I've learned after years of marriage to you is that you act before you think things through. Listen to Mr. Delmont's proposition. See what he has to offer. If we like his deal, wonderful. If not, he joins ranks with that other man and Florianna."

"Nancy, will you please let me handle this?"

That broad's frosty stare would have dropped the leaves off a maple tree in June. She let go of Pinky's shoulder and got nose to nose with Martin. "Martin, if you shoot that man without finding out what he has to offer I'll cut you off forever. You'll never touch me again."

Martin should take her up on that offer I

thought to myself. Shit, with what I knew about Nancy, I wouldn't touch that broad unless I was sealed inside one of those space-guy suits.

Martin sighed, "Nancy, that shrimp lawyer works with Zabarte so it doesn't make any difference how much money he offers. He's going to end up with the rest of them."

Nancy frowned, "What do you mean, the rest of them?"

"Remember? The two I have locked up in the compliance office closet."

"I forgot, how silly of me. I think the temperature in the tank room has frozen my brain. Why is it so cold?"

"Another one of your lover's expensive ideas. Paul demanded complete control of everything. So he made us install airtight weather stripping on the doors. Add that to the low ceiling, no windows and some tanks covered with a sheet of ice and this room is nearly as cold as your bed."

"Martin, that was hitting below the belt, but the cold didn't slow down Paul."

"Touché."

Nancy glanced at her watch. "Damn, I'll never make that hair appointment now. That means we have to get rid of four outsiders plus Florianna. Just how do you plan on completing that formidable task?"

"First, we'll drop the kid into an empty, unvented tank. She'll be gone in less than a minute, then we'll push the woman in—I'll set it up to look like she tried to rescue the kid—then the shrimp—and finally, the big guy. I'm worried about the size of Zabarte's shoulders. Like Paul, he's going to be a tight fit."

"Not a bad plan, but what about your lover,

Florianna?"

"I haven't decided what to do with her."

Nancy pasted on a big grin. "Leave her to me."

That's when I figured out if I didn't do something real fast, me and Flo, Pinky, and the Kid would end up as a winery accident and I was afraid to think what horrible thing Nancy would to do to Florianna. I was pretty sure if Martin took a shot at Pinky right now, with his gun buried in the boss' back, Pinky would be dead before he hit the concrete. So I had to come up with a way to get Martin to pull the trigger, and figure out a way for him to miss the boss from that close. Then, after Martin missed Pinky, I'd grab his gun and turn these wackos over to the Sheriff. Of course, if I screwed this up, Pinky would end up trying to convince old Lucifer that he could get him off with a plea bargain and I'd end up back at the Old Globe tending bar—holding the shitty end of the stick again.

With nothing to lose, I reached behind me, flipped the light switch, and yelled, "Drop, Pinky!"

In a blink of the eye, the tank room got darker than the inside of a crow's guts. I grabbed Florianna and yanked her to the ground, hoping she'd figure out I wasn't just trying to cop a feel.

For a couple of seconds, everything was quiet, almost spooky.

Flash-Bang! That crazy Martin pulled the trigger. For a split second, we could all see each other, kind of like one of those old photos from Civil War times. Those pictures were grainy, sort of like looking through a thin layer of sand—black and white—and the soldiers always looked at you through big, bugged-out eyes. Martin and Nancy stood by the ladder, smoke floating around their heads. But Pinky wasn't standing in front of Martin, or lying in a heap on the concrete floor. He wasn't holding on to the ladder. The little shit was gone!

Just like that, it was pitch black again. Florianna pushed me away and disappeared into the dark.

Nancy's voice cut through the darkness. "Martin, where are you?"

"Still standing next to you. Did I hit Delmont?"

Nancy said, "Go find that switch or open the door. We need some light in here."

I had to move away from the switch, and fast. I slid left along the wall. I wanted to stay close to the switch because if Martin turned the lights on we were goners. I heard Martin's feet shuffling toward the wall near the switch. I figured if I could grab him before he pulled the trigger, and get that gun away from him, we'd be fighting on even turf. In fact, if Pinky were still alive, we'd have the bastards outnumbered.

A couple more shuffles and then Martin yelled, "Ouch! Nancy, I just banged my knee into a concrete tank pad."

"You wimp. If you don't turn those lights on, so we can get rid of these pests, your bruised knee will be the least of your problems. Find that switch and do it now!"

"I'm sure I'm close. Don't worry, I'll have everything under control in a minute."

The sound of Martin's feet got closer, and I was ready to jump him, when Pinky yelled out and did what he usually does, screw up my perfect plan.

"Bear, everything is black. That shot must have blinded me. Where are you?"

Martin's feet stopped moving.

Flash-Bang! In the burst of light, I saw that Martin had turned to shoot in the direction where

Pinky was standing when the lights went off, but I spotted the boss up the ladder, near the catwalk.

Nancy screamed, "Martin, have you lost your mind? That last shot nearly hit me!"

In that last flash, I could see that Martin was about ten feet away with his back to me. I wanted to take him down but it got dark again and he was too far away to make a blind leap into the black.

The sound of his feet moved away.

I slid about five feet to my right and yelled, "Pinky, keep climbing. Once you've hit the catwalk you're safe," and dropped to the floor.

Flash-Bang! Martin fired in the direction of my voice.

My knee! Jesus, he hit me! I felt down my leg and found the bandage the doc had wrapped around my knee was floating around my ankle. My knee hurt like hell, but Martin hadn't hit me. Scooting on my butt, I made my way back toward the light switch.

Starting to sound bored, Nancy said, "I'm growing weary of this game, Martin. Turn on the lights."

"Damn it, Nancy, shut up. I'm doing the best I can."

Something metal clanked against the concrete floor.

"Damn!" cried Nancy. "That little bastard up on the catwalk just threw something at me."

"What do you suggest, my dear?"

"Do I have to think of everything? Shoot the bastard, and be quick!"

"But I can't see him."

"Do I have to do everything? Aim the gun about ten feet above me and fire!"

Flash-Bang! Flash-Bang! The second shot was

followed by a funny twang, like the bullet had ricocheted off something. In the two quick flickers of light I saw Nancy go down, both arms flopping.

I scooted five feet to my left, away from the light switch and said, "Ha-ha, you just shot your wife."

Flash-Bang! A bullet smashed into the concrete wall about a foot to my right and a million needles slammed into my forehead. I blinked and that was a mistake. My right eye felt like somebody had swapped my eyelid for a sheet of rough sandpaper.

The bastard was getting better at shooting in the direction of my voice. As I brushed the sand and gravel away from my eye, I tried to count the shots Martin had left. One shot in the office and six in the tank room. If I had nailed the make of the revolver, that weapon held eight bullets. That meant he had one more left. What the hell, I'd made it this far. I stayed put and laid down flat on the concrete floor. Then I found one of the pieces of concrete wall on the floor and tossed it to my right. It landed real soft, maybe too soft for—

Flash-Bang! The light showed Martin had buried his last bullet, about belt high, into the wall five feet to my right. That dumb little hunk of crap had sealed the deal.

"Sorry, Martin. I'm over here."

His shuffle and his voice moved directly toward me. "Say your prayers OSHA-man."

"Okay, but first let me tell you that I've been counting and I'm pretty sure you've used all eight shots. You dumb-shit, your revolver is empty."

After about ten to fifteen seconds went by, and he didn't pull the trigger, I figured that I had counted right. On one leg I started to move in the direction where I had last seen Martin standing. Then I heard some metallic clicks.

He laughed. "Mr. Zabarte, you were correct, but I've reloaded and unless you are very, very good, I don't think you can dodge another eight shots."

I was positive he knew where I was. I wasn't sure if I should drop, jump to the left or the right when Florianna's voice cut through the black. "Dodge this, you bastard!"

The sound of cracking bone, just like that sickening noise I'd heard when I crushed Jerry Butler's head against a brick wall, filled the tank room. A body hit the concrete floor.

"Mr. Zabarte, we're safe now," said Florianna, "You can turn the lights on."

THIRTY-SIX

Bear-Alexander Valley, California

I flipped the light switch, and as I limped to the door, I yelled, "Florianna, if you've got a working cell call 911. I'm going to get Flo and the Kid."

I crashed through the compliance office door and ran to the closet. "Flo, are you okay?"

From the other side of the door I heard Flo's voice. "We're both fine. We heard some shots. Are you—"

"Except for my knee, I'm good. How much room do you have in there?"

"Why?"

"Damn it, Flo, I have to break the door down and I don't want to hurt you in the process."

"Go ahead. Ettamae and I will stand away from the door."

I glanced around, looking for something heavy enough to break off the door handle. The FAX machine looked like it would do the job. I lifted it up but the damn thing was as light as a feather— probably made out of a hundred percent plastic. I dropped it, grabbed a heavy oak chair, lifted it over my head, and slammed it onto the door handle. Both the doorknob and the chair hit the floor along with a big hunk of the closet door.

Flo ran out and wrapped her arms around me. She looked great, maybe even better than that day I first saw her in LA. "Sweetheart, you don't look so good. Are you all right?"

The Kid said, "Flo's right. Your knee looks like it lost a battle with Grandpa's weed whacker and your right eye looks like you went three rounds with Mike Tyson."

I had forgotten all about my knee. I glanced down and the Kid was right, my leg looked shitty. I rubbed my hand across my forehead and knocked off more sand and stuff. "Hey, if it hadn't been for a little piece of concrete wall, we'd be dead when we woke up tomorrow morning."

"Waking up dead." The Kid laughed. "Flo, did you ever notice that Bear has a unique way of putting things into perspective?"

Flo gave me a big kiss, so big she was getting close to being x-rated. "I have and I love every time he screws something up."

About then it hit me how close we'd all come to buying the farm. I said, "Were you scared being locked in the closet?"

Flo said, "I was okay until I heard the first gunshot. After that, every time I heard another shot I said a little prayer that you were alive and okay." She brushed some dust and knocked some chunks of concrete out of my hair.

"Flo, how's my right eye look?"

"Open wide," She came close and I wanted to hold her again. "There's a lot of junk floating around in there. We'd better have a doctor do the job."

Florianna walked into the office. "I called 911. A Sheriff's deputy and an ambulance are on their way."

I wrapped my arm around Florianna's shoulder. "Flo, she's the reason we made it out of that mess."

"Mr. Zabarte, you did all the heavy work. All I did was apply the coup de gras."

"What did you hit him with?"

"One of those stainless steel fittings hanging on the pegboard."

My head hurt like hell but I couldn't help smile as I said, "A heavy blunt instrument all women carry around in their purse."

Flo pushed me to the side and said, "How's Martin doing?"

Her eyes lowered and she blubbered out, "He's dead."

"What about that bitch, Nancy?"

Florianna said, "She's still alive. I think she's going to make it."

I said, "Thank God for that. If they were both dead we'd have a hell of a time proving they killed Hellman."

Florianna smiled. "Not really. When I'm on the job, I carry a small digital recorder with me so I can make verbal notes as I go through my day. When you grabbed me, and took me to the floor, I turned my recorder on. Frankly, I was recording evidence to be used against you for rape. Then I figured out you were the good guy, but don't worry, I didn't turn the recorder off. Everything Martin and Nancy said concerning Hellman's death has been recorded for posterity."

"I don't know nothing about the dude named Posterity, all I care about is the Sheriff."

Florianna gave me a peck on my cheek. "That's for saving my life. I don't know what I would have done if—"

The door opened and Pinky waltzed in. He was examining his index finger.

"Boss, are you okay?"

"Fine, my boy, just fine. But during that calamitous madness we encountered in the tank

278

room, I seem to have snagged a fingernail. Does anyone here have access to a new emery board?"

THIRTY-SEVEN

Pinky-Alexander Valley, California

Over the years, I had participated in many investigations where the risk of physical harm to my person was a bona fide likelihood. But the few moments I spent in the St. James Winery tank room, locked in a dark world where everyone was blind, was without question, the most alarming time of my life.

As directed by Martin, I stood at the foot of the ladder while he dug his gun into the small of my back. Rather than listen to the harsh rhetoric between Bear and Martin, I substituted their banter with the pleasurable memories of my married days with Willow.

Suddenly, Bear's loud and clear admonition, "Pinky drop," broke through my blissful reverie.

However, in a moment of instant clarity, I ignored Bear's command to drop and jumped straight up. Hand over hand I scrambled up the ladder. A nano-second later, a deafening roar rocked the murky void.

My fingers locked around the rungs, and as I hung on the ladder, while I took shallow breaths, I came to the happy conclusion that once again, I was right and Bear was wrong.

The female voice asked, "Martin, where are you?"

He responded, "Did I hit Delmont?"

Again, I was shocked. Other than Martin St. James, name me one winery owner who desires to murder his top customer.

Nancy said, "Kick your feet around to see if he's on the floor."

My God, what a callous woman. She thought Martin's bullet had hit me, and as I lay in a heap, she wanted him to rub his filthy shoes all over my lifeless body.

Silently, and carefully, I took one rung at a time and moved up the ladder. For the first time since the gunshot, I opened my eyes and I could not see a thing. I leaned my head forward and brushed my nose against the rung of the ladder. The metal cylinder was no more than an inch from my eyes but I could not make out the bar. I pressed my nose against the metal. I felt the cold, and then smelled the metal, but I could see nothing! Pictures of a blind Pinky Delmont making a fool out of himself during his next trial sent waves of humiliation through me. Was it true? Were my glory days as an attorney behind me? I cried, "Bear, everything is black. That shot must have blinded me. Where are you?"

Flash-Bang!

The female yelled something and spotting the flash from the gun informed me that I was not blind. I pulled myself up the ladder until the rungs ended at the catwalk.

Bear yelled, "Pinky, keep climbing. Once you've hit the catwalk you're safe."

Flash-Bang!

Another shot, but this time the flash was aimed in Bear's direction.

The female blathered on about missing her hair appointment as I pulled myself along the catwalk. I started to move away from Martin when my hand bumped into a heavy metal ring, I did not know what it was, but I was positive the device was heavy enough to show that female below me that I was not going down without a fight.

I heard Martin say, "Damn it, Nancy, shut up. I'm doing the best I can," as I calculated the female's position below me based on her last diatribe. I dropped the ring in her direction but when it hit the concrete I thought I had missed her.

"Damn," cried Nancy. "That little bastard up on the catwalk just threw something at me. Whatever it was hit the floor and grazed my ankle. Do something to make him stop at once."

"What do you suggest, my dear?"

"Do I have to think of everything? Shoot the bastard and be quick."

"But I can't see him."

"Point the gun ten feet above me and fire away."

"I'm not sure I'll hit him."

"Martin, we both know you've never been up to snuff, in the winery, or the bedroom, but even you can handle this task. Point the pistol and shoot!"

Flash-Bang! Flash-Bang!

I was lying flat on the catwalk when the first shot buzzed past my left ear. The second shot hit the metal base of the catwalk, below my chest, and ricocheted down. In the fading light I watched the female below me drop to the floor.

Not sure which direction was the safest, I remained wedded to the catwalk.

Flash-Bang!

A bullet smashed into the concrete wall opposite my perch and I could only surmise that Bear was still alive and that was why Martin continued to shoot at him.

Flash-Bang!

"Missed me again Martin," mocked Bear. "I'm over here,"

While Martin concentrated on Bear, I crawled away from the confrontation. I passed what felt like a tank, then a second. I stopped to rest for a moment when the lovely Florianna's voice rang through the tank room, "Dodge this you bastard."

Suddenly the sound of cracking bones assaulted my tympanic membrane. Then a deathly silence followed by a body hitting the concrete floor. Florianna's victorious cry, "Mr. Zabarte, we're safe now. You can turn the lights on," allowed me the opportunity to stand and feel for a ladder.

Later, the medical examiner's report indicated that Florianna's words to Martin St. James were the last sounds his brain processed as we reached the dramatic conclusion of the tragic opera, now known throughout Alexander Valley as the label-switch murder.

The lights went on and my view from above was horrendously magnificent. My ursine investigator stood next to Martin's body. Blood slowly trickled off Bear's face and a crimson stain saturated the jeans above and below his right knee. Martin however, was another matter. A pool of vital fluids spread outward from his head and the crimson puddle grew as I watched.

The female below me lay on the concrete floor, a gunshot wound visible in the vicinity of her clavicle. She was pale and bleeding, but the volume of blood loss was nowhere close to the same quantity as Martin's, leading me to believe that she would survive long enough to go to trial for the murder of Paul Hellman.

In a triumphant state of mind, I rushed down

the metal ladder. The lack of concern for my personal safety caused the tip of my perfectly manicured index finger nail to be torn off, thus placing a damper on my joyful disposition.

THIRTY-EIGHT

Bear-Alexander Valley, California

I watched Florianna take Pinky's injured hand and sit him down next to one of the desks. Then she opened a drawer, pulled out a little stick and the beautiful twin started to do something to his fingernail. I'll never figure out if the boss had more luck, brains, or was he just good-looking. Forget it, he's got good old shit-house luck.

Flo said, "Florianna, you told us you called 911. Did I hear you say you also called for an ambulance?"

Before the babe could say a word, the office door crashed open and Nancy St. James, her right shoulder still bleeding down her dress, and looking like death warmed over, stood there holding Martin's revolver in her good left hand. She looked around, spotted me, and pointed the damn gun at my chest.

Flo screamed and the Kid dropped to the floor behind one of the desks.

I crouched down, getting ready to jump her, but I was as weak as a newborn baby. My head was spinning, my eyes were blurry, and my knee was burning, like someone had dipped my leg into a barrel of gasoline and then lit a match. Damn, once Martin hit the deck with a crushed skull, I thought all I had to do was wait for the Sheriff to show up and then Flo could take me to the hospital. I said, "Nancy, put the gun down. There's been enough killing around here for one day."

Her cold eyes stared at me. She said, "During Martin's last moments, I heard him say to you that he was going to shoot you. One way or another, you're going to die because you caused the death of my husband. So I'm going to put one of these bullets into your chest, or I'll shoot you five or six times depending on your answers to my questions. What I need to find out is who actually crushed my husband's skull? Did you do it, or was it his young lover?"

Florianna looked at me, her eyes pleaded for her life. I said, "Nancy, your husband was going to shoot me. It came down to him or me so I hit him with everything I had."

Nancy smiled. "I thought so. It would take a man of your strength to do that amount of damage to—"

Suddenly the office door crashed into Nancy's left arm. The weapon fired. A bullet ripped through the side of my shirt and into the wall behind me.

In a flash I decided that a woozy head and crappy knee were not as bad as being dead, so I jumped and slammed Nancy to the floor before she had time to squeeze off the second shot. The broad landed on her right shoulder with me on top. She screamed, the same kind of pitiful cry you hear out in the desert from a rabbit when its leg gets snared in a trap.

I looked up and standing by the office door was the Kid. I rolled off of Nancy and said, "Thanks, Kid, I owe you one."

"You're welcome, but between you and me, we're even. I think me saving one big dude equals you saving one grandpa."

Flo said, "I'll find some rope and tie this bitch

up."

I said, "Be careful with her shoulder, you don't want to be accused of police brutality."

Flo looked at me and smiled. "Oh really? What makes you so sure?"

"Because deep down you're as gentle as a pussy cat."

Pinky jumped up. "Bear, I would have helped you in your time of need but you seemed to have the situation under control. Florianna, now that you have contained the wound to my digit, would you care to join me in a glass of Bench-Land cabernet, vintage 2001?"

Florianna smiled and giggled. "Come with me, Pinky. I know where all the good stuff is stored. Mr. Zabarte—"

Flo yelled from the closet where she was scrounging around for a hunk of rope. "Call him Bear. You're one of us now."

Florianna said, "Okay. Bear, let us know when the deputy arrives." She grabbed Pinky's hand. He cried "ouch" but I think he was faking it, and she pulled him out of the office.

"Found me some rope," cried Flo.

I picked up Nancy and set her in a chair. She kept screaming at me while Flo wrapped the rope around her chest and feet. When Flo was done, the bitch was wrapped so tight that the deputy might have to take the chair with Nancy to get her to jail.

The Kid suddenly appeared with a first aid kit. "There's not much in here for a gunshot, but at least we can swab the wound on her arm with some antiseptic."

That was about the time Luciano wandered through the open office door. "Jesus, Bear, you look like you've been run over by a truck." The he looked past me and saw Nancy, bleeding, moaning, and tied to a chair. "What the hell did you do to the boss' wife?"

I said, "Where have you been?"

"Where I told you I was, in the warehouse moving around pallets of wine. What happened here?"

That was the same thing Luciano told the cops he was doing the night Hellman was killed.

I said, "We had a small war in the tank room. Martin's dead. Nancy's been shot, and as you can tell, I'm not in the best of shape."

"I don't understand. What do you mean a small war?"

I heard sirens in the background, and to tell the truth, I was getting dizzier by the second. About that time the office started spinning faster than the dry cycle on a washing machine. "Luciano," I had a hell of a time getting my finger to stop shaking so I could point at the desk next to him. "Hand me that pencil before I puke."

Luciano glanced down and spotted what I was pointing at and gave it to me.

I knelt down, stuck the pencil into the barrel of Martin's revolver and lifted the gun off the floor. "Stick around, Luciano, I'll explain everything when the cops get here."

That's when the deputy ran in, saw me with the gun stuck on the end of a pencil and skidded to a stop. He pulled out his service revolver, pointed the damn thing at me, and yelled, "Drop your weapon."

I let go of the pencil and that's the last thing I remember.

All the stuff that happened after the gun hit the floor and before I woke up in the hospital is the gospel according to Flo. She swears that her story is one hundred percent true. Don't get me wrong. I believe everything Flo tells me, and she's honest most of the time, but she's a broad and sometimes broads have a different way of seeing things.

Once I hit the deck, Flo found an old blanket in the closet and stuck it under my under my head.

Next, one by one, Flo, then the Kid, Florianna, Pinky, Luciano, and finally that damned Nancy told the deputy what happened in the tank room at the St. James Winery.

Then the deputy told Flo, and the Kid, that their stories didn't count because they were locked in the closet the whole time. Flo got really pissed off at the deputy, called him a dimwit, and few other things that me and Flo had agreed we wouldn't say in front of the Kid. After the deputy cooled down, he told Flo to clam up so he could try and sort out what really happened.

But before he could ask another question, the ambulance arrived, driven by the same two dudes that had picked me and Grandpa Ollie up in Rio Nido. The first thing they did was go to the chair where Nancy was and start to take off the rope that kept her tied up. They said she was still bleeding from her shoulder and needed immediate medical attention before they got to me.

Flo screamed at the deputy to throw a pair of cuffs on the broad tell the ambulance dudes to check me out first.

The deputy told Flo to shut up or he'd arrest her. Nancy and me were both injured and he had to let the ambulance dudes to do their job.

That's when Florianna walked in and told everybody to shut up and listen to the recording she had made. Everybody sat down, and Florianna turned her recorder on. For the next ten minutes

Luciano, the deputy, even the ambulance dudes, listened to gunshots, yells, screams, and a pot full of words from Martin and Nancy, telling how they killed Paul Hellman and stuffed his body into the tank of cabernet.

By now, even the dumb deputy figured out that Nancy was guilty of something, so he pulled out a little plastic card and read the murdering bitch her rights.

Then, while Nancy screamed a bunch of dirty names at the deputy, he cuffed the nasty broad to the chair. He told the ambulance dudes that once they slapped a bandage on her shoulder, they had to help carry her, and the chair, to his car. Once they reached the car, the deputy cuffed her in the back seat and drove to the county jail where he booked her for murder one.

Now you know why, according to Flo, it took the ambulance dudes more than ten minutes to get around to looking at me.

THIRTY-NINE

Pinky-Alexander Valley, California

The moment the Sheriff's deputy placed the handcuffs on Nancy St. James, I reached for my cell phone. It was then that I recalled watching my communication device shatter under the heel of Martin St. James.

"Florianna, do you have a cell phone I could use?"

She reached into a pocket just below her left breast, pulled out a cell and handed it to me. Oh to be a cell phone and reside so close to the Promised Land, I mused. Over a short period of time I had become besotted with this female. She had everything a man of my prominence could, and would ever hope for. Her face was flawless. Her body was inviting. Her intellect was stimulating. Florianna possessed all the desirable female characteristics a man needs and wants.

I turned my head and said, "If you will excuse me for a moment, I have an important call to make. It is truly a matter of life or death."

"I understand."

Florianna walked over to Bear, lying unconscious on the floor, and rearranged the blanket under his head.

I keyed in Charles' number. "District Attorney's Office."

"This is an emergency. Tell Charles I need to speak with him at once."

"And just who are you?"

"J. Pinkus Delmont. My good woman, if Charles is not on this phone in fifteen seconds, I can guarantee you will be seeking new employment before morning."

"Yes, Mr. Delmont. I will get him at once."

"Pinky, have you lost your mind. I said you can't call me at my office unless—"

"Not to worry, I have uncovered the smoking gun you required."

"Thank God! You did? Come on, Pinky, cut to the chase, who murdered Paul Hellman?"

"According to the autopsy report Hellman drowned, so the killers are Martin St. James and his wife. Martin knocked Paul out but it took both husband and wife to stuff Hellman in the tank of cabernet."

"And you have irrefutable proof of your claim?"

"That and more. During the past hour, Martin and Nancy attempted to murder my investigator, a winery employee, a woman, a child, and me. Charles, to put it mildly, death was my close companion today."

Charles hesitated, as I thought he would. Friendship only goes so far, and I was asking the man to risk his career, as limited as it was, on my phone call. "Pinky, it's not that I don't believe you, but—"

"Charles, have I ever stretched the truth to feather my nest?"

"Are you kidding me? Remember that day near the end of our—"

"Do you want to hear the rest of the evidence, or spend my valuable time recounting a day from our past?"

"I apologize, Pinky. Please go on."

"I have a recording of Martin's and Nancy's conversation explaining, in detail, how they killed Hellman. Their attempt to shoot both me and my investigator is also on the recording."

"As you are aware, recordings are not always accepted in court. Do you have anything else?"

"My investigator, Bear Zabarte, and Florianna, she works at the winery, were both present during the event."

"And they are willing to stop by my office and record, on video, a deposition to verify this story?"

"Charles, you wound me with your arrow of doubt."

"Pinky, listen to me." His voice took on a strident tone. "If I discover that you have embellished any facts in order to satisfy an agreement you made with Ben Hamilton, you'll face a charge of obstruction of justice. You will go to trial and the jury won't be happy with a Nevada lawyer who fooled around with the California justice system. Do I make myself clear?"

"I'm shaking in my Nevada boots. Now, before you have me arrested, stick around for few more bombshells. Martin St. James is dead."

"Oh my God!"

"His wife Nancy is in the custody of a Sheriff's deputy and the deputy is transporting her to the county jail in Santa Rosa."

"Why didn't you tell me this before I risked making a fool out of myself?"

"Charles, it has been a very long day. Now that I have your full attention, I need to add that Florianna, the woman who killed Martin, did so in self defense."

"Pinky, I will need to talk with Florianna."

"I understand. I will bring her to your office at ten o'clock tomorrow morning and sit with the woman as she recounts her harrowing experience."

"Pinky, please accept my apology. You accomplished the impossible and found the smoking gun to clear Enrique Flores. I'll call the judge and tell him that new evidence has been uncovered, and in the mind of the District Attorney, the new evidence casts doubt upon the guilt of Enrique Flores. Your man will be released as soon as I can corroborate your story."

"Has our relationship come to this, Charles? You need to corroborate my story? You are treating me no better than a reprobate who walks into your office, drunk and disheveled, accusing a local man for the murder of John Lennon. Contact the deputy who placed the cuffs on Nancy St. James. Ask him why he arrested the woman. Charles, I am shocked by your conduct toward me and from this moment on, I formally cut all the ties of friendship we forged at law school."

"What do you want me to do?"

"Call Ben Hamilton, tell him my outstanding news, and inform him that his nephew will be released immediately."

Charles paused, then he said, "I can't go that far, but I'll ask the Judge to place Enrique Flores under house arrest and restrict his movements to his home. Flores will be required to wear an ankle bracelet until we complete the paper work. And don't say another word. You've just used up all your good will in this county."

"Thank you, Charles. It's been a pleasure doing business with you."

"I'm sorry that I can't say the same."

The line went dead. I was a touch surprised at Charles' initial reaction to the conclusion of our joint venture. A short while ago, he had pleaded with me to extricate an innocent man from incarceration. I did as he asked while maintaining Charles' political standing with the bigoted voters of his county. What more could I have accomplished for my old friend?

"Are you finished with my phone?" asked the lovely Florianna. "I need to check in with my sister."

"Of course, my dear. I have another extremely important call to make, again bordering on a matter of life or death, but you take all the time you require."

I picked up a dusty phone that sat on one of the desks. It was dead. While the only working cell phone was being used, I walked over to Bear, who was stretched out on the floor. His hands were neatly folded on his chest, as if he had passed on to the Basque dream of lush, green pastures where newly born lambs wcrc safe, because in Basque heaven, vicious wolves were not allowed.

"Can't you see he's unconscious?" The overly endowed Florence Sonderlund pushed me away from my recumbent investigator. "Get away. He needs fresh air."

"My good woman, I do not see the need for—"

"I'm not your good woman, and never will be, so stop calling me that. Who were you talking to on the phone?"

"That, my good woman, is none of your business."

At that moment Florianna took her cell away from her ear. I returned to her side, snatched the phone and forced a smile. "My turn."

Florianna's lovely forehead creased into a frightful frown. "I just talked with my sister and learned of the shameful way you treated her when you dumped her. Pinky, what you did to her was unconscionable. Arianna and I are identical twins, and emotionally, we're very in tune. We both get physically ill when somebody like you uses us and tosses us away, like one would throw away a disposable cup from the corner coffee house. Will you dump me, just like you did to my sister, in the near future? I don't think so. In case you've forgotten, I just killed the man I had been sleeping with for the past year. I guess you could say I don't get sick I get even! Make your phone call, return my cell phone, and then get out of my sight."

"As you wish, my dear."

I was not going to allow Florianna's rant at mankind drag down my soaring spirit to her level. As I keyed in Ben's number, I realized that my bright future with Florianna had come to an abrupt end. The woman seemed happy that a quirk of fate had given her the opportunity to crush her lover's head. In fact, she seemed pleased. While waiting for my call to Ben to go through, I made a mental note to discuss with Charles the possibility that Martin's death at the hands of his ex-lover might not be self-defense after all. Florianna could be unbalanced, perhaps criminally insane.

"Hello, Ben? I have great news. Charles is going to release Enrique from jail and place him under house arrest."

"That's wonderful. Hold on, what do you mean, house arrest?"

"That's just a formality, until Charles has the time to look over all the evidence. Trust me, your nephew is a free man."

"Outstanding. This was a well-spent hundred thousand dollars. How do you want me to handle this transaction?"

Perhaps I was exhausted, or in a bit of shock due to my near-death experience, but I neglected to check my surroundings before I said, "Make out a check for one-hundred thousand dollars to me, J. Pinkus Delmont. Indicate in the notation line at the bottom of the draft a single word, bonus. Date it, sign it, and mail the check to my office. Ben, it has been a pleasure worki—"

"Bonus?" Flo's cry assaulted my right ear. "A hundred-thousand dollar bonus? My man lies on the floor. He nearly gave his life in the tank room to save your worthless butt. Pinky, before I do anything rash, such as turn you over to the Nevada Bar Association, I'm going to give you one chance to do the right thing."

I returned my attention to my phone call. "Ben, as I was saying before I was rudely interrupted, it has been a pleasure working with you. If you ever require legal representation in Nevada, please feel free to call on me anytime."

I closed the cell, handed the instrument to Florianna, and turned to face Bear's woman. "My good woman, we are standing on California soil. I am here as a wine-loving citizen, not as an attorney. What makes you think the Nevada Bar is concerned about my present activities?"

Flo walked over to Bear. Other than his taking sporadic breaths, the man exhibited few indications of life. The skinny child sat down on the floor and took hold of Bear's hand.

"It doesn't have anything to do with you practicing law in California, it has to do with failing to do your job back home. You lied to the court concerning a fake illness, the reason you were unable to meet your court date. You lied to Willow, your ex-

297

wife, and the District Attorney, concerning your physical condition. Don't forget, I was the one who, following your explicit directions, made the phone calls to the court to seek an extension for a false cause. Florianna, if it's okay with you, I need to borrow your phone for a couple of important calls."

My God, once again I had underestimated the level of treachery in this female. I raised my hand. "Enough. Provide me with your definition of 'my opportunity to do the right thing'?"

"Place seventy-five thousand dollars of your bonus into a trust fund of my choice for Ettamae's education."

I rapidly considered my alternatives and found none. I was doomed to negotiating with this witch. "Thirty-five."

"Sixty."

"Forty-five."

"Damn it, Pinky, fifty thousand and that is my last offer. Take it or leave it, but if you leave it, my next call is to the Nevada Bar."

"Fifty it is. Now, I assume we are done here."

Flo reached down and stroked Bear's chin. "Not quite done. Ettamae is a growing child. She needs a place to live, food to eat, and clothes to wear. My best guess is that two-thousand a month will cover her financial needs until she reaches the age of twenty-one."

The corner of my lip quivered slightly as I struggled to control my rage. This woman had just cost me a lump sum of fifty thousand dollars and now she was angling for more. She reminded me of my least favorite ex-wife. That female took me for a cool million, and those were the days when a million dollars was a lot of money. "How old is the child?"

"Ten."

I required time to think. I calculated, twenty-four thousand a year for eleven years would equal two hundred and sixty-four thousand. That was outrageous. I willed myself to remain composed. "I was led to understand that the child has a living grandfather who would be responsible for all her expenses."

"Pinky, just like Willow has said all along, you are a unique piece of work. The old guy is blind, has two broken legs, and presently owns a business that's probably floating down the Russian River. Ollie's only concern over the next few years will be to recover the use of his legs, not worry about where the next nickel will come from to raise his ten-year-old granddaughter. Since Ollie's accident, it has been my intention to take care of Ettamae while he recovers. If and when that happy day occurs, Ollie will need the extra money because his Social Security checks won't be enough to pay for a new pink dress, shiny new shoes, school supplies, or all the other items a growing girl requires."

"Five hundred a month."

"Pinky, this has been a tough day for all of us, and that even includes you. My final offer to you is one thousand dollars a month. The money will be deposited into a special checking account of my choosing. The account balance will be open twenty-four/seven to you in case your sick mind thinks that everyone is as untrustworthy as you are. Take it or leave it. I'm too tired to fight with you any more."

I considered negotiating further, but at the moment, she was correct, I was exhausted. "Madam, we are in agreement. You supply me with the bank routing number and checking account number. I will instruct my accounting firm to transfer one thousand dollars each month into the child's account. And, don't think you can come up with a way to play fast and loose with that little girl's money. I will instruct my accounting firm to review her account on a quarterly basis and each year they will perform a surprise audit in a randomly selected month."

The witch stuck her hand in my direction. "We've got a deal."

I ignored her feeble attempt at congeniality. "Madam, deal or no deal. My accountants will be monitoring every penny."

"Whatever." She handed me Florianna's cell. "Now, while I'm standing next to you, call Lu and instruct her to transfer fifty-thousand dollars to Bear's checking account. Within the month, I will give your bean-counters the information concerning Ettamae's educational trust fund so you'll sleep well each night knowing that there's no hanky-panky going on."

"Madam, in the months, no years, we have know each other, the only positive quality I can ascribe to you is that of perseverance. However, I find that this time you have taken what most feel could be a positive quality and carried that trait to the point of agitation."

FORTY

Bear-Healdsburg, California

According to Flo, once I passed out, I was totally zonked 'til I woke up in the emergency room at the Healdsburg Hospital. The first thing I saw was a bright light in my eyes—a dude dressed like a doctor—and his hands were close to my right eye.

The Doc said, "Ah-ha, Mr. Zabarte, we meet again. Now that you're awake we need to discuss the latest reasons for your visit to my charming base of operations. Yesterday, you were lucky when I was able to patch-up your right leg. Had the trauma occurred a bit higher you would have lost your kneecap. Today, it seems that lady luck kissed you again. But I am curious. Was today's knee trauma caused by a lack of understanding or shear madness on your part?"

"It was my fault, Doc, but I had to hit the deck. The bastard had a bead on me."

"A bead on you? Let me move on. I was able to repair your knee, for the second time, and feel you still have an excellent chance for full recovery. Next, concerning your right eye. What caused that injury?"

"I was leaning against the wall and the bastard's shot hit the concrete a few inches from my head. That's when concrete crap hit my eye."

The Doc shook his head, like he thought I was bull shitting him. "A gun shot? I need to report this injury to law enforcement."

"Don't worry. A sheriff's deputy helped me into the ambulance."

"Thank you, but I'm required by law to report all gun shot injuries. Now, that gravel and sand you called concrete crap caused multiple corneal abrasions. They should heal within a week without leaving a scar but each time you blink you will feel some pain and the sensation that you have sand in your eye. The main concern with corneal abrasions is infection and that could cause permanent damage to your vision. Before you leave today I will give you a small bottle of antibiotic eye drops. Take two drops directly into your right eye, three times a day, until all the drops are gone. If you fail to use all the eye drops you could lose the sight of your right eye. Do you understand?"

"Yup. All the drops in my right eye."

"Finally, it's time we discussed the hole in the side of your shirt, the general area where you have a horizontal burn mark a quarter inch below your first rib. I have no doubt that hole in your shirt, and a bullet caused the burn on your skin. Did that bullet come from the man you were talking about earlier?"

"Nope. That happened ten minutes later when Nancy tried to shoot me and she missed."

"Mr. Zabarte, I am a skilled emergency room physician, not a career counselor, so you can take my advice or ignore it. I believe the litany of assaults on your person in a single day are a sign that it is time for you to seek a safer profession."

"Thanks for the heads up, Doc. God knows it's tough being an investigator for Pinky, but it beats the crap out of mopping barf off the floor in the men's can at the Old Globe."

Flo stuck her head around the curtain. "Got him

302

all patched up, Doc?"

"And you are?"

"She's all mine, Doc," I said.

Flo smiled. "Like he said, I'm all his. Is he healthy enough to talk business?"

The Doc sighed, like I wasn't the only crazy one. "Go ahead, but he needs his rest so hold your visit to no more than five minutes."

He got up and left me and Flo alone. "Babe, what's going on?"

She told me how Pinky gave fifty big ones to Ettamae. Knowing that cheap bastard, I couldn't figure out how Flo did it, but she did. "Hey, that's great. Now the Kid can afford a really good car, like a Porsche, or a—"

"Bear, that money will be placed into an educational fund, for her college."

"Oh. But what if she doesn't want to go to college. I know when I finished high school I was ready to hit—"

"Bear, you are not the norm when it comes to the educational system. End of discussion. Ettamae goes to the university of her choice."

"Okay, anything else?"

Then she told me about the grand a month Pinky popped for and that Ettamae was going to live with us until her grandpa got well enough to take care of her.

I sat up, felt a little woozy for a second, and then I slipped my feet onto the floor and stood up. My knee felt like shit, and my head hurt like hell, but I had to stand up and face Flo because she had just dropped a big bomb on me.

For a second, I wished I was back home in the empty waste of northeast Nevada so I could think. I didn't know what to say to Flo, but I knew I wasn't ready for the Kid to live with us. Shit, I'm still trying to figure out how to live with Flo, but I was afraid to tell her that there was no way the Kid was going to move in. Or ask her if she had lost her marbles. Or tell her to go find herself another dude, one that likes to be around kids.

Like I said, I was hurting and tired, so I didn't say any of those things I was thinking because I knew that would piss Flo off. "Go over that again."

"Bear, like it or not, Ettamae's going to live with us. We are not going to send that sweet child into the Foster Care system."

Flo started to blubber and it didn't take a genius to see she wasn't fooling. I sat on the edge of the bed, to take some weight off my knee. Flo sat down next to me, took my hand, and we didn't say anything for a couple of minutes. Then, it was sort of like Flo became a big lake and her damn broke. She cried, and cried, and cried. I put my arm around her and after the sobbing slowed down, she wiped her eyes on my shirtsleeve.

"Bear, I've never told you this, but I spent three years living with foster parents. Don't get me wrong, I'm not saying that they were bad people, but there's no substitute for your real mom and dad."

"Babe, I'm sorry. What happened to your parents?"

She leaned over to give me a hug and banged my knee.

"Ouch."

"Sorry. I didn't mean to hurt you."

"Babe, there's a lot of stuff I don't know about you. I tell you all those stories about my Mom and Pop, living back home in Elko, growing up with my buddies, Pop taking me on camping trips. It's your turn now. What happened to your parents?"

She sat for a long time, longer than I ever heard her stay quiet. Then she kissed me. "I'll tell you the whole story later. We're discussing the future of a ten-year-old girl."

"Right." I stood up and put all my weight on my good leg, then shifted some to my right leg. Not great, but I could live with it. "Flo, I'm not much of a catch. After living with me for two years you know all my bad habits. I swear too much, stare at girls, work for Pinky Delmont, fart when I shouldn't, and scratch myself in all the wrong places. Babe, I'll do what I can to get better, but I'm a dude who's been living that way all his life. The Kid—"

"Ettamae. Her name is Ettamae."

"She told me I could call her the Kid. She told me doing that was en, en . . . . something."

"Endearing is the word, but it's just a nickname. Bear, a nickname is okay for a child but our girl is on the verge of becoming a woman. Promise me you'll try to address her by her given name."

Our girl? Almost a woman? Damn, I haven't gotten past a little girl living with me. Oh shit, in a couple of years I'll be living with two women. No wonder all those dudes spend all their time at the Old Globe. "Like I said, I'll do the best I can. Now let's get out of this place, pack up our free toothbrush and head home. I'm starving for a big meal at the High Roller buffet at the Nugget."

"Thank you, Bear. She's a good kid. I'm confident in a month you'll think that Ettamae's lived with us all her life."

That's what I'm afraid of!

FORTY-ONE

Pinky-Alexander Valley, California

I was packing my suitcase and feeling a touch nostalgic—my week in the wine country was coming to an end—when I heard a knock. I opened the door and there stood the ferret- faced Bliss. Behind him stood Thor, the muscular bartender from the Downtown Pub. Since I had moved into the Red Rose, Bliss had haunted my every move. But Thor? What could this genetic throwback possibly want from me?

"Bliss, I am busy packing. What do you want?"

Thor pushed Bliss aside. "Mr. Delmont, we met before. Remember? My name is Thor."

Of course I remember, you dimwit, I thought. How could I forget the name of a thug that threatened my very existence by holding a knife to my throat? I flashed Thor an exasperated expression. "And what brings you to my doorstep today?"

"It's the old problem of deadbeats, Mr. Delmont."

"I do not understand. Explain yourself."

"Mr. Delmont, we get a lot of tourist trade in Healdsburg and once in a while, one of those tourists skips town without paying their B & B bill or their bar tab."

My anger rose as I came to the conclusion that the deadbeat he was talking about was me. But before I could correct his error Thor pulled out his knife and stuck the weapon under my nose.

"So a couple of years ago, we businessmen in town started to keep our ears to the ground and if we picked up a vibe that one of those tourists was going to take a powder, we'd call around to warn each other. Mr. Delmont, does that remind you of anyone we know?"

Keeping my head very still, I cried, "But you know me!"

"You told me you worked for a movie company. That was bullshit! You told me you were going to make Arianna a movie star. More bullshit! Hell, I know I'm not the brightest bulb in town, but I don't know how you make your money—or if your real name is Delmont, so don't give me that 'you know me' crap. From our way of thinking you are one hundred percent bull shit, right Bliss?"

I shuddered and a sharp pain shot through me when Thor's blade sliced a tiny piece of skin off the tip of my nose. I cried, "Ouch! . . . Thor, please don't hurt me any more. Granted, I may have invented a few fabrications, but they were necessary under the circumstances. However, I remain in the dark concerning your need to bother me today."

"The word is out that you're going to skip out on your bill at the Red Rose."

"What word?"

"Someone in town, we'll call him Mr. B, got a phone call from a certain Las Vegas gentleman you talked to a couple of days ago. I think we both know the Las Vegas gentleman I'm talking about."

My stomach tightened as a drop of my blood hit my chin. "Go on."

"The gentleman told Mr. B that he was upset. Come to think of it, I think Mr. B forgot to add the word 'very' in front of the word 'upset'. The gentleman was *very upset* by the large wad of lettuce you billed him for legal services."

My mind raced back to my phone conversation with Macario, and to the best of my recollection his exact words were, "I would presume that the bill will be reasonable, and the definition of reasonable is left to my discretion." It was now obvious to me that Macario's definition and my definition of reasonable were different.

I said, "Thor, you and your fellow businessmen are mistaken. My disagreement with the Las Vegas gentleman amounts to pennies. I will call him and settle this matter at once."

"Mr. Delmont, the gentleman led Mr. B to believe that you only had a couple of minutes to live and Mr. B should collect what you owe him, in cash, before you leave the building."

My heart was pounding so hard that I could barely catch a breath. "Besides losing my nose what could possibly happen to me in the next few minutes?"

Thor lowered his knife. "Take a look out the window and find out."

I walked over to the window that faced the street. The enforcer from Las Vegas was sitting on the hood of his black Cadillac and in his right hand he held a pistol with an excessively long, cylindrical barrel. He looked up, saw me at my window staring at him, jumped off the hood and started toward the B & B's front door. I considered calling the local police, but I knew my clock would run out before anyone could arrive to save me.

The armpits of my shirt were soaked with sweat. "Thor, the mysterious Mr. B is Bliss. Am I correct?"

"The gentleman told Mr. Bliss that he was giving you a last chance to correct the legal services billing problem. The gentleman said he would transfer one thousand dollars into your checking account as soon as your secretary emails him a bill, with the words, PAID IN FULL in caps. The gentleman's last word to Mr. Bliss was that he would give you ten minutes."

My mouth became so dry that I struggled to ask my question. "When did Mr. Bliss receive the call from the gentleman?"

Thor checked his watch. "About five, no, it was four minutes ago." Then he handed me a slip of paper with an email address. "He told Mr. Bliss he'll call off his dog as soon as he gets the email from your gal."

"Thor, Bliss, do either of you have a cell phone I could borrow?"

Thor handed me his. Fighting to control my shaking hands, I keyed in my office number. Lu answered on the second ring. "Law offices of—"

"Shut up and listen!" I yelled my instructions and the email address. "Lu, you have no more than three minutes to send the email. When you have completed that task call me back at," I thrust the phone at Thor's face. He gave Lu his number,

I watched the second hand on my Rolex count my life down to one minute and five seconds when Thor's cell played, "Take Me Out To The Ball Game".

I cried, "Yes?"

Lu said, "Pinky. I did everything as you instructed. What happens next?"

I tossed the cell to Thor and ran to the window. I watched the hit man return to his Caddy while he talked on his cell phone. He nodded, got into the car and backed into the street.

I watched the Caddy drive west toward the plaza, then sat down and took a few deep breaths. Then I punched in my office number, to apologize to Lu for my shortness with her a moment ago. I counted eight rings before she answered. "Yes?"

That was not like her. Lu was always so prompt. "Lu?"

"Mr. Delmont, I boxed up my belongings and was walking out the door when your call came in. I'm happy I decided to return to my desk and pick up your call. As of this moment, I quit. If you're wondering why, yesterday you told me to transfer fifty thousand dollars into Bear's account. You told me a cock and bull story that the money was for a child's education, but you didn't fool me. Your investigator's a nice guy but I'm a college graduate and there's no way that man's more valuable to this enterprise than I am. The least you could have done was give us each twenty-five thousand. But that's not all. A few minutes ago you told me to shut up, in fact that's happened twice, and no one on this earth talks to me that way. And if that wasn't enough, you are an immoral human being. There were days when the first thing I did when I got home was to take a shower, trying to wash off the corruption I had picked up as your employee. I leave you with this final thought: the moment I walk out the door your office is unattended."

The call went dead. I glanced out the window. The black Caddy was nowhere in sight. I pulled out my pocket calendar, found the number for the Rapid Replacement Agency, and placed the call.

"Louis?"

"Yes, this is Louis Loomer. Who's this?"

"J. Pinkus Delmont. Louis, I am calling you from Northern California. It seems that I will require a person immediately. Nothing complex, just someone to go to my office, answer the phones, and take down messages."

"Mr. Delmont, I will be able to provide you with a qualified person first thing tomorrow morning."

"Not tomorrow, you dolt! My office is empty and at present, no one is answering my phones."

"Did you just call me a dolt?"

"I apologize, Louis. During the past thirty minutes I was nearly executed, was called an immoral human being, and, finally, told I am a corrupting influence."

"Mr. Delmont, I can't comment on your near death experience, but a few personal insults do not give you the right to verbally slur an innocent party such as myself. But I'm a professional and you need my help. Insults or not, I am here to take care of your replacement needs. Moving on, will you be seeking a permanent replacement for your secretarial position?"

"Yes, I am afraid I will."

"Mr. Delmont, I might be treading on thin ice, so to speak, but this is the second secretary to walk away from your employ in less than a year. Perhaps I will require more input from you concerning special talents, or the willingness to work long hours, or—"

"Mr. Loomis. I run a tight ship and the demands on my employees are high."

"The last girl I sent you was young, energetic, and extremely talented. A woman like that will not be easy to replace on such short notice. Perhaps I could find you an interim surrogate while I search for your permanent replacement?"

Short of finding Mable, and convincing her to return to the fold, I could only think of one person. Could I, for a day, a week, or longer, coexist with

Bear's woman? What horrible deed had I done to extract so much retribution? "Mr. Loomer, did I understand that your search for my permanent replacement would take twenty-four hours?"

I detected a chuckle on the far end of our discussion. "Mr. Delmont, I didn't say twenty-four hours; my exact words were, a woman like that will not be easy to replace on such short notice."

A premonition of pending doom settled upon me. "My good man, begin your search. I have a woman in mind who will take care of my office during the interim."

FORTY-TWO

Pinky-Carson City, Nevada

A week passed, during which time neither Flo nor I had raised our voices in anger or threatened each other with immediate death. In fact, the woman acted toward me in a civil manner. She was efficient, competent, and accomplished her required tasks with little or no complaint. Of course I was paying her handsomely for her time. In fact, as a little bonus, I presented Flo with the eleven bottles that were leftover from the mislabeled case of Bench-Land cabernet. Obviously, I kept the two legitimate cases of the 2007 Bench-Land and immediately added them to my nearly full wine cellar.

All in all, beyond acquiescing to a single demand, the Flo experiment worked and for a week my office functioned without any emotional eruptions on her part. The demand? A minor change of operation in my office procedure. I was forced to make my own coffee, a duty I rapidly discovered was beyond my sphere of expertise. I made a quick switch to hot water and tea and that solution immediately remedied the problem.

One quiet morning, while I sipped my tea, Flo walked into my office. "Pinky, take a look at these." She handed me two 8x10 glossy photos. The first one showed the twin sisters dressed in the first costume Arianna wore when she served me beer at the

Downtown Pub. The second showed the girls dressed in identical gray, business suits, the type Florianna wore while working at the St. James Winery.

I said, "Who sent these."

"I don't know. The pictures came in an envelope without a return address. Pinky, I think they're both nuttier than a fruitcake. It's obvious to me that they could do both jobs and no one would ever know. Think of what could happen to a guy dumb enough to get married to one? What do you want me to do with the photos?"

"Rip them up and burn the pieces." Flo shook her head and left me alone while I finished my tea in peace.

On the final day of our détente, Flo buzzed my intercom. "A man named Charles is on line one. He claims he is the Sonoma County District Attorney."

"His claim is valid." I punched a key. "Hello Charles, what can I do for you?"

"Nothing, really. After you returned home I talked with Ben. Pinky, I know you charge your clients large retainers, but I was shocked to discover that you ripped off my old friend."

"I told the man my price. The decision to accept was his."

"True, and I guess we'll all sleep better knowing that an innocent man was freed. I suppose I should thank you for everything you accomplished."

"Charles, I am very busy. Beyond your expression of gratitude, do you have anything else?"

"Yes. After you left the fake election memo on the desk at your B & B my opponent cancelled his TV ad campaign. I hit him hard with a media blitz and now I'm up seven points in the polls. It looks like I'm a shoo-in for re-election."

"Charles, I am pleased that you are satisfied

with your elected position but that sort of post is not for me. I would seek another calling—a door-to-door vacuum cleaner salesman, for example—before I would attempt to live with the boredom you are forced to deal with on a daily basis. From what I understand your job consists of managing a passel of lawyers. My God, that is tantamount to herding a hundred cats across a river. My good man, I salute you, but thank my lucky stars that I remain in an efficiently run private legal practice."

"I heard your investigator was injured prior to the arrest. Will he recover?"

"Yes. He was wounded, but his leg will heal and do not forget, I was also wounded, and I have fully recovered."

"Glad to hear that. Pinky—"

"Charles, your question brought everything back. There was danger at every turn that fateful day at the winery. Bear, my investigator, was at my side, but I accomplished all of the heavy work. The final assault in the tank room was my plan. Then, thinking outside the box, I created a diversion in the dark so Martin would run out of ammunition. While I was risking my life to save the others, my investigator—"

Flo burst through the door and threw the office keys on my desk, narrowly missing my cup of tea. "Before you ask, yes I was eavesdropping on your phone conversation and heard everything you said about that day at the winery. Tell Charles from me that you are a lying bastard. Never mind . . ." The witch grabbed the phone out of my hand. " . . . Listen up, Charles, this is the straight scoop. The plan to go to the winery and collect hard evidence was Bear's idea. My man threw the light switch so Pinky could hide in the dark and not get shot. Dragging his bad

315

leg all over the tank room, Bear dodged shot after shot 'til Martin ran out of ammo."

Flo handed me my phone. "Pinky, speaking of plans, I hope you have something in mind for running your damn office. A female just walked in the front door. Her name is Kimberly Stuart. She's your new secretary, so I'm out of here. While you sit on your butt with a phone to your ear, two lines are ringing. And the best part? You and Kimberly don't have a clue of how to access or print out your daily calendar. Bye now."

The door slammed as I heard Charles' laughter coming through my receiver. "Pinky, sounds like the wheels of your efficient, one-man practice have come off. Perhaps I could send you a few of my unherdable cats? By the way, I heard through the grapevine that you were considering making an honest woman out of Arianna so I'm positive you'll enjoy the two photos I mailed to you."

I slammed the phone down and walked through my private office door. The outer office was empty except for a small-framed female, immaculately dressed in a navy blue suit, who stood next to Lu's desk. Wait, I thought, that desk does not belong to Lu anymore, that desk belongs to . . . what was that woman's name? . . . ah yes, Kimberly Stuart.

"Ms. Stuart?"

"Please call me Kim."

The woman's facial skin was heavily made up in a futile attempt to cover over the miles. My first guess placed her somewhere north of forty and south of fifty. Her hair was the ubiquitous copper-blonde that many aging females seek to mask the aging process. Her ring finger was empty, but I detected a faint white line that informed me that one had previously been worn, and for some time. "Kim, when a phone rings answer it and say 'Law Office of J. Pinkus Delmont.'"

She nodded, answered the first line, and said, "Excuse me, there's a lady on the line who wants to speak to you."

What else could happen today? "Hello?"

"Pinky, it's Willow."

"My love, how delightful to hear your mellifluous voice. What can I do for you?"

"Who was that female that answered your phone?"

"Willow, hold on. I am returning to my office where we can continue this conversation in private."

I walked in and picked up my phone. "The woman is new and she answers to the name of Kimberly Stuart."

"How old is she?" The concern in Willow's voice jumped a notch.

"Not to worry. At least forty-five, perhaps more."

"What happened to Lu?"

"We decided to part ways. Willow, beyond expressing my undying love, what else can I do for you today?"

"I wanted to congratulate you on your new-found attitude toward people less fortunate than yourself."

"My dear, to the best of my knowledge I have always been tolerant toward the poor and dispossessed, so I remain confused by your statement."

"Hey, all you had to say was, 'thank you. I've turned over a new leaf and I'm pleased that you noticed.'"

I sighed. "My love, this has been a particularly harrowing day and you have me at a disadvantage. Explain what you mean by my new found attitude."

"It's too late to hide your generosity. I'm talking about the educational trust fund you set up for that cute little girl, Ettamae. The child who lives with Flo and Bear. I thought I knew you, but then this happens and I see you in a whole new light."

How do these confidential agreements become public knowledge? "Before I go any farther, I must know how you discovered I was involved. The fund was set up on the condition that the money for the child's education was donated by that prolific benefactor known as Anonymous."

"I promised her I wouldn't tell, but seeing that she doesn't work for you anymore, the information came from Lu."

"My God, I can only guess at what other confidential information she disseminated to the populace of Carson City."

"Besides you, and possibly Flo, I'm the only one in this town who cares about your secret. Don't worry; your cynical, hard-shelled persona will remain in place. Lu also told me about the thousand a month you're contributing to support the child. Pinky, those acts of kindness have made me reconsider you and our past problems. Is it possible that the old Pinky has changed, like Scrooge changed on Christmas Eve? I don't know how you feel, but I am willing to give our relationship another chance."

My thoughts flashed back to my new secretary, Kimberly Stuart, and her empty ring finger. That ring finger told a story, perhaps sad, perhaps not, but a tale of a lost love nonetheless. "My dear, I would desire nothing more. I suggest we meet at my place for dinner."

"I'll be there. By the way, yesterday I received a letter from my first cousin in Scotland. He posed an interesting question, and because I value your

318

opinion, I want you to read the whole letter."

"I will do that, but after breakfast."

"Breakfast? I'm ready to give our relationship a second chance, but don't you think that's moving a little fast?"

I fully understood that earlier, my motives toward Ettamae's future were less than charitable, and the only person that knew my true feelings was Flo. A possible reconciliation with my ex-wife hung in the balance, an equilibrium that would only remain in place at the mercy of Florence Sonderlund, a woman who detested me.

Then I reconsidered Willow's words, "Pinky you have changed." Was it possible that she was right? Had I truly changed, or was I just looking for a quick roll in the hay with my favorite ex-wife? Only time would tell. "Willow, the faster we find out if you can stand living with me again, the better. Since our divorce, every night, without fail, your face is the last thing I see before the veil of slumber descends."

"Pinky, that's the nicest thing you've ever said to me."

"Thank you. One last thought, would you stop by The Wine Shop and pick up a couple of bottles of St. James Bench-Land cabernet for tonight's dinner?"

"What year?"

"Any year before 2009."

"Hold on! Didn't you tell me six months ago that you had a cellar full of the world's best cabernets?"

"I did, but since that conversation, my stockpile of the world famous Bench-Land cabernet has dwindled."

"Are we talking about an expensive wine?"

"Of course, but the cost of true love has no bound.

AUTHOR'S NOTES

It all started on at five hundred watt radio station in Bakersfield. The work was . . . wait, that's the beginning of a different book—this book's about wine.

Okay, it all started in 1977. Life was good. Mental stress was almost non-existent. So what did we do? Bob and I built a winery! We had the love of great wine. We had made amateur wine. What more could it take to build and run a successful winery?

Over the next seven years we found out that not all of the madness turned out good, or bad, but the reality was, as we all eventually learn, that life is not the destination, it's the journey.

It didn't take us long to figure out that coming up with the idea of a winery was a lot easier than getting a use-permit from the county. The area was zoned for agriculture, some grapes but mostly apple trees, so wineries were an acceptable use. However, one of the neighbors didn't like wine, and his father had been a high-level county official, so the hard fought battle for our use-permit was a long one.

Once we won the use-permit war, our next task was to construct the winery building, pour concrete tank pads, buy four 5000 gallon stainless steel tanks to bolt to the concrete pads, plus six twenty foot hoses, fittings to connect the hoses to the tanks, a commercial refrigeration unit so we could control fermentation temperatures, thirty brand-new, French oak barrels, a crusher-stemmer, a press, a bottle filler, a cute little device to pop the corks into each bottle, and a label machine.

Speaking of a label machine, we had to name the winery and design a label. The name? That was pretty easy. The winery was surrounded with apple orchards so we chose Pommeraie, a French word meaning apple orchard. Our label turned out to be a very unique oval shape in red and gold for the cabernet and green and gold for the chardonnay. In a word, our label was a real eye-catcher.

Now, once our wallets were nearly empty, it was time to look for grapes.

We contracted with a cabernet grower who had ten tons to sell, and a chardonnay grower who had five tons to sell.

We fixed the last refrigeration problem an hour before the first grapes were delivered. I sat back, the muscles that had locked my stomach onto a ball, started to relax.

That's when the last shoe dropped. The neighbor who didn't want the winery filed a formal protest with the state to stop the issuance of our "Winegrowers License." The state set a date in January for the hearing. That created a minor problem. We had crushed ten tons of cabernet grapes. We had three tanks full of grape juice, seeds and skins. Without a license, we couldn't allow the juice to ferment into wine. I talked with a guy from the state and told him we were storing grape juice in temperature-controlled tanks so fermentation was not possible. The state guy said, "Sounds okay to me."

That day, we locked the gate into the winery, took the phone off the hook and hunkered down.

In January, the state hearing sided with us and the winery was now allowed to ferment wine. We were pleased to hear that the winery was now legal because in mid-December, after a power failure, nature took it's course and the wine started to ferment.

Would I do it all again? As I said, life is not the destination; it's the journey, so the answer is yes.

One more note on the wine business. In the book I write about a St. James Winery Bench-Land cabernet that sold for $140 per bottle.

The question is: How does a winery set a price for a bottle of wine?

Read on and you'll find out the answer.

Unlike many other products we buy, there is no, I repeat, no correlation between the price of a bottle of wine and the cost of the liquid inside the bottle, the bottle, the cork, the foil, and the label.

In case you think I'm crazy, consider the famous, "Two-buck Chuck" that you can buy at any Trader Joe's store. Their cabernet sells to the public for $1.99 per bottle and don't forget, Trader Joe's makes a profit and the winery that made the wine makes a profit.

Are there really cabernets that sell for $140.00 a bottle? Is water wet? Of course there are and many sell for much more than $140.00.

So with all your newfound knowledge you now know the answer—A winery will charge whatever they think a customer will pay for their wine.

If you have any questions concerning, wine, or my books, email me at ken@kendalton.com.

Ken

September 2011

www.kendalton.com
www.facebook.com/KenDaltonMysteryWriter